D1398799

Voices of Shadows Past

Secrets of Scarlett Hall

Book 3

Jennifer Monroe

This book, *Voices of Shadows Past*, the third installment of the Secrets of Scarlett Hall Series, can be read as a standalone novel; however, it is important that you know that it takes place concurrently with the second book in the series, *Echoes of the Heart*. If you have not yet read the previous books in the series, I would highly recommend that you do so.

Secrets of Scarlett Hall

Whispers of Light

Echoes of the Heart

Voices of Shadows Past

Prologue

Scarlett Hall, January 1806

Lady Eleanor Lambert held many secrets close to her heart. And although many had caused her great anxiety, there were in fact some which had brought an abundance of joy. Her life thus far had been anything but perfect; in fact, some moments had been painful beyond belief. However, she took pride in concealing that pain from her children in order to ensure they lived a happy life, a life better than the one she had lived, for they were all in life that truly mattered.

Some secrets are meant to be told when the time is right while others are meant to be kept for eternity, yet she had been forced to reveal two secrets, one to each of her two eldest daughters. They were told in necessity, as a means to right a wrong, and she had no regret in their telling. Regret that the secrets existed, certainly, but not that they were revealed.

She picked up the quill and dipped the nib in the ink. Whether it be an entry in her journal or a letter to a loved one, Eleanor found comfort in putting to paper her thoughts and concerns, to release the worries that plagued her, and she was finding the need to do so more often as of late. It was as if she were writing to a close friend without the worry of being rebuked for her thoughts and feelings.

Scarlett Hall had almost been lost; however, it was Laurence Redbrook, Duke of Ludlow, who agreed to marry her eldest daughter, Isabel, in exchange for his help in that matter. It had been Isabel's strength that Eleanor leaned on in the worst of times, and her daughter had agreed to marry for convenience. However, much like a flower in spring, Isabel's love for the man bloomed, and Eleanor was pleased that Isabel and Laurence had come to love one another, for a marriage without love is not much of a marriage at all.

That crisis was averted only to open yet another. Hannah was readying herself to leave for the season in just a week, and the girl argued against going as fiercely as a woman being asked to throw herself into the mouth of a volcano, as the ancient tribes in South America of which Eleanor read had done.

Although she had quashed any notion of her daughter missing her debut into society for the second year in a row, Eleanor could not help but worry about how miserable the poor girl truly was. It was her hope that, under Isabel's guidance, Hannah would put the absurd notions of becoming a spinster to rest. Now, all Eleanor could do was hope for the best.

Her youngest daughter, Juliet, however, was another matter. Although the girl would be joining Hannah and Isabel for the season, and therefore leaving the house empty, Juliet had a fiery temperament that concerned Eleanor more than Hannah's reserved nature.

Sighing, Eleanor returned the tip of the quill to the parchment to complete the letter she had been writing before her thoughts had carried her away.

As for Juliet, she continues to remain as wild as the wind in a storm. She has grown to be a beautiful young woman, a fact she understands all too well and uses it to her advantage whenever possible. She may be prone to telling great tales, but her heart remains pure despite her deception. Although it may not be right of me to do so, I find that she holds a special place in my heart. I cannot explain my reasoning, Charles, although you should know. However, that is perhaps a secret meant only for my heart and not that of any other.

Although I shall never tell you or anyone this particular secret, I will tell you this. For all the hurt you have caused me, the grief you brought upon me during our marriage, in the end, you allowed me the most beautiful and strongest of daughters. And for that gift, you will always have my gratitude.

Eleanor looked down at the parchment and smiled. The letter was not complete, and it was time for her to retire for the night. It would be added to the many letters she had written to her husband over the course of the past four years since his death, and she was certain it would not be the last.

She rose from the chair and yawned. Her bed was calling to her.

However, before she could make her way to her bedroom, the sound of cry of pain resounded in the hall, causing Eleanor's skin to go cold, and she recognized it as Juliet.

Chapter One

Two things existed in the world that Miss Juliet Lambert hoped to accomplish. The first was to attend her first season, for which she would leave the confines of her Wiltshire home in just a week's time. Granted, she loved Scarlett Hall with its jutting parapets and grand towers, but so much more could be had in life beyond its walls, and she was determined to experience all she could. Parties, balls, dinners, dancing; to be a part of such a grand spectacle was a fantastic dream, and she could barely keep her excitement under wraps.

Her second goal in life was proving to be a greater difficulty. It was not the type of challenge that would last her a lifetime, for it had more to do with the sport than the prize. Daniel Haskins, one of the handful of stable hands at Scarlett Hall, was of the lower class; however, Juliet found him handsome in his own way with his dark hair and brown eyes. Yet, for some reason the man barely showed her an ounce of interest, and for the life of her, she could not reason out why.

It was not for lack of trying that the man paid her little heed. She had batted her eyelashes at him in some effort to appear demure. She had dropped her handkerchief on the ground, and although he had retrieved it for her, he turned away almost immediately, much to her chagrin. She may as well have been one of his horses for all the interest he showed in her!

The fact of the matter was, how could Juliet expect to catch the eye of some noble duke or earl if she was unable to catch the eye of a lowly stable hand?

It was this frustration that had Juliet sitting in the drawing room with her sister Hannah, who was a year older and could not have been more different from Juliet. Whereas Juliet welcomed the idea of attending the season, Hannah had little interest in going to London. So much so that she had feigned an illness the year before in order to remain home. Juliet could not fathom any woman of the *ton* wishing to remain home when she could find such wonderful entertainment elsewhere.

"It will be the reason she gives her heart to him," Hannah was saying, speaking of the characters in a book she was penning.

Although Hannah's usual drivel about her writing typically bored Juliet, Juliet allowed it this evening. She was well out of ideas on how to gain Daniel's attention, and since Hannah enjoyed romantic novels—a strange phenomenon since she cared little for romantic notions in her own life—perhaps an idea on how to catch Daniel would take root.

"That is fascinating," Juliet replied. "Tell me again."

Her sister smiled and smoothed the white skirts of her dress, a stark contrast to Juliet's red. "In her defiance, Christine shall attempt to remove the ivy that has obscured her view from the window. Then she will slip and fall into the arms of Percival, who will be there to catch her when she falls."

Juliet could not help but sigh as she thought of such a notion happening to her. It would be Daniel catching her in his strong arms, and she would reward him with a kiss. Of course, such an action on her part would be unladylike, but would it not be warranted for such a brave act? Daniel would be so overcome with her beauty that he would whisk her off to marry her, and he would find joy in working in order to buy her gifts, thankful that a man of his station had been fortunate to marry a woman such as she.

"It is the proposal about which I worry," Hannah said with a shake to her head. "Would he make the request in a place that has some special significance, or should he speak to her outside her window as Romeo did with Juliet?"

Juliet clicked her tongue. "That is of little importance," she said as she rose and walked over to the liquor cart. "What is important is the part when she falls." She perused the numerous bottles until her eyes fell on a red wine lying in one of the slots on the side. She poured a glass and turned around, the bottle still in her hands.

"What are you doing with that?" Hannah demanded. "You do not mean to steal it, do you?"

Juliet laughed. "Steal it? My dear sister, how can one steal what one already owns?" For all the intelligence Hannah purportedly had, this riddle seemed to stump her. "I am merely going to allow myself a drink or two."

Hannah glanced at the closed door. "I do not believe you should do that," she said in that incessant admonishing tone she tended to use with Juliet. "If mother were to catch you drinking, she will be quite unhappy."

Juliet returned to her sister and placed a hand on the woman's shoulder. "My sweet, innocent sister," she said with a sigh. "Mother is busy in the office, hiding away as she oftentimes does. She takes no notice of what we do, nor does she care."

Although the words were true, saying them aloud pained Juliet. Over the past year, their mother had become somewhat of a recluse, and she spent less time with any of her three daughters. Juliet was glad their brother Nathaniel was off at boarding school, for he was not home to endure the neglect. When Isabel married Laurence, Juliet had to admit that she and Hannah had become quite jealous of the time their mother had spent with the new couple.

"I hate to admit it," Hannah replied, "but you are right. It hurts me that Mother has ignored us." She sighed, and Juliet's heart went out to her sister. Hannah was by far the most attached to their mother, and Juliet knew the woman hurt the most. "Juliet, may I ask you something?"

"Yes, of course."

"I...what I mean to say is the season..." Hannah sighed. "If I do not meet a gentleman, what do you suppose will happen?"

"You will meet someone eventually," Juliet replied. "That is, after all, the true purpose of men and women." She walked over to the fireplace and looked into the dancing flames. "We are to find love, if there is any to be had, of course. To court, to marry and to produce

6

children faster than hats at a millinery."

Hannah gasped. "Children? I do not want to have children."

Juliet could not resist the urge of mischievousness that came over her. "Have you not heard the latest fashion of the *ton*?" she asked. Her sister replied with a shake to her head. "Why, women are now expected to have at least a dozen children."

"This cannot be," Hannah replied. "That many children? I cannot imagine! From my understanding, the pain of one childbirth is bad enough, but a dozen?" She looked up at Juliet. "And you? Will you do the same?"

Juliet laughed. "I? Children? I think not. No man will put such a burden on me."

"Not even Lord Parsons?" Hannah asked with a wicked smile. "I saw the manner in which he spoke to you at the Wilson Party."

Juliet clenched her fist. They had attended that party three weeks earlier to celebrate the upcoming season. Lord Hugh Parsons, although a handsome man, was by no means a man she wished to court her. Her mother had accepted his first card, and Juliet found the man such a bore, she had almost fallen asleep. When he sent another card last week, Juliet had promptly refused before her mother had even seen it. Thankfully, her mother never learned of it, and Juliet had sworn the maid who had received it to secrecy.

"Not even Lord Parsons," Juliet replied firmly. "That man is not worthy to look upon my beauty."

A small smile played on Hannah's lips. "And yet Daniel is?"

The words hung in the air, and Juliet felt her heart skip a beat as she thought of the stable hand. "That is silly even for you, Hannah," Juliet retorted. Yet, the words were true. The idea that she was attracted to the man caused her great confusion. If only he was of noble blood! Regardless, there were plenty of gentlemen nearly as handsome and with far more wealth than he could ever dream of possessing. Yet, she could not stop herself from attempting to gain his attention.

Looking down at the bottle of wine she still held in her hand, Juliet knew it was time to implement the plan she had been devising for the past few weeks.

"Daniel is a stable hand," she said with a jut to her chin. "Therefore, he stands among some of the poorest in England."

"Then why do you spend so much time with the man?"

Juliet tightened her grip on the bottle. "If you must know," she said with as much haughtiness as she could muster, "he has requested to gaze upon my beauty daily." She gave a dramatic sigh. "It was a request about which I considered telling Mother, for I believed his intentions ill. However, then I realized that, as he said, there is no woman as beautiful as I."

Hannah's smile faltered, and Juliet seized the moment. She did not enjoy telling tales; however, at times, they were necessary.

"So, yes," Juliet continued. "I do allow Daniel to gaze upon me, for it gives the man the strength to complete his work."

"It sounds odd," Hannah said.

Juliet shook her head in disbelief and headed toward the door.

"Where are you going?"

"To the stable," Juliet replied. "My horse has not been well, and I must check on her."

Without waiting for a response, Juliet hurried down the hallway, the bottle clutched to her breast. The servants, including Forbes, the butler, would more than likely have retired for the night, and with her mother busy in the office, it was the perfect time to escape.

She glanced around as she wrapped her cloak over her shoulders, and with the bottle of wine now hidden beneath the heavy wool, she made her way out the door. Yes, now was the most opportune time to implement her plan. For, if someone as well-respected as Lord Parsons had an interest in her, then a simple stable boy had no excuse not to, as well.

**

The horizon was a beautiful red, much like the wine in the bottle Juliet carried as she made her way to the stables. Her mind and heart both raced with excitement at what she planned to do.

The story Hannah told had been brilliant, and for a moment, Juliet regretted the many tales she had told concerning the season. Poor

8

Hannah was anxious enough about attending without Juliet's help. Her sister would see that there was nothing about which to concern herself once they were there.

Yet, Juliet worried. Although she desperately wanted to go to London, the idea of not seeing Daniel for so many months did not sit well with her. It was strange that she had these feelings, for a woman of her station did not cavort with men from his. Despite the fact he had not shown any interest in her as a man would have for a woman, they had shared in many talks that she found rather intriguing. Her mother and Isabel had warned her that spending too much time in the stables was unbecoming of a lady; however, that advice, much like any other she received, went unheeded. She was intelligent enough to get out of any situation that might occur, despite the warnings.

Slipping through the white painted wooden door, Juliet glanced around. The horses were locked away in their stalls, and the stench of the place made her feel ill. The stables were well-maintained, but even the slightest odious odor could shake the countenance of any young lady. However, she had a plan to fulfill, and she would not leave until she saw it completed.

She narrowed her eyes in the dim light searching for someone particular, a beast much like the horses. She strained to hear any sounds of the man, but only the light neighing of horses or faint movement from their stalls was all she heard. At the end of the long corridor, a smaller hallway branched off to the right and led to a large room. There was where numerous saddles and blankets were kept, and at one of the several tables sat Daniel working on a saddle. As she drew closer, she realized it was hers.

Her legs grew weak as she watched the man. His shirt drew tight across his broad back, and that might have been enough, but it was the hands that worked the saddle that made her heart flutter and her face burn, for the muscles under his sleeves relaxed and contracted with each movement he made.

"It's an honor to have you here again, Miss Juliet," Daniel said without looking up from his work. "To what do I owe this pleasure?"

Juliet swallowed hard in an attempt to bring moisture to her suddenly dry mouth. "I-I came to check on my saddle. Have you fixed it according to my wishes?"

"I have," he replied. "Or rather I'm almost finished."

"Please," Juliet said, "continue as if I were not here."

The man nodded, his dark hair bouncing from the movement. His arm muscles bulged as he pulled tight one of the knots.

How could a man such as he be awarded with such a strong body?

Juliet started when the man stood and faced her. With brown eyes and a strong jaw and cheekbones that highlighted a rare smile, the word handsome did not do him justice. In truth, Juliet had never seen such a finer man as he. However, she would never admit as much to him.

"I've finished your saddle," he said with a bow. "I hope it's to your liking."

Juliet swallowed hard again, reminding herself of her position in life. Although winning the man's gaze was of the utmost importance, she had to maintain a ladylike stance. It would do no good giving the poor man any ideas. Well, perhaps a few ideas, but she could not allow it to go too far; she had to respect her position in society.

"I would like to see it now," she replied as she walked over to him. The dark brown leather had light tan strips, giving it a far different appearance from those of her sisters. In all honesty, it was the most beautiful saddle she had ever seen in her life. "It is acceptable," she replied, although keeping her excitement hidden was difficult.

"Acceptable?" Daniel asked in shock. "I'm sorry. Doesn't it make you happy?"

Juliet turned to the man and looked into his eyes. A woman could become lost in them if she did not keep her guard.

"Miss Juliet?"

She shook her head to clear it. "Yes. It is fine. Thank you for doing the work I requested."

"I'll try harder next time," he said sadly, his eyes lowered. "I think my craftsmanship is getting better, though, don't you?"

Juliet sighed. "A lady such as I has high standards. I realize that you, unlike Lord Parsons, understands those standards." The man raised his head and smiled, and Juliet had to suppress a grin. Men were so predictable and easy to manipulate! "Yet, I find your willingness to please me admirable."

"Thank you, Miss Juliet," he replied. "I'm happy to hear that. I'll do better next time, I promise."

Juliet turned and walked over to one of the worktables where various tools lay. She placed the wine bottle she had brought with her on the table and picked up one of the tools with a pronged end that reminded her of a fork. "You recall me telling you of Lord Parsons, do you not?"

"Yes," Daniel said. "He's the gentleman from the party you went to with your sisters and Miss Annabel, if I remember."

A streak of jealousy rushed through Juliet at hearing her cousin's name. Annabel was beautiful with her wheat-colored hair and blue eyes, and Juliet could not help but worry that perhaps her cousin had caught Daniel's eye when she, herself, had not been successful.

"You are correct," she responded as she replaced the tool and chose another, as if that were the object of her discussion. "He sent me another card last week, as well as a letter."

"I'm happy to hear it," the stable hand replied, much to Juliet's frustration. "From what you've told me about him, he's a respected gentleman."

Juliet clenched her fist. Was the boy daft? Could he not see she wanted him, not Lord Parsons, to look her way? She turned and allowed a moment to take in his strong features. "I, too, believe the same," she replied. "Or I did until I received his letter. I must admit it frightened me and…" She paused for dramatic effect. "Oh, I suppose my safety holds little concern for you."

"Miss Juliet, I'm very concerned about your safety. And your happiness. You may tell me if you'd like."

Juliet pressed a hand to her breast and sighed. There were times to tell tales, and now was indeed one of those times. "I will because I trust you. Can I trust you?"

The man nodded. "Of course."

11

"Well, you see, at the party, when Lord Parsons spoke to me, he told me I was the most beautiful woman in all of England. However, the card that came with his letter held such vile words..."

"What did it say?" Was that anger in his voice? Oh, she hoped so!

"He wishes to kiss me, to press his lips to mine," she said with feigned modesty, as if such an act was beyond her senses. "That such an honor was worthy of payment. He then offered me the sum of five thousand pounds and the deed to a parcel of land near Dover." She looked up. "I have never been more offended in all my life!"

"I think," Daniel said, taking one step toward her, her heart racing, "that a woman of society shouldn't be treated that way." He paused and frowned. "I-I should get back to working on your saddle."

Juliet could not stop her mouth from falling open as the man returned to his stool and leaned over the saddle once more. What had happened? At one moment, he was moving toward her, and in the next he was once again focused on his work! Why could he not admit that he found her beautiful? Well, she would get him to admit as such one way or another!

Taking the wine bottle, it was time to execute her plan. Without another word, she walked over to a ladder that led to a loft above them. Mostly filled with straw, the loft was for storing old saddles and other items that were no longer used. Her plan was simple. She would entice Daniel to join her in the loft, where he would finally admit to her beauty. They would drink in celebration that she had finally caught his eye.

She climbed the ladder in silence, and when she neared the top, she reached up and placed the wine bottle on the landing. Then she turned and looked down at Daniel. "I am going to enjoy a drink to ease the pain in my heart. Perhaps you would like to join me?"

Daniel looked over his shoulder. "I must regretfully decline, Miss Juliet," he replied. "It wouldn't be proper for me to drink with you."

Juliet snorted. "Are you certain?" she asked, attempting to keep her tone cordial but failing miserably. "I do have wine and more secrets to share with you."

"I can't," the stable hand replied as he returned to his work.

Juliet was now past frustration. Why should a lady such as she work so hard to gain the eye of a man such as he? Did he not see how lucky he was?

The story Hannah had told about the woman falling from the window had been silly, but Juliet was at her wit's end. She had to do something to gain this man's attention!

"I am in charge, as you know," she said with a jut to her chin, which likely did not have the same effect from where she stood perched on the rung of the ladder as she grasped the top rung with her hands, "and you must obey my wishes."

"Your words might be true, Miss Juliet," Daniel replied, although he did not look up from his work. "But this request I cannot obey."

Juliet pursed her lips. "Fine. Then I shall have to tell Mother." As she began her descent, she kept her eyes on Daniel in hopes he would change his mind before she reached the ground. However, he did not even look up! "I could let..." Suddenly, her foot slipped off the next rung, and she cried out as she grasped the rung above her. However, her hands were too weak to hold her weight, and she came crashing down to the ground. A shot of pain raced through her foot and up her leg, and she could not stop a cry from erupting in a very unladylike manner.

"Juliet!" The stool flew back as Daniel rushed to her side.

Juliet grasped her ankle as pain like nothing she had ever felt in her life pulsed through her.

"Daniel!" she said with a groan, and she could do nothing to stop the tears that flowed down her cheeks. "It hurts so terribly."

He squatted down beside her, his eyes wide with concern as he pulled a piece of straw from her hair. "You will be all right," he said. "I'll take you inside." He placed a hand around her waist and one under her knees and picked her up as easily as if she were a sack of oats.

"Do not try to have your way with me," she whispered, for she had never felt more comfortable in all her life—barring the pain in her ankle, of course. "My weakness is not a means for which you may take advantage."

"I would never hurt you," he replied as he made his way to the house.

"Thank you." She looked down at her foot that pained her as if a carriage had run over it, and she pressed her face into Daniel's chest. Despite the pain, she enjoyed being in his arms more than she would have imagined; her fall had been well worth the pain if it meant having this moment. His chest was strong and firm, and although she knew she should not, the temptation was too great. She touched the muscle in his arm with the pretense of keeping herself from falling.

"Your mother'll wonder why you were in the stables," Daniel said as they approached the house. "What should I tell her when she asks? She'll throw me out for allowing you to be hurt."

Juliet sighed as he ascended the steps to the portico as she reveled in the boulder that was his arm muscle. "Do not worry about employment," she replied. "There is nothing I will not do to keep you here with me."

When he looked down at her, Juliet received that which she had been searching, for in his eyes was a glow she had not seen before, and she knew it was she who had caused it.

Chapter Two

D aniel Haskins had first come to work at Scarlett Hall when he was only twelve years of age, and it was within a few days that Miss Juliet Lambert began coming by to talk to him. Her visits, however, were becoming more frequent as of late, and her mother, the Lady Lambert, did not approve of this particular pastime for her daughter. Daniel could not agree with the woman more. Miss Juliet was a lady and, therefore, much too good to be in a place that smelled of manure and horseflesh.

Now, as he picked her up from the floor after she had taken her horrible fall, he wished, as he often did, that the woman would have listened to her mother.

As he stepped out of the stables with Miss Juliet in his arms, her head resting against his chest, he could not help but worry. Not only was he concerned for the wellbeing of the woman he currently held, but he was displeased with himself that he had not done a better job of keeping an eye on her. If he would have done as she asked in the first place, he might have been there to catch her when she fell.

No, he could not have done as she asked. If he were caught with her alone in the loft, not only would he be sacked, but Miss Juliet would be faced with a great shame. And that was something he would never allow.

"Thank you," Miss Juliet whispered.

Daniel said nothing, for he was only doing what was right, but when she squeezed his arm, he had to fight back the urge to throw her to the ground—and an urge to hold her tighter.

He hurried his step. What he needed was to see Miss Juliet safe inside the house, and he hoped beyond hopes that Lady Lambert would not be standing in the foyer waiting for them.

"Your mother'll wonder how you ended up on that ladder, which will get her to wonder how I let you climb up there. Then that'll make her wonder why I didn't stop you. I'll be sacked for certain." He had no family and nowhere else to go. What would become of him after so many years working in a place as grand as Scarlett Hall? He'd never have such fine living quarters as he had in the rooms he shared with the other stable hands!

"Do not worry," Miss Juliet said as she placed a hand on his chest. "There is nothing I will not do to keep you here with me."

The words were kind and they soothed his worry even as they sent a shiver down his spine. Not of fear, but of wonderment. Never had she been so kind to him. As a matter of fact, he rarely saw much in the way of kindness from her at any time.

He sneaked a glance at the face of a woman he considered beautiful beyond words. It was strange, but a yearning came over him, a strange feeling he had never felt before, but he pushed it away. No stable hand had the right to have such feelings for a woman like Miss Juliet.

It was a relief when she removed her hand from his chest. Having her in his arms was bad enough; one less body part touching his was a relief.

Daniel shifted her weight when they reached the stoop, and he was able to grasp the doorknob and push the door open. Inside was dark save one candle left on a small table at the bottom of the stairs. He had to stop himself from gawking at the interior, for although he had been in the employ of the Lamberts for seven years, he had never been inside the great house before.

"Ahh!" Juliet cried. "The pain is worse now!"

"Where am I to take you?" Daniel asked. "Your mother? Should I call for her and ask?"

The sound of hurried footsteps made him turn to find Lady Lambert rushing toward them, a candle in her hand.

"What is...? Juliet?" Her skirts flowed around her as she hurried to them. "What has happened?"

"My Lady," Daniel said, debating if he should bow or not with his burden, "Miss Juliet fell and hurt her foot."

When Lady Lambert looked up at him, he knew she was displeased. Well, this was it. He would be out in the cold before he even got Miss Juliet to her room.

"I will explain everything," Miss Juliet said, although her words were strained. "But for Daniel's sake, and for mine, I must sit."

"To the drawing room," Lady Lambert commanded. "Follow me."

Daniel followed the baroness down the hallway and through a door where a large fire burned in a massive fireplace. He had never seen any room like it with its fine furniture and opulent rugs. Opulent? That was the word, was it not?

"Place her on the couch," Lady Lambert said.

"Yes, my lady." Daniel did as the woman asked, passing a large cart filled with all sorts of bottles of spirits. He suspected that was from where Miss Juliet got the bottle she had taken to the stables.

As he lowered her to the couch, Miss Juliet surprised him by batting her eyelashes so quickly, he wondered if she got a bit of dust in them. Well, he could not help her with dust in her eyes. It was bad enough he was not able to do more than carry her inside.

Finally relieved of Miss Juliet, he bowed deeply to Lady Lambert. "I-I suppose I should go now."

"No. Remain here. I would like to speak to you before you leave."

Daniel could do nothing more than nod. Leave. Yes, he was definitely going to be sacked.

"Here, let us remove these," Lady Lambert said as she began to unbutton Miss Juliet's shoes.

Daniel thought the skin would burn off his face at that moment. She was going to remove her shoes while he was standing there?

However, such thoughts disappeared and concern returned when Miss Juliet cried out in pain once more when her mother removed the shoe on her hurt foot.

"Mother!" Juliet shouted. "It hurts!"

Lady Lambert clicked her tongue as she continued to remove the shoe, although she moved more gingerly now. Daniel almost cried out himself when he caught sight of the woman's ankle, for it was red and swollen.

"I cannot endure this pain, Mother," Miss Juliet said. "I may need a drop of brandy to ease the pain."

Although distressed over all that had happened, he could not help but return the smile of mischief Miss Juliet gave him as her mother walked over to the liquor cart.

"What were you doing in the stables alone?" Lady Lambert asked. "We have spoken about this before, and now I find you have disobeyed me once again."

"I cannot, nor will I, lie to you," Miss Juliet said as she rearranged the pillows behind her. "I went to check on the saddles."

"Whatever for?" her mother asked as she returned with two glasses of brandy. She handed one to Miss Juliet, and much to Daniel's surprise, she handed the other to him. "A man carrying such a burden is well deserving of a drink." She gave him a faint smile, and Daniel could not miss the twinkle in her eye.

"Thank you," he replied, taking the delicate glass from her. *What a kind woman she is,* he thought. To have him in her home and then give him a drink? No one would believe him if he told such a story. Not that he would. He was not one to tell tales, true or not. Nothing came from it anyway. If the tale was true, no one would believe it, and if it was not true, it was simply a lie and nothing more. And if there was one thing Daniel did not do, it was lie.

Lady Lambert went to sit beside her daughter, leaving Daniel unsure what to do. Did he allow Miss Juliet to drink first? Did he take a seat without being offered? No, that was just silly. Luckily, the younger Lambert did not wait to take a sip of her drink, and he did the same.

He had never tasted anything so wonderful! It was rare that he drank any type of spirits, but nothing he had drunk in the past ever tasted as marvelous as this. Although, it still burned as badly as it went down as what old Liam kept under his bed for special occasions.

Wishing to draw out the experience, he took another small sip. The longer it lasted, the longer he could enjoy it.

"The saddles, Juliet?" her mother said. "What was so important that you went to check on them?"

Daniel curled his toes. Now was when he would be sacked for sure.

"Lord Parsons mentioned going riding," Miss Juliet said, "and I had requested that Daniel make sure mine was ready for the man's arrival."

"His arrival?" Lady Lambert asked. "I did not know he had requested to call over."

"Why, yes. I may have forgotten to mention it to you, but in my excitement over him sending me a card, I had completely forgotten."

Lady Lambert sighed. "So, you do have an interest in the man?"

"Oh, very much so," Miss Juliet replied.

Daniel could not stop the bolt of jealousy that ran through him. Then he remembered that Miss Juliet was crafting a story, as she was wont to do. She had no interest in Lord Parsons. Or did she?

When the door opened, Daniel nearly jumped out of his shoes. Miss Hannah, dressed in a white dressing gown, entered the room, her eyes falling on Juliet.

"What happened?" she asked with a gasp. When she saw Daniel, she screamed and crossed her arms over her breasts.

"I'm sorry!" Daniel said as he squeezed his eyes shut and spun around to face away from her.

More footsteps resounded in the hall.

"Is everything all right?" That was Forbes, the butler, if Daniel guessed correctly.

He sneaked a peek over his shoulder. If Forbes could be in the same room with Miss Hannah half-dressed, and able to keep his eyes open, Daniel could take a quick glance.

"Yes," Lady Lambert replied. "Hannah, return to your room. Forbes, I shall speak to you in a moment, once I am finished with these two."

As Miss Hannah and Forbes left the room, Daniel wondered once again if this was the moment he would be out on the streets. What would he do then? Where would he go? Would he be given at least a

19

reference? Despite his concerns, he turned back to face his future; he was a man, not a mouse!

"Now," Lady Lambert said to her daughter. "Go on."

Juliet sighed. "I thought I heard a noise, like heavy breathing in the loft. So, I climbed the ladder, but there was no one there. However, as I went to climb back down, I slipped and fell."

"And you were there?" Lady Lambert demanded.

How Daniel wanted to tell the truth, for he admired the woman greatly. It was Lady Lambert who had brought him a piece of cake whenever they had a party in the great house. Or she would offer him a kind word after her husband berated him for one thing or another. Yes, he would tell the truth.

"I was..."

"Speaking with one of the servant girls from Lord Briny's house, I suspect," Miss Juliet said, interrupting him.

Lady Lambert narrowed her eyes at him. "Is this true?"

Daniel could do nothing more than nod.

"I know he goes there every Monday," Miss Juliet continued. "And I know he goes to meet up with several of the servants to play cards, or so is the excuse that is used. Although, I find gambling a poor use of one's time." She hung her head as if it was she who carried the shame.

Lady Lambert sniffed derisively. "I could not agree with you more, but how do you know about all this?"

"The servants gossip worse than men."

The older woman gave a tiny snort. "That is also true. So, how was it Daniel came to find you?"

"Lady Lambert," Daniel replied, "Miss Juliet was on the floor when I returned to the room. I picked her up and brought her straight to you. I'm sorry I was not there to stop her from being hurt." What bothered him most was that the lie burned his tongue worse than the brandy burned his throat no matter how quickly he spoke the words.

The older woman sighed as she stood and collected his glass. She walked back over to the cart and surprised him by refilling it. "You have nothing for which to apologize," she said as she returned the glass to him, full once more. "The woman you saw tonight? What is her name?"

"Oh, her name?" he asked. For a moment, his mind drew a blank. Then he said the first name that came to mind. "Elizabeth."

"I see." The woman wore a sly smile. "I shall ask Daniel to carry you to your room. Tomorrow morning, I will send for the doctor." Then she turned to Daniel. "Will you help once again?"

Daniel nodded, and for the second time that night, he carried Miss Juliet in his arms.

***

Carrying Miss Juliet up the stairs was much more difficult than carrying her across the drive and into the house. With each step, his back groaned and his calf muscles threatened to tear. It was not that he did not perform heavy tasks every day, but climbing steps carrying someone was not something he did on a regular basis.

Lady Lambert walked in front of them, the candle in her hand lighting the way.

"It is a good thing we keep the staff well-fed," Juliet said halfway up the stairs. "Daniel has the strength of a young stallion."

Daniel felt his face heat, and he knew he had to be a bright red. It only worsened when she reached out and touched the muscle on his arm once more.

"Quite strong, in fact."

Daniel swallowed hard and hoped Lady Lambert did not turn around at that exact moment.

"Indeed," the elder Lambert replied with irritation in her tone. "We are thankful for our servants. And we do *not* refer to them as stallions."

When they reached the top landing, they turned right and passed several doors, one which opened to a peering Miss Hannah.

"Do not worry for me, dear sister," Juliet called out. "Although he is a brute, his strength serves a purpose. Plus, Mother will protect me from him."

Lady Lambert spun around and glared. "Juliet!" she gasped. "Conduct yourself as a lady! You are embarrassing not only me but yourself far more than you realize."

"I am sorry, Mother," Miss Juliet murmured.

They stopped at another door, and Lady Lambert opened it and stepped aside to allow Daniel to carry his burden inside.

"Place her on the bed."

He gazed at the bed for a moment. It was massive, almost as large as his entire room, with heavy drapes tied back to each corner post. Several pillows were piled up at the head, and he laid Miss Juliet into them with as much care as he could. He tried his best not to touch the blanket, but his hand brushed the smooth fabric, and he wondered what it would be like to be covered in something so exquisite.

"I hope your injury isn't too bad, Miss Juliet," he whispered before he stood back up and looked around at the rest of the room.

What he saw was as formidable as the bed itself. A vanity with a large mirror sat against one wall between two large windows, perfume bottles lined up on one side and a variety of jars on the other. A wardrobe sat on the opposite wall, and a chest at the end of the bed would have been too big to hold everything he owned in the world.

Miss Juliet let out a heavy sigh. "I may lose my leg and forever be stranded in this room. I shall grow old and wither away..."

"I believe it would be best if Juliet remain quiet and rest," her mother said, interrupting her daughter. "Let me walk you to the door."

Daniel gave Miss Juliet a fleeting smile before following Lady Lambert out into the hallway and down to the foyer. However, rather than taking him to the door that led outside, she continued to the drawing room.

"Lady Lambert," he said as the baroness walked over to the cart of liquor bottles once more, "might I ask something?"

"Yes, of course," the woman replied. "What is it?"

"If I'm to lose my position, I understand. I'd just ask if I could have time to say goodbye to the others."

Lady Lambert turned and gave him a shocked gaze. "Lose your position? Whyever would that happen?"

He shrugged, suddenly uncomfortable. "I don't know. I thought with Juliet being hurt..." he allowed the words to trail off when she walked over and offered him an entire decanter of brandy. Not only because it was brandy, but because the bottle was worth more than his boots!

"Take it," she said when he hesitated. "Please. It is a gift of celebration for you and Elizabeth."

What an odd comment, he thought. Why would this woman be happy for him and a woman who did not exist?

"Thank you," he said as he took the bottle, although a bit of guilt tugged at him at accepting on such terms. "I've never owned anything so...nice." It was true, for although she paid him fairly for his work, he had never spent even a farthing on himself, except on necessities such as a new shirt when he needed one. Otherwise, he saved everything he earned.

"As to your work here," the woman continued, "I see no reason you should not remain. If that is what you wish, of course."

He nodded emphatically. "Oh, yes, I would."

"I believe that, in time, Juliet shall marry Lord Parsons. What do you believe? Will he be a good suitor for her?"

Daniel did not know much, but he knew that a stable boy was the last person a lady went to for advice. And the question she asked did not sit well with him for all too many reasons.

"Surely for all she has spoken of the man," Lady Lambert continued, "you must be pleased he will be joining her for the season?"

A strange sadness came over Daniel, and he could not for the life of him understand why. "I didn't know that," he replied.

"In truth, neither did I," Lady Lambert said. "However, if Juliet wishes the man to call, I am certain they will see each other often while they are in London." She walked over to stand in front of Daniel. "Then she will be happy."

"Well, if she's happy with him, then that's all that matters." Silence filled the room, and Daniel cleared his throat. "It's the same as I feel for Elizabeth. I hope one day to win her heart." He was unsure why he lied. Perhaps it was hearing the stories Miss Juliet had told over

23

the years that propelled him to embellish on his story.

Embellish? he scolded himself. *You outright lied to a lady!*

Much to his relief, Lady Lambert smiled. "You do care for her, do you not?"

He nodded. If he spoke, he would confess it all. Lying never came easy to him, but now was not the time for repentance.

"That is wonderful," the woman said, her smile widening. "Simply wonderful!"

Why was this woman so happy that he had an interest in someone? Well, if it meant him keeping his position, he would boast of this imaginary woman forever.

"Now," Lady Lambert said, "allow me to walk you to the door."

Soon, Daniel was outside, a bottle—no a crystal decanter!—in his hand. When he returned to his quarters behind the stables, he sat down on a low stool and tried to unravel the riddle that made up the events of the evening.

There was Lord Parsons, who Miss Juliet claimed had tried to buy a kiss from her. Then Daniel had told a bald-faced lie right to Lady Lambert that he cared for a woman who did not exist. And, between all that, Miss Juliet had fallen, and both he and she had told lies about how that had come about. Then there was Miss Juliet touching his arm like she did, and mother and daughter both giving him bottles of drink...

He sighed. None of it made sense as far as he was concerned, and he stared at the crystal decanter, the nicest thing he now owned. Blowing on the inside of the metal mug he took down from a hook on his wall, he poured the smallest amount of brandy, returned the stopper, and placed the decanter on a shelf as if it would break by simply setting it down.

As he sipped at his drink, he shook his head. Although he tried, he could not solve the riddle of all that had happened this night.

Chapter Three

Since Juliet was young, she had anticipated her debut to the *ton* during her first London season. However, fate had played a horrible trick on her in the form of a fall in the stables, and now she would be unable to attend. Her life, now overwhelmed with misery, consisted of lying in bed and missing out on everything that was happening outside her bedroom door.

She was angry at Hannah, who had faked an illness the previous year in order to miss going to London. Now, that same sister would be leaving today with their eldest sister, Isabel. Together, the two women would attend the finest parties, buy the most exquisite of dresses from dressmakers known worldwide. And Juliet would be stuck here at Scarlett Hall.

This was supposed to be Juliet's time to be introduced into society, to be admired and complimented on her beauty. Yet, none of that would happen because of her injured foot, an injury that had come about by her own silliness in a weak attempt to fall into the arms of Daniel the stable hand.

Her plan had been simple. She would lure the man to the loft, where they would share in the wine she had brought. The shock of his refusal to do as she ordered had not only embarrassed her, but it had caused her to lose all awareness of where she was, which, in turn, had caused her to fall from the ladder. She had not expected to break her ankle in the process!

When Doctor Comerford had suggested bed rest, she had been angry, but now her anger turned to jealousy as her sisters entered her bedroom to bid her farewell. They wore beautiful traveling dresses — Hannah in green and white print and Isabel in a blue that matched her eyes — and beamed with excitement. Isabel was positively glowing, and Hannah offered a half-smile. Oh, why had she encouraged Hannah to go? In the beginning it had been to lend aid to Isabel and her mother, but now Hannah would be experiencing everything that Juliet could not. And the woman did not even want to go!

"Oh, Juliet," Isabel said with a sad frown. "I do wish you were going with us today. It will not be the same without you."

Juliet swiped at the single hot tear that escaped her eye. "I know." She turned to Hannah. "The amount of attention the men would have given me would have elevated you in status."

"Perhaps," Hannah replied before taking a seat on the bed beside their cousin Annabel. Isabel joined her on the opposite side. "I am going to miss you, and just as Isabel said, it will not be as fun without you there."

Juliet sighed as she looked at her sisters. They were kind, and she could see the pain in their eyes. The pain of knowing that the most beautiful daughter of the Lambert family was to be left behind. It would not be the same without her there, that much was certain. For wherever Juliet went, be it a party or a shop in the village, she was the focal point of both men and women alike. It was a burden brought on by her beauty and station, and one she carried with as much grace as she could.

"I do have to admit..." Juliet clamped her mouth shut. It was not fair to make her sisters suffer any longer. She did love them and she regretted allowing her anger to get the best of her. Her mother had scolded her often as of late, telling her that she needed to mature. Although Juliet had ignored most of the advice the woman had given, she had to admit that, in this, her mother was correct. "I admit that I am happy for you both. May the season be the best ever."

"You are too kind," Isabel said before leaning over and kissing Juliet on the forehead. "We really should be on our way. I believe

Hannah needs to speak to Mother."

Juliet looked at Hannah, who gave a nod. Hannah had been caught sneaking out of the house, and Juliet had found it extremely amusing. Hannah always acted the innocent, but it was a relief to learn she was not as prudish as Juliet had always thought.

After a few more hugs and goodbyes, the others left Juliet alone with her thoughts. She sighed and leaned back into the mountain of pillows behind her as Daniel came to mind, and she recalled how it felt to be in his arms.

Her goal that night had been to catch his eye, and although she had accomplished her task, it had come at a great cost. Yet, was it enough? She wanted more from the man, but she could not for the life of her figure out what that something was. Perhaps it was a kiss. She could not help but grin as she thought of him kissing her. The poor man would be so overjoyed! However, she would soon grow tired of his ongoing thankfulness.

Despite how appealing kissing the man was, she reminded herself that she was making every attempt to obey her mother's wishes, which came down to one single command. Behave. That was easy for anyone else to say, but for Juliet, she knew she had an impish bone, one that had brought mischief to her at every turn since she was a very young child. Now, as a woman of eighteen, she knew it was high time to put those ways behind her.

Glancing at her wrapped foot propped up on its pillows, she sighed. The doctor had insisted she remain in bed for several days before she could be up and about. He had suggested she use a convalescent chair, but that would require the presence of someone to push her about at all times. Therefore, she had convinced him that she would be better served using a pair of crutches. Her mother had been beside herself at the thought of her daughter using such primitive accessories, but Juliet would not be reliant on another person to move about!

Having an entire week in bed gave her plenty of time to think, and she found her mind thinking of her past and, more importantly, her future. Since she was missing the season, and the doctor had ordered her to be off her feet for several weeks, she had convinced her mother that she would attend any local parties. Although few men remained in the country, most having gone to London themselves, a few she deemed handsome enough remained.

Yet, none compared to Daniel.

It was a shame, really, for if he had money and came from rich stock as she did, perhaps they might have had a future together. However, the man was a child of servants, and she the offspring of the best of society. No, it would never be a successful match, and she found it saddened her somehow.

The door opened, and Juliet smiled as her cousin Annabel returned to the room.

"Oh, Juliet," Annabel fawned, "it pains me to see you in such distress!"

"Fear not. The pain in my foot is nothing compared to the pain in my heart, which comes from knowing that my sisters care nothing for the sacrifice I made in order to ensure their safety."

"The highwayman," her cousin whispered in awe. "You are so brave."

Juliet smiled. Not wishing to reveal the truth to her sisters and cousin, she had told them a tale of a highwayman she saw sneaking onto the property. Following the man to the loft, she found he had disappeared and had called out for Daniel to save her. However, rather than waiting for him to help, she had made the attempt to climb down on her own, thus leading to her fall and subsequent broken ankle.

"I am brave," Juliet replied with a sigh. She looked over the dress Annabel wore. "That dress. Is it new?"

Annabel nodded, her blond curls so much like Isabel's bobbing. A year younger than Juliet, her resemblance to Isabel was almost uncanny with her elegant face and pretty blue eyes. "Your mother purchased it for me. My parents were upset, especially Mother."

Juliet nodded as her cousin lay on the bed beside her.

"Mother does spoil you," Juliet said. "And for good reason. Your parents do not realize what a wonderful daughter they have."

Annabel turned a bright pink. "Thank you," she whispered, although the pain in her eyes was evident. "I hope you do not mind the company. I may be here for a few weeks."

Juliet turned her head to stare at her cousin. "Your parents are leaving again?" she asked in shock. It was true Juliet's mother always spoiled Annabel, but Juliet understood why. Annabel's parents were often away traveling the world. They preferred to leave their only child either with a governess or with the family of her father's brother. She was in attendance at Scarlett Hall so often that she was considered more a sister than a cousin most of the time.

"Well, I do not mind," Juliet said. "You will be able to assist me in the coming months. In exchange for your help, we shall adventure."

"An adventure?" Annabel asked. "What sort of adventure?"

Juliet grinned as she reached under her pillow and produced a bottle of wine. "My innocent cousin," she said, "we will not have just one adventure, but many." She removed the cork and took a sip directly from the bottle before passing it to Annabel.

The girl hesitated only a moment before taking a drink and passing the bottle back to Juliet. "I cannot wait! I think my life is due some excitement."

Juliet sigh. "So is mine," she said, her mind drifting. "Although, I must admit, after Daniel carried me to my room…" She allowed the words to hang in the air, and her cousin gave an expected gasp.

"Carried you to your room?" she asked as she sat up in the bed and stared wide-eyed at Juliet.

"Oh, yes. Did I not tell you?" Juliet asked, and Annabel shook her head. "It was at his insistence. And I was shocked when Mother allowed it. Although I am thankful for what the man did, it was humiliating the way he stared at me." She felt that all too familiar mischievous bone take over as Annabel's face filled with shock.

"How did he stare at you?"

Juliet glanced around the room conspiratorially. "With lust," she whispered. "Drool dripped from his mouth, and he was breathing heavily. Thankfully, Forbes was able to compel the boy to leave."

For some time, Juliet elaborated her tale of Daniel and his rescue of her, and when she spoke his name, it did not escape her notice that her cheeks burned hotter each time.

***

The following morning, Juliet, with the help of Annabel and her mother, rose from the bed and stood on her uninjured foot. She accepted the crutches, which had been delivered the night before, and placed one under each arm. It took her several attempts, but soon she was moving around the room with relative ease.

"Very good," her mother said as Juliet showed off her new skill. "You seem to have little issue with them."

"It is simple, really," Juliet said. "Now I can be free once again to explore the grounds and not be confined to my room."

Her mother gave her a reproachful look. "I am uncertain you should..."

Juliet sighed. "I promise I will take the best of care, and Annabel will be with me. If I find traversing the grounds too difficult, or if I feel it will be overly dangerous, I promise I will ask Annabel to bring me out with the convalescence chair."

"Oh, very well," her mother conceded. "By the way, I will be going into the village today. I shall not be back until dinner, so do spend your time wisely." Her raised brow told Juliet exactly the meaning of her words, which was to keep out of trouble.

"I will mind Annabel," Juliet said with a grin. "Do not worry about her behavior."

Her mother's smile had a strange sadness to it, and the woman placed a hand on Juliet's shoulder. "You were once a tiny spark, but now you are a raging fire." She shook her head. "I will see you this evening."

As soon as she was gone, Juliet turned to her cousin. "Whatever did she mean by that?" she demanded. "I would expect such words from Hannah but most certainly not from her."

Annabel shrugged as she picked up one of Juliet's bottles of perfume. "I believe she means to say that you are wild."

Juliet snorted. "I may not be as tame as other women, but I am by no means wild." She paused. "Am I?"

"I do not think she meant it as an offense," her cousin replied. "In fact, I am certain of it. What she means is that you are a wild fire lighting up the rooms in which you walk. Perhaps in that way you are untamable.

Juliet considered this for a moment. "Yes, that makes sense. It is my spirit combined with my beauty that was once a spark that has now turned into a raging fire." This made her smile all the broader. "I do feel bad for being so beautiful…and for the men who will fail in their attempts to tame me."

"But what of a proper gentleman?" Annabel asked as she returned the perfume bottle to the vanity table. "Will he not be able to tame you?"

Juliet could not help but laugh. "Men are fools," she replied. "Although I do not wish to do so at this moment, I will tell you every secret there is to know about them later."

"I would like that," Annabel said with a smile. "I will need to know as much as I can before my first season next year."

"There is plenty of time to prepare for that." Juliet repositioned the crutches and made her way to the door, her legs reminding her of the pendulum on the large wall clock downstairs. Although—and she would never admit this aloud to a single soul—she did not move as elegantly as the pendulum.

She stopped at the door. "If you would please," she said to Annabel, who jumped forward and opened the door with a quick apology. Juliet stepped through the door and took a deep breath. "It is nice to be free again. Now, let us go straight outside for some air."

They made their way down the long hallway, the paintings on their right depicting several generations of Lamberts, all looking at Juliet with clear admiration for her courage despite her current predicament. In all honesty, that was always how they viewed her, and she could not have felt prouder. Convalescent chair indeed!

When she reached the top of the main staircase, however, her heart skipped a beat. The stairs looked far more imposing than they had since she was a young child. One slip and she would surely break more bones.

"How do you propose going down?" Annabel asked. She glanced over the railing. "Do you suppose I should ask Forbes to help?"

"I can do it," Juliet said defiantly, although her heart was pounding in her chest. "Stand in front of me so that if I do fall, you will be able to help."

Annabel nodded and went to the step second from the top.

Juliet placed one of the crutches, the one on the same side as her uninjured foot, on the next step down. "Do not let me fall, or mother will blame you for my death." Annabel's jaw dropped, and Juliet laughed. "I am only teasing." She returned her concentration to moving the other crutch beside the first and swinging her body down.

"You did it!" Annabel exclaimed with a clap of her hands. "One more!"

Juliet nodded, a bead of sweat forming on her brow as she repeated the same motions with success. Glancing down at the bottom of the staircase, she saw Forbes waiting.

"Miss Juliet," the man said, a look of concern on his face, "may I be of assistance?"

"No, thank you, Forbes," Juliet replied regally. "The doctor advised me to do what I can to regain the strength I lost from so long in bed. I must do this lest I become lame."

The man gave a nod but did not leave. Although each step was difficult to maneuver, and Juliet grew weary with each movement, she managed to make it to the main floor without incident.

"Well done," Annabel said with a tight hug. "I was unsure if you would be able to do it."

Juliet smiled and turned to the butler. "And what do you think, Forbes?"

"In all my years I have never seen such bravery," he replied. "Miss Juliet, your desire to do as you wish amazes me daily."

Annabel snickered, and Juliet frowned. What did he mean by that?

Before she could respond, however, Forbes added, "Would you care to eat? I will bring it to wherever you wish."

Juliet's stomach rumbled in reply, overriding her desire to go outside. "Please," she said. "I suppose we can eat in the drawing room. It will be much more comfortable there."

With a nod, Forbes turned and walked away as the two women made their way to the drawing room. Once there, Juliet tottered to the couch, leaning her crutches on one of the side tables and plopping herself into the cushions with a sigh.

"What shall we do today?" Annabel asked. "Mother has been after me to complete some pieces of embroidery; although, I must admit I find it a bore."

"Embroidery?" Juliet asked with a laugh. She leaned in and lowered her voice. "We are close, would you not say so?"

"Oh, yes," Annabel replied emphatically. "In truth, I must admit that I feel closer to you than your sisters. However, do not tell them so; I would not wish to hurt them."

"I would never do such a thing," Juliet said, and she meant it. It was no surprise she was the favorite, but there was no sense in hurting others by stating the obvious. "As I was saying, embroidery is for old maids and spinsters. We are meant for adventure."

Annabel giggled. "And will we adventure today?"

Juliet smiled. "Oh yes. And you will also learn a bit about men at the same time."

Chapter Four

After a small meal of a selection of fruit and cheese, Juliet donned her favorite coat and made her way down the two steps at the front of the house. With Annabel at her side, she looked around the large property and breathed in the clean air. Numerous trees bereft of leaves lined the drive, and behind them sat rolling hills, the summer green now dormant.

Annabel shivered. "It is cold," she said, her breath creating tiny clouds. "Have you ever wondered how the servants stay warm?"

Juliet paused. "No, I cannot say that I have." She moved the crutches forward. "I suppose they have fires like we do."

Her cousin jumped in front of her, almost making her fall. "I have a secret!" she whispered as her eyes darted around them. "But you must not tell a soul. Please, swear this to me."

Juliet sighed. Such theatrics! "We have already made a pact, or have you forgotten?" She and her sisters, including Annabel, had promised to always love and protect one another for the entirety of their lives. "A bond formed between sisters can never be broken."

"No, I have not forgotten. However, please, swear, for I am all aflutter at speaking about what I must tell you."

Juliet smiled. Although she loved her sisters, Annabel she loved the most. They were beyond cousins; they were true sisters, and Juliet considered the younger girl her closest friend and confidante. "I swear that if I were to tell a single soul what you reveal to me, my foot will rot off and be taken away by a ghost."

Annabel's eyes grew wide, and then both women laughed.

"Now, tell me this secret before we freeze."

Annabel glanced around once more. "I overheard a man speaking in the village not five days ago," she whispered. "It was outside of one of the shops."

"Which shop?" Juliet asked, her curiosity piqued. She was not one for gossip, but a tale or two never hurt anyone.

"There is a new cobbler beside the jeweler's," Annabel replied. "It is not yet open, but that does not matter. What matters is that one of the men said that on cold days like this one, servants..." her voice trailed off and her cheeks became so red, Juliet reached out and confirmed they were burning.

"What?" she demanded, barely able to contain herself. "Do tell me!"

"They get into the same bed and hold one another! Can you imagine?"

Juliet shook her head in disgust. What rubbish! Everyone knew that men and women did not share a bed. Ever.

"Do you think our servants do the same?"

Juliet went to reply no, but she paused. Would Daniel do such a thing? No, of course not. Although the man was a fool at times, he certainly would not participate in such debauchery. "I say absolutely not. Our servants are the most upstanding of their kind. Now, let us continue, for I have much to tell you."

They made their way to the stables, Annabel shivering despite her warm wrap and Juliet keeping warm with the effort of managing the crutches.

"There are two things a woman must understand about men," Juliet said as they traversed the drive, taking care not to misplace one of her crutches and send herself crashing to the ground. "If she understands both of these rules, her life will be filled with jewels, dresses, and invitations to the most important of parties."

"What rules are these?" Annabel asked with clear interest.

"The first is that men must be jealous of any man who wishes to speak to you," Juliet said. "The second is that it is your obligation to make them feel guilty."

"Guilty? Guilty for what?"

Juliet sighed. The poor girl knew nothing about men! It was lucky that she had someone like Juliet to guide her. "Guilty for not adhering to the first rule, which is jealousy. Once they become jealous, you make them feel guilty for feeling so."

Annabel frowned. "But if they are jealous because you want it, is it not wrong to make them feel shame for doing what you want?"

"My dear child, rather than explain this simple notion all day, I shall demonstrate for you. Would that help?"

"Yes, I believe that would," Annabel replied.

Juliet motioned to the smaller of the two doors that led into the stables, and her cousin gasped as if just realizing her error of not opening the door for her. Once inside, the animal stench almost overwhelmed Juliet.

"Now, keep your voice down," Juliet whispered. "The stable boy is often sleeping instead of working, and I do not wish to alert him of my presence."

As they made their way down the central corridor, Juliet was indeed shocked to find Daniel wrapped in his coat and sleeping on a pile of straw in one of the stalls. She could not help but stand gazing at him. He really was a handsome man, especially when he was asleep.

"You were right," Annabel whispered. "He does sleep when he is supposed to be working. What will your punishment be for his idleness?"

"Mother has allowed me to whip his backside," she said, which drew a gasp from Annabel. "However, I will show him mercy just this once. He did carry me to the house when I fell, after all."

When they moved to turn away, Daniel smacked his lips, causing both women to stop in their tracks. Then he turned onto his back and produced a snore loud enough to rattle the floorboards.

Juliet could not cover her mouth fast enough to keep the laugh from erupting from her lips, and she dropped one of her crutches in the process.

Daniel bolted up and swiveled his head back and forth muttering, "What?"

This, of course, sent Juliet into a fit of laughter that caused her side to ache as she leaned against Annabel for support. "That is the funniest sight I have ever seen!" she said through titters. "You snored so loudly, we thought thunder was trapped inside the stables."

The man's face turned a deep crimson and he scrambled to his feet. "I'm sorry, Miss Juliet," he said, keeping his eyes downcast. "I worked late into the night and needed a short rest."

"Do not worry," Juliet said with a wave of her hand before taking her dropped crutch from Annabel. "I am in a good mood today and therefore will be kind."

He nodded with clear relief, and Annabel smiled. Juliet could see the admiration in the girl's eyes.

"Do you like my crutches?" she asked Daniel.

"I do," he said, bringing his eyes up to meet hers. They stood staring at one another for several moments before he looked at Annabel. "Miss Annabel, it's good to see you."

"Thank you," Annabel said, her voice as timid and kind as always.

For a moment, a bolt of resentment coursed through Juliet. Why was Annabel smiling like that at Daniel? She went to say something but stopped. No, this was silly. She had no reason to be jealous of Annabel and Daniel! However, as she looked at one and then the other, she could not stop herself, even when he returned his gaze to Juliet.

"Lord Parsons sent me another letter," she said haughtily. "This time he has increased his offer. I must admit the sum would be sufficient to buy me enough dresses for five seasons, but I am not to be bought."

"I didn't think you could be either," Daniel replied as he walked over to his worktable. "I should get back to my duties for today."

Juliet glanced at Annabel. The girl did not seem all that impressed. What was wrong with her? Well, she would change that immediately. "My foot," she said as she looked down at her wrapped appendage with sadness. "I still cannot fathom you not catching me."

The man remained quiet for a moment and then turned to face them once again. "I have only one regret in life," he said. "That I've failed you." He then gave her a deep bow.

Juliet had always been prone to tales and games such as these, and although they typically brought her joy, she found she did not enjoy it as much in this instance. The man genuinely appeared to be bothered by her words, and it somehow saddened her to see it.

She cleared her throat in an attempt to regain her composure. "I have already forgiven you. Please, return to your duties."

He thanked her and turned back to face the table. He did not even bother to bow one last time as a farewell! The ingrate!

"He does seem upset by what he did," Annabel whispered as they left the stables. "You could see it on his face. I understand what you mean now about guilt."

Juliet nodded. However, her plan had failed once again, for now she was the one who felt guilty, and picturing the sadness written on his face only made her feel worse.

***

A fire roared in the fireplace in the drawing room, and Juliet watched as flames danced around the logs. Her mother had said that she, Juliet, was like a fire, wild and untamed, and Juliet found she had to agree with the woman. Although a member of the *ton*, she had always felt different from the other women. Granted, she enjoyed much of the finer things in life, such as jewelry and gowns, just as her peers; however, there were times when she felt distinctly different.

Whenever she attended a party for one of the other young ladies she knew, they often spoke of becoming wives and baring children. Julie agreed with this aspect of a woman's life, but there was plenty more to do before then. She wished to go on adventures, perhaps to travel abroad and see other places, not simply sit at home and do embroidery. Yet, when she spoke of such dreams with others—bar her sisters and cousin Annabel—they simply politely nodded and promptly changed the subject.

If that was the only thing bothering her at the moment, she would have considered herself content. However, something else prodded at the back of her mind, and if the previous ideas did not shock her peers, this particular idea would have them apoplectic.

The fact of the matter was, over the course of the past year, Juliet was finding herself wishing to be in Daniel's presence more. That in itself would not have been an issue, but rather than spend time telling her tales as she had done since childhood, she found herself watching him as he worked. The more she observed him—sometimes up to an hour at a time—the more she found him fascinating. More often than not, they sat together saying very little. In truth, he was a kind and handsome man; everything a woman would want in a man—except the fact he was of the lower class, of course.

Although she ordered him around like a personal slave, he always did what she requested. He had arranged a meeting place in the forest for Juliet and her sisters, started a fire to welcome them, and even allowed her to pat his head like a dog. Of course, Isabel and her mother had given her a look of scorn, and rightfully so now that she looked back on her actions.

However, it was the manner in which the man had finally looked at her a week ago as she lay cradled in his strong arms for which she had been hoping, and now she wanted to see it again.

Voices from the hall had Juliet sit up straighter, as did Annabel. Her mother entered the room, a beautiful woman despite her age. When she was younger, Juliet had wished she had her mother's light hair and blue eyes, but she had received her father's darker hair and eyes instead, the only one in the family burdened with such striking features. A burden she was well-able to manage.

"How was your outing, Mother?" Juliet asked as her mother joined them in the sitting area. "Did anyone inquire after me?"

"Yes. As a matter of fact, Lord Parsons did."

Juliet thought her heart would leap from her throat, and she grasped her skirts in her fist to keep her features calm. "Oh? And what did you say?"

"I told him about your accident and that you would not be going to London this year. When I mentioned his card, he said he had yet to receive a reply."

That is because I threw the blasted card in the fire, Juliet replied silently. She could not tell her mother the truth in this instance. "The man has probably sent out so many cards he cannot remember which ones have been returned to him," she said aloud. "It does not matter; he will be leaving for London soon, anyway."

It was the manner in which her mother smiled that made Juliet's skin crawl. "I told the man as much," she replied. "What a shame after all the interest you spoke of him."

"You did not share that with him, surely!" Juliet said.

Her mother chuckled. "No. That is not ladylike. However, when I mentioned that you would not be attending, he replied that he has also had to delay his departure."

Juliet shot a glance at Annabel and then looked back at her mother. "I suspect he will be quite busy before he leaves."

Her mother rose from her chair. "I invited him to call over Wednesday next. It will serve as an opportunity to show Annabel how a lady conducts herself in the company of a gentleman."

"Thank you," Annabel said.

Juliet shot her cousin a glare. This was the last thing Juliet wanted! She had no interest in Lord Parsons, nor would she develop any feelings for him. Not as long as Daniel was in her sights.

"You seem anxious." Her mother walked over and placed a hand on Juliet's forehead. "Do you have a fever?"

"I do not believe so," Juliet replied. There had to be a way to keep Lord Parsons from calling. "It is that I am injured, and I do not wish to look unsightly."

Her mother gave her a small upturn of her lips. "I do not believe the man will mind. You should smile, though. I thought the news would make you happy."

Juliet forced one of her best smiles. "I am happy," she said. "I suppose I could say that I am overwhelmed with joy."

"Good," her mother said with a nod. "Lord Parsons is a respectable man, and I am certain an afternoon with him will be enjoyable." She walked to the door and then stopped. "Dinner will be served soon."

Once she left, Juliet let out a heavy sigh.

"Oh, Juliet," Annabel lamented as she reached over and took Juliet's hand in hers. "You must be so happy. Lord Parsons is very wealthy, and I have heard other women speak of how handsome he is."

"Yes," Juliet replied absently. "He is handsome and wealthy." However, that did not intrigue her as it once had. One day, perhaps soon, she would be forced to marry a man of title and wealth, and although the thought of the fine things a man such as Lord Parsons could give her did pique her interest, she knew it would not be Lord Parsons himself who would do the providing. The man was arrogant and spoke too much about himself. Yet, Juliet knew she had to be on her best behavior when the man came to call, for although her mother could be lenient in many ways, this was one time she would not be.

"I will find a gentleman next season," Annabel said as she rose from the couch. "A man unlike any other, who will buy me beautiful things and love me."

"Love," Juliet repeated as she also rose with the aid of her cousin. "That is what all women want, is it not?" Annabel nodded, and Juliet wondered why, after having quite a few gentlemen call and meeting others at parties, she had yet to find it.

Chapter Five

Daniel brushed Penelope, Miss Juliet's horse. Although the woman rarely rode, he always made sure the animal always looked its best. He would never admit it to anyone, but Daniel found great satisfaction in bringing happiness to Juliet, even though doing so in itself was a chore.

As he moved the brush across the horse's flanks, his mind wandered. He had done so much for the young woman in the course of the years he had been in the employ of the family. He had aided her in escaping into the night, performed menial tasks for her, and listened to her endless supply of stories, and the fact was that he was very much inclined toward her. Oftentimes he even imagined himself being married to her.

"But that is a dream for fools," he whispered to Penelope. The horse whinnied in response as if to say she agreed with him.

Although Daniel could not read or write, he was smart enough to know that Miss Juliet was only playing with him with all her requests and elaborate stories. He would never dare call her a liar, but he was sure most of her tales were not entirely the truth. Especially those that were so farfetched, such as highwaymen hiding in the lofts of the stables, or men offering her vast sums of money for a kiss, or princes from faraway lands wanting to marry her.

He did not care that those tales were fabricated. Just listening to the sound of her voice was enough to bring him joy, for much like her spirit, it was simply beautiful.

Thinking of her made his heart happy, but he knew the truth: a stable hand and the daughter of a baron had no chance of a life together, not in the matrimonial sense, that is. She was a woman who lived a life of luxury, who had the finest of clothes and the best of everything. A life he could never afford to give her even if she looked his way. Scarlett Hall had a drawing room with far more wealth than he could have earned in his entire lifetime! No, he could never come close to providing for her to the extent to which she was accustomed.

"Those foolish dreams are nice enough," he whispered as he patted the horse. "But it would be like you standing beside a donkey. And I'm that donkey."

The horse nodded its head, and Daniel laughed. Yes, even she agreed with him.

Walking back to his work area, he returned the brush to its shelf and thought about what more he needed to finish for the day. He had already completed his usual chores.

Then his eyes fell on the saddle he had been working on when Miss Juliet fell from the ladder. The woman had not seemed overly pleased with his work thus far, and he knew he had more to do. So, he grabbed the necessary tools and a few strips of leather, pulled the stool in front of the table, and studied the saddle.

His plan was to emboss her name on the flap on either side, and he smiled as he thought of her reaction to his work.

Before he could begin, however, the sound of a horse approaching made him stand. He buttoned up his coat and hurried to the stable door. Before him stood a large chestnut mare, the owner of the animal perhaps two or three years older than Daniel's nineteen years. With his strikingly blond hair and upturned nose, the man reeked of arrogance.

"Well, do not simply stand there, boy," the man said. "Guide my horse in so it may rest."

"My apologies," Daniel said. He took the reins and led horse and rider into the stables. As he waited for the man to dismount, Daniel could not help but wonder who he was. But, it was of no concern to a stable hand; his only job was to see the horse cared for while the man called at the great house. The coat the man wore was one of the finest

Daniel had ever seen, and not for the first time, he felt ill at ease in his own coat.

"Does the lady of the house not pay you enough?" the man demanded as he looked Daniel up and down.

"She does, sir."

"My dogs sleep in better clothing than what you wear," he said with a shake to his head. "Stable my horse and be certain she is fed and watered."

"Yes, sir."

"Lord Parsons," the man said smugly.

Daniel stopped and looked at the man. It was the same name Miss Juliet had given as the man who wished to buy kisses from her, if Daniel remembered correctly. Well, he might not believe the story about the kisses, but the man was certainly real.

"You stare at me as if you have heard my name before," Lord Parsons said as he came to stand in front of Daniel, his hands on his thighs. Although they were of the same height, the man's obvious wealth made Daniel feel smaller somehow. "Well, speak, boy!"

"Yes, Lord Parsons. I have heard your name."

"From Miss Juliet?"

Daniel nodded.

"Ah, so you eavesdrop, then?"

"No, my Lord," Daniel replied with a shake of his head. "Not exactly. It's just that Miss Juliet tends to speak aloud. I can't help if I happen to hear some of what she says."

The man's solemn face changed, and he barked a loud laugh. "That is true," he said and then clapped Daniel on the shoulder. "Women are prone to such things." His breath smelled of alcohol, and Daniel had to fight himself from taking a step back. "Is there anything else you heard her say?"

"No, my lord."

"Well, you be sure to tell me anything you happen to hear. Miss Juliet is very important to me, and I can pay well if you relay any information you might learn."

"Yes, my lord," Daniel replied, although it was a lie. Something about the man did not sit well with him, and Daniel would tell him nothing.

Lord Parsons turned and left the stables, leaving Daniel to care for his horse. As Daniel poured oats into a feedbag, he thought about the man's words. Lord Parsons was interested in Miss Juliet, and by all accounts, he wanted to make her happy. However, did the man actually accomplish this?

Once the horse was placed in one of the stalls, Daniel returned to his worktable and traced a hand over the saddle. Just minutes before, he had been excited to put her name on the leather, a sign of his dedication to making her happy. That joy, however, had faded as reality seeped in.

Daniel might care for Miss Juliet, but Lord Parsons was the kind of man Daniel could never be—a man of title and wealth who could provide a life Daniel never could. For he was the son of a barmaid, and he did not know his father. When his mother died, Daniel had only been ten years of age, and had been forced to live in the streets. However, he had survived on luck and perseverance.

Well, he might not be able to have the pleasure of taking Miss Juliet as his wife, or of enjoying the feeling of her lips upon his, but he could still make her happy.

So, with a smile, he picked up his tool and leaned over the saddle. He would make sure it was the finest work he had ever done.

***

As Lord Parsons prattle on about nothing of any particular interest, Juliet could not keep her mind from wandering. Although she often thought of herself as the wisest, not only of her sisters but of all women of the *ton*, a realization hit her so hard that she almost spit out her tea.

Her mind had somehow returned to the night when she injured her foot and her mother had questioned Daniel. Juliet had thought it odd when her mother gave a sigh of relief followed by a proclamation as to the wonderfulness of Daniel caring for this other woman, this

Elizabeth. Who was Elizabeth, and why was her mother so interested in a relationship between servants?

Now, as Lord Parsons droned on about yet another meeting in which he had been involved, Juliet realized she had puzzled out this particular riddle. Her mother was not as naive as Juliet had suspected, and the woman had become aware of Juliet's growing interest in Daniel. It had been Juliet's hope that, by swearing off any such notion, her mother would leave it at that. Granted, Juliet would never engage in any romantic notions with a stable boy, but she also did not want her mother to keep her from spending time with him. He *was* her only form of entertainment!

The fire crackled, and Juliet smiled at Lord Parsons in order to study him. She supposed he was not unfortunate looking, and his coat was, in fact, very nice. And as Annabel had mentioned before, the man was indeed wealthy, so he did have some good qualities. All those combined meant one thing: Juliet needed to convince her mother that she was, indeed, intrigued by this man in order to keep the woman from learning the truth about her infatuation with Daniel. It was as simple as that.

"And now I find myself not in London as I had hoped to be," Lord Parsons said, breaking Juliet from her thoughts. Had he changed topics again? She was uncertain, for she had not been listening once again. "I must admit, however, I do find myself in much better company."

Juliet glanced at her mother, who gave her a nod of encouragement. Earlier, Juliet had sworn to appease the woman, but now she had to do more to keep her mother believing she had no interest in Daniel.

"Lord Parsons," she said in a sweet tone she knew he enjoyed, "may I ask a question?"

"Please do," the man replied. He sat with his back so straight, Juliet wondered if his clothes ever wrinkled.

"How does a gentleman ever find the time to seek his own pleasure in sports or other activities when he is always conducting business?"

The man sighed. "That is the problem, is it not? It is that exact issue that prevented me from attending the season thus far. Yet, my plan is to work and grow my business now in order to allow myself more time for leisure once I am married."

His eyes locked with Juliet's and a small smile played on his lips. Although she returned his smile, she did not like the look in his eyes. It made her feel as if he was peeking at her through her bedroom window as she dressed, and she was glad when he turned his gaze to her mother.

"Lady Lambert, are all of your daughters this wise? Truly, I must admit I have never had a more engaging conversation than I am at this moment."

"You are kind," her mother replied. "Unlike some women of our station, Juliet has been allowed to seek knowledge, something both myself and her father encouraged all our daughters to do."

For a moment, Juliet's heart pained her at the thought of her father. He had been a kind and caring man, and she missed him terribly. She would never admit it to her sisters, but she was well aware that she had been his favorite.

"Ah, yes, Lord Lambert," Lord Parsons said with a sigh. "He was an honorable man and one worthy to always be spoken of in reverence. I only had the honor of meeting the man once when I was younger, but his demeanor was always one to which I aspired."

Juliet found his words kind, and yet somehow she did not believe them. That was unfair. Perhaps the man meant what he said, and she misinterpreted his tone, which was highly likely since her focus was on maintaining her composure for her mother's sake.

They continued with polite conversation. Annabel, who sat beside Juliet on the couch, remained quiet. How difficult it must have been for her to endure a man calling on Juliet. However, she was only a year away from her debut into society; she would simply have to wait just as Juliet had.

Lord Parsons set his teacup on the table and smiled at Juliet. "Do you know when you will be able to walk again; without the aid of crutches of course?"

Finally, the man asked a question about her! "Doctor Comerford believes perhaps another month," Juliet replied. "That is my wish, for I desperately need to leave the house." She smiled, but it slipped when she glanced at her mother and saw the frown the woman wore.

"Not that I mind being home, mind you. I simply miss being outside."

"I understand," Lord Parson replied. "Perhaps I might be of help."

Now it was Juliet's turn to frown. *Oh, bother. Now he believes he must save me. How tiresome!*

"Lady Lambert, I must leave tomorrow for business but will return in a fortnight. I would like your permission that, upon my return, I take Miss Juliet for a ride in my carriage."

Juliet had to bite her tongue to keep from screaming. This was *not* what she had in mind!

Her mother, unsurprisingly, replied, "That is a wonderful invitation. I think it would be a grand outing. Do you not believe so, Juliet?"

All eyes turned to Juliet, and she felt as if her veins had filled with ice. If she refused or made any excuse, it would only grow her mother's suspicion. However, if she agreed, it might give Lord Parsons the idea that she did, indeed, have an interest in him. *Oh, bother!*

"Juliet?"

Juliet swallowed hard and turned to the man. "My apologies. I was just thinking how lovely that would be. I would be honored to go on a carriage ride with you." The lie burned worse than the brandy she was determined to drink when this blasted encounter came to a close. However, she had no choice but to agree. For now. She would come up with one excuse or another when the time came to actually go with the man.

"Excellent," Lord Parsons replied. He rose from his chair. "I shall call over in two weeks this Sunday." His eyes met Juliet's and she could not help but tremble with uneasiness. "Lady Lambert." He gave her a bow. "Miss Annabel." Another bow. "It has been a pleasure."

Juliet's mother rose, as well. "Thank you for calling. We look forward to seeing you upon your return." She led him from the room, and when the door closed, Annabel placed a hand to her breast.

"How wonderful!" she squealed. "He is very handsome, and did I mention he is well-off? But he wishes to go on an outing with you!"

"Yes, wonderful," Juliet mumbled, but when her mother returned, she forced her smile back onto her face. "I am so happy," she said.

"What a fine gentleman. And to think he wishes to see me again! I did not believe he would."

"It is because of your beauty," her mother said as she took Juliet's hands in hers. "You are bright and intelligent, and that did not seem to deter him one bit. Perhaps, in time, he may wish to court you."

Juliet nodded. "I would like nothing more," she said, although her stomach was flopping around inside her. Just the thought made her feel feint, and she was not prone to fainting spells. She attempted to get moisture back into her mouth. "Thank you for arranging this day. It means much to me."

Her mother hugged her and surprised her by whispering in her ear, "I was worried that...No, it does not matter. What does matter is that you have got the eye of a gentleman."

"Yes, I suppose I have," Juliet replied, although when she said so, she thought of Daniel.

Chapter Six

S now fell overnight a week after Lord Parson's visit, leaving a light dusting for as far as Juliet could see from inside the carriage. With Annabel at her side, the two women were on their way to Rumsbury to look at the new plates at the dressmakers in hopes of ordering one or two new dresses and perhaps a new gown each.

At first, her mother had told her she could not go, but Juliet persisted, assuring the woman that her foot was neatly wrapped and she would take the utmost care while traversing the footpaths. Forbes had also wrapped the bottoms of her crutches with rags to keep them from slipping on the already drying paths.

Juliet attempted to push away the thoughts of Lord Parsons' return, which would be in nine days, but to no avail. The thought of being with the man made her want to sick up, for she had no interest in him whatsoever. However, she had no one to blame for her current predicament than herself, for it was her stories—others would call them lies but she knew better—that had landed her in the fire. She had yet come up with a plan that was feasible enough to get her out of the outing with him, and she rarely failed in getting her way. This would be no different, but she would have to devise the perfect plan, for her mother would accept nothing less than perfect.

As the carriage trumbled down the road, she found her mind turning to her sisters. Hannah had accompanied Isabel and Laurence to London, and she felt a pang of jealousy at the fact they would be soon readying themselves for one party or another while she remained home awaiting the arrival of a man she could barely stand.

"Do you believe my parents love me?"

Annabel's question caught Juliet off-guard. "Yes, they love you. Why would you ever ask such a thing?"

The girl did not turn her gaze from the window. "It is that they are always away and leave me at Scarlett Hall." She turned, and Juliet was shocked to see tears rimming her eyes. "Not that I do not enjoy my time there, mind you, for you are all like sisters to me. But I do not understand why my parents always leave me behind. It is as if they do not want me with them."

Juliet's heart went out to her cousin as she tried to determine how best to respond. It was no secret that Juliet and her mother disapproved of the manner in which her uncle and aunt treated Annabel, but they also would never tell Annabel their feelings. And although Juliet had learned her lesson as of late concerning the telling of tales, she knew in her heart that, in this instance, it was necessary.

"I must confess something I overheard nearly a year ago," she said with a small smile. "Now, I was caught eavesdropping and therefore sworn to secrecy, but I believe our pact is stronger than my oath to them."

"To whom?" Annabel asked. "What did you swear to keep secret?"

Juliet shifted her body so she could look directly at her cousin. "Your parents and my mother, of course. I was on my way to the drawing room from the garden when I heard voices in Father's office. I overhead your parents voicing their concern for your beauty."

"My beauty?" Annabel asked with a gasp. "They do not believe I have any?" She had a panic to her voice, and Juliet reached over and grabbed her hand.

"Not at all," she said with a laugh. "In fact, quite the opposite. You see, there are women such as myself and you who are so beautiful, they cause parents to worry. If your parents were to allow you to go with them on their travels, they are afraid a gentleman would take you away from them. So, in their great wisdom, which I understand quite well, they decided to leave you with us."

Annabel smiled. "Is this true?"

Juliet nodded, but she could not say the words.

"So, I am beautiful and not a burden on them?"

Juliet sighed. "Of course you are beautiful. I must admit, and it pains me to say so, but I oftentimes am envious of your beauty. Look at the lovely color of hair with which you have been blessed! And your mind and heart are so appealing, I am surprised you are not already married."

The smile Annabel wore was well worth the story, for all of her sadness disappeared, replaced by a joy that made her face brighten. "Thank you. And I believe your hair is beautiful, as well."

"It is 'the color of the night sky'," Juliet said, quoting her father. "A gift only I received, much to the dismay of my sisters."

The carriage came to a stop, and Juliet could not wait to exit the vehicle. It had been over a month since she had been to Rumsbury, and she had no doubt many passersby would stop to inquire as to how she injured her foot.

The door opened, and Annabel helped Juliet alight from the carriage. When Juliet had the crutches placed under her arm, she glanced around expectantly but was disappointed at the number of people out and about. Granted, it was a chilly day, and many people would have left for London for the season, but that did not say there would be so few doing some sort of business in the village.

"Wait here," she said to the driver. "We will only be a few hours."

The driver bowed as Juliet repositioned her crutches. Then, she and Annabel began the slow amble down the footpath, which had already been cleared of the bit of snow and was as dry as if it had never snowed at all—much to Juliet's relief.

They stopped and looked through the window of the butcher's shop. A man in a white apron, as wide as he was tall, sliced at a piece of flesh.

"Did you know the man had eleven children?" Juliet asked. Annabel shook her head in reply. "They all went missing. Every single one of them. Although," she glanced around them and lowered her voice, "I heard he killed them."

Annabel's eyes widened. The butcher turned toward them, the knife raised above him. Annabel let out a shriek so loud that Juliet was overcome with laughter.

"Come," Juliet said. "Let us leave before he decides to kill us!"

"You are incorrigible," Annabel said, although she also laughed. "I can never determine when you are telling the truth or when you are lying at times."

The dress shop was ten shops ahead, but Juliet enjoyed stopping and peering into every shop along the way. The stopped in front of one that had been empty for several years. It had no signage, and the facade was an odd gray, as if it had not been painted in several decades, which more than likely it had not. In the one large window was a display of women's shoes—some with numerous buttons, others simple slippers, as well as the finest riding boots Juliet had ever seen.

"This is the new cobbler's about which I spoke," Annabel said. "Shall we go in?"

"Oh, yes," Juliet replied.

Annabel held the door as Juliet managed the single step through the door. She glanced around, but no shopkeeper was in sight. Along one wall sat two benches upon which clients could sit to try on shoes and be measured for others. Along the opposite wall were several shelves with more samples of the wares. A simple unpainted wood counter was at the end of the short room, a white door behind it.

"Ah, good morning!" a man said as he came through the white door. He was close to forty with dark hair and eyes and a kind smile. However, for a shopkeeper, his clothes were of poorer quality than most, covered with patches and tattered hems. "My name is Robert Mullens, and I am your faithful cobbler here to serve you." He bent to give them a bow but then pretended to lose his balance, his arms flailing at his sides as he wobbled from one leg to the other.

Juliet and Annabel giggled as the man straightened himself with a wide grin, as if entertaining them gave him as much enjoyment as it gave them.

"Forgive me," he said. "It is not every day ladies such as yourselves enter my shop. I am overcome with honor at your presence."

"Thank you, Mr. Mullens," Juliet said. She was unsure why, but she immediately liked the man. "My cousin, Annabel, mentioned your shop to me. I believe you have a fine selection of shoes. I am particularly interested in a new pair of riding boots."

"You're correct, Miss," the man replied as he walked over to a shelf. "My wares are of the finest craftsmanship." He looked down at her foot. "Oh, begging your pardon, but may I ask what happened?"

"It was a highwayman," Juliet replied. "I chased him into the stables and thought I had him cornered in the loft. I climbed up the ladder only to find he had escaped, and from there, I am afraid I fell."

The man shook his head in apparent sympathy. "My shop is now inhabited by women of great bravery," he said in a diffident tone. "I presume you are brave as well?" he asked Annabel, who simply nodded. "Very well, then. Please have a look at my wares. I am able to craft any shoe you would like. And because of your bravery, I will spend extra time to be certain they are perfect."

"You are kind," Annabel said. "Thank you, Mr. Mullens."

The man clicked his tongue. "Please, call me Robert. All my friends do."

Juliet glanced at Annabel, who was looking at her. Only close friends and family called each other by their Christian name, but the man seemed kind enough. And he did insinuate that they were friends.

"I am Annabel Lambert," her cousin said before turning toward Juliet. "This is my cousin, Miss Juliet Lambert."

The man's eyes went wide for a moment, but then he was all smiles and bowing once again. "You are the daughter of Lady Eleanor Lambert of Scarlett Hall, I presume?"

"You are correct," Juliet replied with a wide grin. "I assume you have heard of me?" She was not surprised, really; most people knew of her.

The man replied with a nod but remained staring at her for several moments before replying. "I am new to Rumsbury, but I have heard much of Lady Lambert and her daughters, all women of great renowned beauty and minds." He looked at Annabel. "And their cousin, of course. I am humbled to be in your presence."

Juliet's spirits had been lifted higher than she had expected when she left the house this morning. "Please, there is no need to compliment us on our minds and beauty. It is a burden we both share."

Annabel nodded her agreement but did not respond.

"Well, then," Robert said. "Why do you not have a seat on the bench while I collect a few samples of shoes I believe will interest you. I will only be gone a moment."

Juliet smiled and moved to the benches, relieved to be able to sit once again.

Annabel sat beside her and leaned in closer. "I do not believe that man's words were appropriate."

"What do you mean?" Juliet asked. She enjoyed what he had to say immensely, so she could not understand what concerns her cousin would have. Well, she was a young girl still, after all.

"Speaking of our beauty?" her cousin asked. "No gentleman speaks to us so openly, not one we have just met, anyway. I do not think him civil."

Juliet glanced at the white door. "My dear, he is merely a cobbler, a common man. Do you not recall what I told you in the carriage of our beauty, or more so yours?"

"Yes, but…"

"Did you not hear the man's words?" Juliet interrupted. "Words of your beauty have already reached him. If he wishes to gaze upon us, although it makes him appear a fool, then we should allow him to do so."

Annabel pursed her lips. "I suppose there is no harm in it. His words were not crass, after all."

"That is what I meant. As long as we conduct ourselves as ladies, we have nothing to fear."

"You are right," Annabel replied, although she still appeared dubious. "Forgive me for worrying, as I tend to do."

Juliet gave her cousin a smile. "Do not worry. If the man behaves as a beast, I shall protect you." She raised one of the crutches and jabbed it in the air like a sword to punctuate her words, which made Annabel giggle.

"You are the brave one," Annabel said and then giggled again.

When Robert emerged from the other room, he carried a single riding boot in his hand. "Miss Juliet," he said, coming to stand before them, "this is the latest fashion from Paris, and I have not made a pair for anyone yet. May I humbly ask your thoughts?"

"Yes, of course," Juliet replied, elated he thought her opinion would be so valuable. The boot was impressive, made of soft brown leather that changed from light to darker tones top to bottom. "I wish to be the first to own them," she said firmly, although she would be unable to wear them for some time. Plus, she did very little riding as it was. Regardless, she would be the envy of the other women of the *ton*. "You will be willing to bill my mother, will you not?"

"I am afraid I cannot charge you," Robert said.

"Whyever not?"

Robert laughed. "What I mean is, may I ask a favor?"

Juliet nodded. What could this man wish from her?

"As I said before, ladies such as yourself have not yet graced my shop. If I were to make a pair of these boots for you, at no charge, of course, would you be kind enough to tell the women who admire them where you purchased them?"

Juliet could not believe her good fortune. Although she had always looked down on the common people, this man was far wiser than any she had ever met. Not only did he recognize her status and beauty, he somehow knew how others looked to her in admiration.

"I believe we have an agreement," Juliet replied. "Although, with the many parties and other events I must attend, I may require more shoes."

She thought the man would laugh at her suggestion, but instead he smiled. "It would be an honor," he replied.

Juliet glanced at Annabel, and for a moment she felt bad that the man had not offered her the same. However, it would be rude to ask him to do so. Furthermore, the girl would never be able to handle the attention she would gain from their peers; not in the same way Juliet could.

"Allow me to measure your foot," Robert said.

Juliet could not help but smile. When she turned to Annabel, she was pleased to see that her cousin was smiling as well. It was smiles such as these to which Juliet looked forward.

Chapter Seven

Juliet stood beside Annabel in the drive of Scarlett Hall, the afternoon sun melting away any remnants of snow that remained. Although Juliet had returned home with her spirits lifted at the prospect of new riding boots, the sight of the stables brought a sorrow to her heart. She had not ventured inside them to see Daniel since Lord Parsons had called the previous week. It was as if her agreement to accompany the man on an outing had brought about a bout of guilt and somehow broke a sacred bond between her and Daniel.

"Did you wish to go to the stables?" Annabel asked, a package of brown wax paper containing the new gloves they had purchased in her hands.

"I was thinking of Penelope," Juliet lied. "Come, I would like to check on her."

Annabel glanced at the front door of the house. "Your mother will not mind? I thought she warned you about going there."

"Alone, yes," Juliet replied with a jut to her chin. "However, you are with me, so there is no need to worry. Besides, the woman is probably locked away in her office again, so there is little chance she will learn of it."

"Why does she do that?" Annabel asked. "I remember her always being happy and spending time with us. What has changed?"

"It is the worry Hannah causes her at the moment, I am certain," Juliet replied. "Before that," she shrugged, "I am uncertain, but I suspect it had to do with Isabel. My sisters have always caused her great heartache. However, it does not matter, for all she cares about now is that I entertain Lord Parsons."

"You speak as if you have no interest in the man," her cousin said as they reached the door to the stables. "I thought you liked him."

Juliet snorted. "He is a fool, a man consumed with brandy and arrogance. I only agreed to his invitation to please Mother." When Annabel pursed her lips, Juliet spoke before the girl could ask another question. "Let us see what the stable boy is doing."

Annabel opened the door and they entered the stables. Juliet searched for Daniel, but when she could not see him, she led Annabel further down the corridor. More than likely he was in the back at the worktables.

When they rounded the corner, Juliet felt a sense of pleasure when, indeed, Daniel sat at his table, this time with a book in his hands. Then she frowned as he spoke, his voice loud.

"'J. This is a J.'"

Juliet took a moment to look the man over. Why did he not buy himself a new coat? The one he wore was as tattered as that of a street urchin.

"'This is a...'" He slammed the book shut. "I can't do this. I'll never learn."

"You are reading?" Juliet asked.

Daniel jumped from the stool, his eyes wide with alarm. "Miss Juliet. Miss Annabel. I did not hear you come in."

Juliet smiled, her heart warming at seeing his face. "We are quiet when we walk, a trait we were taught by a scoundrel from Scotland."

Daniel smiled and clasped his hands in front of him, but he said nothing.

"Were you reading?"

"I..." He glanced at the book he had thrown on the table and then looked back at them. "I don't know how to read. I mean, I know some letters, and I'm trying to learn, but it's hard to remember what I learned when I was young."

"That is a noble effort," Juliet said. "Although, I do not believe it will be of much good to you, especially one of your position."

Daniel reddened further and looked down at the floor as he nodded.

Juliet studied the man. How was it that she, the most beautiful woman of the *ton*, could stand before him, yet he spent the majority of their time together looking down at the floor? Granted, he did speak to her when she asked a question, and she caught him sneaking glances at him when he thought she was not watching. However, it made little sense that he was not awestruck enough by her beauty to be unable to keep his eyes off her. Never had he ever even commented on such an important aspect of who she was.

Well, she would get him to admit that which she wished to hear! She took a step toward him, her crutches making a light *thump*. "I have good news to share. The new cobbler in the village? When we introduced ourselves to him, he nearly fainted from shock for having ladies of beauty in his presence. Did that not happen, Annabel?"

"It most certainly did," her cousin replied with a proud nod.

"That's nice to hear," Daniel said.

"Indeed," Juliet replied. "However, that is not all. The latest fashion in riding boots has arrived from Paris, and he is not only making a pair for me so I am the first to own them, but he says he cannot charge me, for my beauty is that great."

"I'm happy for you," Daniel said, although he did not appear all that happy. "I should return to work; my break is over."

As he turned his back to her and reached for a tool on the table, Juliet felt a bolt of anger course through her. Why did the man not smile at her as he once had? Her last few attempts at getting him to do so had failed, and it annoyed her greatly.

She gave him a derisive sniff. "You must buy a new coat. Yours is far too worn and makes you look dreadful."

As soon as the words left her mouth, she regretted them and even more so upon seeing the man turn and face her. His eyes were filled with pain as he brushed at the tattered material.

"You're right," he said. "Lord Parsons told me the same. I suppose I should heed his advice, and yours, and buy one when I have enough money."

Guilt coursed through Juliet. Why did she say such things? "I am sorry," she said, taking another step toward him. "I did not mean to speak to you in such a horrible manner. Please, forgive me."

"No, you're only saying what's true," he replied. "And Lord Parsons is a man of stature. I should be thankful he thought enough of me to point it out."

Annabel moved closer to one of the work benches and began fiddling with some of the tools, but Juliet barely took notice.

"Your coat will do," Juliet said, lowering her voice so only he could hear her. "May I ask something."

The man frowned. "You can ask me anything, Miss Juliet."

Juliet's heart beat against her chest, and she felt lightheaded. "These men, they tell me I am beautiful, but I am curious as to what you believe."

When he looked back up at her, he had an earnestness she had rarely seen in him. "Those men are right, Miss Juliet. I've told you before, and my answer remains the same."

She sighed. Why did he not simply say the words? "I ask you again. What do you think? Am I beautiful?"

All went quiet except the light whinnying of the horses and the rattle of one of the shutters that covered the windows. After what seemed like years, Daniel finally replied, "Lord Parsons is a fortunate man to be in your company. I hope he appreciates it." He returned to his worktable, turning his back to her.

Juliet shook her head. What was so difficult about saying a woman was beautiful? Even the lowly cobbler, a man she had never met before today, said the words. Yet, this man before her, who she had known since they were children, refused to speak them.

There was a far greater question, however. Why did it matter so much to her? Why did she need confirmation from a stable boy when she already knew the truth herself?

Regardless, his unwillingness to say what she wished pained her, and so, she decided she would pay him in kind.

"I am leaving with him next week to go on a carriage ride. I will have to endure his speaking highly of me for some time."

"That's good." The boy did not even bother to turn to face her! If her foot did not pain her so much, she would have stomped it.

Annabel joined them, and Juliet did her best to flounce on her crutches. "Have a new coat by next month, or Mother will have you thrown out into the streets," she called over her shoulder as she fought back tears that filled her eyes. Then with a quick nod at Annabel, she headed to the stable doors, leaving the blasted stable boy to whatever work he had to complete.

***

Large snowflakes floated to the ground as Juliet gazed out the drawing room window. The landscape was a blanket of white, and tree branches hung low with the weight they carried. Five days had passed since she had said those horrible words to Daniel, and the guilt had plagued her since. Her reaction confused her, for she did not understand what could possibly compel her to want to hear him call her beautiful. His status was much too low to consider his opinion of any importance, and few men or women of the *ton* would take a moment's notice of the man.

Yet, that was how she was different. She had a desire to look upon his handsome features, even if he was only a stable hand, and all she asked in return was for him to tell her that he thought her lovely. Although his eyes had sparkled the night he carried her into the house after her fall, he had not looked at her that way since, and that, too, bothered her.

Despite her concern for his lack of admiration, something else, something quite strange and unfamiliar, bothered her. What had driven her to be so cruel? By all accounts, she should apologize to the man. It would not be the first time she had made her apologies for unkind words; however, in the past she had only spoken such words to men of greater standing. Daniel was a simple servant and she a lady.

In fact, her words had been in direct frustration of being reminded that she was to accompany Lord Parsons, and therefore she had been heartless. It was not Daniel's fault she had agreed to the outing, but he had broad shoulders that could carry the burden of her frustration.

She remembered watching the poor boy attempting to read. He was nineteen! How was it he was in the employ of one of the greatest families in England and he had never learned to read?

The door opened and she watched the reflection of her mother entering the room.

"There are many activities to keep a young lady busy. Surely gazing out the window for hours is not one of them."

Juliet wanted to remind her mother that she had done the same on many occasions over the last few years, but she bit back the retort. "I have been thinking."

"Of what?"

Juliet sighed. "A gentleman."

"Would this gentleman be addressed as Lord Parsons?" her mother asked as she joined Juliet beside the window. She wore a wide smile, and Juliet did not have the heart to tell her the truth.

Juliet nodded, but her thoughts were on Daniel.

"And what, pray tell, would be in your thoughts concerning him?"

"When does a man tell a woman she is beautiful?" Juliet asked.

Her mother smiled and put her arm through Juliet's. "A time comes when a man realizes how he feels concerning a woman, but it depends on the man. When he is ready, he will utter the words from his heart."

"And what if he does not? Does it mean he does not care for her?"

Her mother sighed. "Men often find it difficult to speak of their feelings. Lord Parsons does not know you well enough to express such sentiments. Do you wish him to do so?"

Juliet nodded. "I do."

Her mother chuckled. "You have never been one for patience," she said. "Do not worry; in time, Lord Parsons will come to feel for you as I suspect you do for him."

"My feelings…" She focused her thoughts on Daniel once again, exchanging his name for that of Lord Parsons in her mind. "I do wish more than anything to hear him speak those words. I just know it will bring me the greatest of happiness."

"I imagine it will. For love is a beautiful thing."

Juliet shook her head. "I believe you may have misunderstood. I do not have any notion of love toward Lord Parsons." *Or even Daniel*, she amended silently. "I simply wish him to call me beautiful."

"My sweet Juliet," her mother said as she brushed a strand of hair from Juliet's face, "the fire inside you rages. You hold such passion, and although you do not realize it yet, what you are wanting just happens to be the first step toward love."

Juliet nearly fell over and had to adjust her crutches. She, Miss Juliet Lambert, perhaps the most beautiful woman the *ton* had ever laid eyes on, falling in love with a stable boy? The idea was ludicrous!

However, as her mind went over the many conversations she and Daniel had shared over the years—not her admonishments but the true conversations they had shared--she had to wonder if there was not a bit of truth to her mother's words. Whatever she asked, Daniel did without hesitation. Yet, he was her servant and was meant to do as she requested. Was that not to be expected? Therefore, did he do so out of obligation or because he cared?

The more she considered it, the more confused she became.

"Juliet?"

"I am sorry," she whispered, frightened of the prospect of having feelings for Daniel, a man who was not of her station.

"Do not worry," her mother said as she patted Juliet's hand. "There is plenty of time to spend with Lord Parsons. Once your foot is healed, I had hoped to visit your sisters in London. I imagine that, now that you have gained an interest in Lord Parsons, perhaps you will wish to remain here rather than accompany me?"

The parties, the dresses, all of London was eagerly waiting for Juliet to arrive. However, as she thought of those things, an image of Daniel came to mind. No, she needed to remain and work out her feelings.

"You are correct, as always," she said. "I will remain here in order to continue seeing Lord Parsons."

Her mother smiled. "You have no idea how happy it makes me to hear you say that. I thought perhaps..." Her words trailed off, and Juliet frowned.

"Thought what?"

"That you had an admiration for the stable boy," her mother replied with a small laugh. "Now I realize it was simply company you sought, and I am pleased you found it with Lord Parsons."

Juliet smiled. So, her suspicions of her mother had been correct. The woman had taken notice of her actions toward Daniel. At least the ruse of holding an interest had removed all suspicion.

"Mother," she said with a laugh, "I am many things, but to believe I would lower myself to consider a servant in that way? They are far beneath us, and he is lucky I even take the time to speak to him at all. In fact, I often wonder about those without the blood we carry through our veins."

Her mother turned and looked at her. "What blood?" she asked.

"Why, that of society, of course. That is what makes us far better than those equal to the animals." She clamped her mouth shut when she saw the anger in her mother's features. She had not meant the words, only speaking them as a way to ease the woman's suspicions and to keep her from examining the possibility of Juliet's interest in Daniel. And now that she had said them, she felt a shame she had never experienced in all her life.

"We are fortunate to be in the position we are in life," her mother admonished. "The servants may be in a lower station than us, but they are just as human as we are. Humans who suffer, who laugh and who cry, and who dream of better lives for themselves and their children. It would serve you well to remember that. I never again want to hear you speak of them with such harsh words."

Juliet had never seen her mother so angry, especially over the servants, but she nodded, nonetheless. "Yes, Mother. I am sorry." In truth, she was.

"It is not good enough to be sorry," her mother scolded. "You must understand their position, as well. Do you believe they do not have their own dreams? Futures they wanted...or did not want? Dreams that their children have a better life than they had been forced to live?"

Juliet stared at her mother, her eyes wide. "I suppose I have never considered it."

Her mother took a deep breath, as if to calm herself. "You are my daughter, and I love you. Consider taking this next hour before dinner to think on what we have discussed, for it will be one of the greatest lessons a woman of your station could ever learn."

Without another word, her mother stormed from the room, and Juliet stood staring at the empty doorway before hobbling over to the couch. She studied the fire and wondered why she had said such hateful things. Granted, she oftentimes considered herself far above those of common stock, but never had she ever thought of the servants as animals.

As she thought about what her mother had told her, her shame grew, much like the guilt she had felt in her harsh words to Daniel before. In all reality, not once had she ever asked the man about his dreams, for she had spent all of their time together speaking only of herself.

Letting out a sigh, she promised herself that she would apologize for her comments about his coat, and then perhaps she would ask him about his dreams. She could not imagine what sort of dreams a stable boy could want—was not possessing a position at Scarlett Hall the pinnacle of dreams? However, if what her mother said was true, he must have a greater wish for his life.

And as she thought on that, she then thought on her own dreams and realized that, in truth, she had come to be uncertain what her dreams truly were.

Chapter Eight

The carriage ambled down the road Sunday morning just before noon, the now melted snow leaving behind ruts deeper than usual. Lord Parsons sat across from Juliet and Annabel, both of whom chose matching blue dresses with dark blue coats and gloves.

"If I may ask," Juliet said when there was a lull in the man's incessant chatter about business, "do you have any dreams?" An hour locked inside such a confined space with the man was making her nearly mad, thus the reason for her question. Anything to change the topic of conversation away from that of business.

The man stared at her as if she had offended him with some vile curse word. "Dreams? I am afraid I do not understand the question."

"It is the dreams one has in life and what they wish to do with it," Juliet explain, unable to fathom how the man could have not understood in the first place. "Some dream of travel while others…"

"Ah, yes," he interrupted. "I have many aspirations in life. The first is to increase my business ventures." The man leaned forward, his dark eyes meeting her own. "Were you aware of my land holdings in this area?"

Juliet stifled a sigh. "No, I was not." She was thankful that Annabel was beside her, for the man peered at her as if he expected her to be one of his holdings very soon.

He snorted. "I am not surprised. Most women typically have no knowledge of such things. However, for some reason I think that you, Miss Juliet, are not like most women. In fact, I believe you are far wiser."

Although men were drawn by her beauty much like Lord Parsons was now, Juliet marveled that yet another man noticed her wisdom, as well.

"The land I own," the man continued, "is vast. However, I own lands in other parts of England, as well. Why, I have properties in Dover and Birmingham, for example." He leaned back in his seat, looking the pompous fool he was. "Now, at the age of four and twenty, I am by far one of the wealthiest barons of the *ton*. I even exceed several earls with what I possess."

Juliet forced a smile as the carriage turned down a lane. "You spoke of other aspirations, my lord?"

"Indeed," he replied as if it had slipped his mind. "However, do you not find the use of titles in such an intimate setting to be a bore? How about you address me by my Christian name, Hugh, while we are not out in public. I believe it would make us both feel more comfortable."

Juliet wanted to laugh. Well, this certainly was a change! Perhaps this man was not as pompous as she had previously believed. "Very well, Hugh, you may address me as simply Juliet, if you would like."

"I would like that very much," Hugh replied. "One day I shall marry a woman of such beauty that every man and woman will marvel at her. Her dresses will come from the finest shops in London, the jewels round her neck imported from faraway lands."

As the man continued with his rant of what he could give the woman who accepted his proposal of marriage, Juliet realized that the idea of possessing all these things he mentioned no longer held the same attraction as it once had. This was what she had always wanted in a suitor, a man who recognized the finer things in life and was able to provide them for her. Now, however, nothing stirred inside her, and she did not understand why.

"To that is what I aspire," the baron stated, bringing yet another rant to an end, "or rather, as you say, dream." He tilted his head and smiled. "And now, Juliet, may I ask about what you dream?"

Juliet smoothed her skirts. "Well, I have always thought traveling would be interesting, perhaps even by ship to new lands. Beyond that, if I am honest, I am uncertain."

The carriage made another turn and then circled around, and Juliet glanced out the window, pretending to be interested in the passing hills. It was not that she did not enjoy conversation with Lord Parsons, but she preferred to relegate these types of discussions to those times she spent talking with Daniel.

"What do you wish for in a husband?"

Juliet looked at the man, amazed by his bold question.

"Forgive me," he said. "I am not proposing marriage." He laughed. "I must learn that the forward tactics I use during business negotiations cannot be implemented in civil conversation."

Juliet gave him a smile. "As I have no plans to marry anytime in the near future, I will answer that question. I want a husband who will allow me to pursue my own interests and not only expect me to be in charge of the house and home."

"That is a reasonable request," Hugh replied. Then he sighed. "I must admit, however, that most men are so full of themselves, they never think of what possible interests a woman could have." He winked at her, which caused her to give a true smile.

Yes, she most certainly had misjudged the man. Thus far he had remained a gentleman, even though his eyes wandered at times, and she decided to engage with him more in order to appease her mother. At least it would not be a complete bore after all.

"I see," she said with a coy smile. "So, you agree that men are beasts?"

"Juliet!" Annabel said in a whispered gasp accompanied by a pointed elbow, but Juliet ignored her.

"Not at all," Hugh said as he raised his hand. "Juliet is quite right, Miss Annabel. My kind are prone to keep our attention on business. Why, we can talk about it for hours on end if we are allowed to do so. Much like I have done today."

"We have had a pleasant conversation thus far," Juliet replied. "I have thoroughly enjoyed it. I must admit, I do tend to find discussion of business a bit boring on most occasions, but your talk of it was intriguing." She sat back in the seat with a satisfied smile at being able to give the man a compliment that was only partially true, knowing full well he would accept it as full truth.

The man indeed returned her smile. "Intriguing enough to perhaps speak about it again?"

She should have known better! Giving a man a compliment was like feeding a stray cat; it would return every day after in order to be fed once again. However, she could not deny him calling over, for her mother would force her to go with her to London and away from Daniel.

At least this man would be pleasant company; he was far more pleasant than she had first assumed. "I would like that," she replied. "Please send a card."

Hugh's smile broadened. "I most certainly will."

The door opened, and as Annabel alighted first, Juliet's heart skipped a beat when Hugh grabbed her by the wrist.

"I almost forgot," he said with a sly grin.

"Almost forgot what?"

He produced a gold bracelet from the inside pocket of his coat. "A woman of such beauty deserves the finest jewelry."

Juliet gasped as the man clasped the bracelet around her wrist. "This is very kind of you," she said, "but I cannot accept such a gift."

"I realize it may be a bit much, but I could not help but think of you when I was away."

Juliet was uncertain what to say and therefore replied with a simple "Thank you" before handing her crutches to Annabel.

Hugh then helped her alight from the carriage, and once she had her crutches positioned correctly, he bowed and said, "I look forward to seeing you again."

"As do I," Juliet replied with a smile. She waited until the carriage pulled away before turning to her cousin and putting out her arm.

Annabel gasped. "That is lovely! Why would he give you such a gift?"

"Because he said I was beautiful," Juliet whispered. "Many men have said it, and it has always brought me great joy." Then she bit her lip as Daniel came to mind, the only man who had yet to speak the words and who she truly wished to hear say them.

"Juliet? What is wrong?"

With a wave of her hand, she moved toward the stables. "Oh, nothing. Come, I must speak to Daniel."

***

The mid-afternoon sun warmed the air, and Juliet paused when she and Annabel reached the door to the stables. Her goal was to apologize to Daniel for her harsh words concerning his coat, and she preferred to do so without her cousin as a witness.

"Wait for me here," she said. "I am afraid the man may cry when I scold him, and it would be unfair to have him seen in such a condition."

Annabel nodded and moved aside. "I understand."

Juliet waited for Annabel to open the door and then entered the stables, the crutches making the now familiar *thunk* on the floor as she made her way down the long corridor. The first thing she noticed when she reached the backroom was the large saddle blanket covering a bulky object on one of the tables in the middle of the room. Daniel was pacing back and forth, his hands clasped behind his back as he mumbled to himself.

"Daniel?"

The man stopped and turned toward her. The smile he had worn all the years she had known him had returned, and it warmed her heart. She had not realized how much she had missed it since her fall.

"Miss Juliet," he said with his awkward bow. "I'm glad to see you."

"Thank you," she replied, feeling her spirits rise. "I wish to speak to you concerning a few matters."

"Yes, of course," he replied. He took a step toward her, his hand now in the pockets of the coat that was well past the condition that even a servant should wear. "If this is about my coat, I swear that I plan to buy a new one soon. My month isn't up yet."

The old guilt returned, and Juliet said, "No. Or rather, yes. What I mean to say is that it is concerning your coat, but I wished to say that my words to you were cruel, and I wish to ask for your forgiveness

70

for speaking so horribly to you."

He gave her a surprised look. "You don't need to apologize to me," he said. "I'm the one who should be embarrassed by offending Lord Parsons."

Juliet sighed. "I care nothing for what the man thinks. Do you forgive me or not?"

"I do, but a lady doesn't need to owe a stable hand any apologies. But if it makes you feel better, I accept your apology and forgive you."

The words were like magic lifting a sorrow she had not realized lay on her heart. As he gazed at her, she glanced down at her wrist, and that need to hear Daniel tell her she was beautiful returned. Perhaps today would be that day!

"Lord Parsons gave me a gift," she said, lifting her hand to show him the bracelet.

"It's a worthy gift," Daniel replied, although pain flickered in his eyes. "It's surely fitting for a woman such as you."

A horse whinnied, but otherwise no other sound echoed in the room.

"He said I was beautiful. Therefore, I must ask you, what do you think?"

The man looked down at the ground, and Juliet looked over his clothing. Although his work trousers and boots were well worn, somehow this time they looked different, not as offensive. Or perhaps she no longer cared how old they were.

"I don't doubt the man tells no lies," he said.

Frustrated, Juliet went to say more, to get him to say what she wished more than anything to hear from him, but when he raised his head once again, his eyes looked into hers.

"If I may say so, and I know my opinion doesn't matter all that much, but the man's right. There's no one who can compare to you in all of England, or anywhere else in the world as far as I know. You're most definitely very beautiful, Miss Juliet."

As the last of his words left his lips, Juliet felt her heart soar and her limbs go weak. He had finally said what she had wanted to hear from him for so long, and the feeling it provided was unlike any she had ever known.

Her elation was short-lived, however, when he added, "I'm glad Lord Parsons can give you things you need."

Juliet shook her head. "I care nothing for this," she said, motioning the wrist with the bracelet. "It is..." Her words trailed off. How she wished to tell Daniel that his words meant more to her than any expensive piece of jewelry. That she found him far more handsome than anyone she had ever met. However, she could not form the words, and with panic in her veins, she turned to the blanket. "What is that?"

Oh, bother! Once again, she did not say what her heart wanted her to say. How had she become such a ninny?

Daniel turned to look at the table. "It was a surprise for you," he said. "It doesn't matter much now; it's foolish really."

"Do not say such a thing," she said, moving toward the table. "This is a surprise for me?"

Daniel nodded. "Yes, but I promise it's nothing that compares to the gold on your wrist." He snorted. "I find it silly now."

"I would like to see it nonetheless," Juliet said. "Let me be the judge as to what is foolish and what is not."

Daniel sighed but did as she bade. When the blanket had been whisked away, she gasped.

"Your saddle," he said, his face a bright red to his ears. "I know you weren't happy with what I'd done, so I tried to make it so you would approve."

Juliet was stunned. The man had outdone himself. The craftsmanship was better than she would have ever expected, even from the finest of leather workers. Even her name had been beautifully carved into the leather on the side.

"Oh, Daniel," she whispered, "it is beautiful!"

"You're just being kind," he replied. "I know it doesn't compare to Lord Parson's ..."

Juliet turned to give the man a glare. "It does not compare to Lord Parson's gift, that is true." When Daniel looked back at the ground once more, she smiled. "It is far better. I assume it comes from the heart?"

He nodded. "It does."

"Mother has told me often that the finest of things cannot be purchased from a shop but rather they come from the heart." She turned back to the saddle. "I can see that in your work." Then a new thought came to her. "You cannot read. How did you do this?"

"One of the house servants can read and write." He reached into his pocket and pulled out a small scrap of paper. "I asked him to write your name for me, and I copied the letters."

Juliet took the crumpled parchment from him. Indeed, scrawled in a meager hand was her name. "This is what you have been doing this past week?" she asked. So, he had not been avoiding her!

Daniel nodded. "I know I embarrassed you but didn't know any other way. If I don't know my letters, then I can't read or write. And if I can't read or write, then I won't be able to put your name on the saddle."

A month earlier, she had wanted to touch the man for her own thrill, but now she wished only to give him comfort as she placed a hand on his arm. "You have never embarrassed me," she whispered. "To know you went to such lengths for me." She removed her hand and wiped a tear from her eye. "It is the most wonderful gift I have ever received."

"I'm glad," he said, and as he stood looking down at her, Juliet could do nothing more than stare into his dark eyes, eyes within which she could become lost. What she wanted to tell him was that she wished only to be near him, yet she still could not find the words to express her thoughts.

She glanced down at the gold bracelet once more. Although it had been a costly gift, it did not come from the heart. Juliet was no fool, and she knew Lord Parsons had presented her with it only as a means to an end. An end in which she had little interest.

"I will never wear this again," she said.

Daniel's eyes went wide as he looked first at her wrist and then her face once more.

Juliet glanced around and then lowered her voice. "May I share a secret with you?"

"Of course."

Her heartbeat increased, and she had to take a deep breath to keep it from exploding from her throat. "I care nothing for Lord Parsons. I only agreed to the carriage ride to keep Mother happy."

Daniel presented her with one of his small smiles. "Miss Juliet, it's none of my business who you spend time with, and you certainly don't need my approval."

"You are right, of course," she said with a light chuckle. "I do not need your approval. Regardless, I do not wish to see the man ever again. I think he is a bore." She searched Daniel's face for any reaction to her words and found none. "He is certainly not the man you are." Ah, there was a reaction! His eyes widened in surprise. "Therefore, I shall not allow him to call over nor will I join him for any outings. Now, tell me, does that meet your approval?"

The man went to speak, and Juliet raised a single eyebrow at him, daring him to disagree with her. He paused and then nodded. "Yes, it meets my approval."

They stood staring at one another for some time, although Juliet was not sure how long. She had finally caught his eye and got him to admit she was beautiful, but now she found she wanted more. What that 'more' was, she was uncertain, but the fact she would remain at Scarlett Hall rather than join her sisters in London allowed her the remainder of the season to figure it out.

Chapter Nine

It had been several days since Juliet had received her gift from Daniel, and she still felt as if she were walking on clouds. Or rather, hopping on clouds with her crutches hindering what was typically a wonderful gate.

When she had returned to the house, she showed her mother the gift Lord Parsons had given her, and of course, her mother's reaction confirmed Juliet's assumption that the woman hoped the baron would call over again.

She had not lied when she told Daniel she hoped to never speak to Lord Parsons again; however, she did not mention this to her mother. The truth of the matter was, she did not wish to hurt Daniel; she had done so enough in the past. From the day he presented her with the saddle and every day forward, she was determined to turn over a new leaf. She would treat Daniel, and all the servants, with kindness.

Today, she and Annabel were in Rumsbury, the sun high in the sky and the weather unusually warm. Soon, March would be upon them, and before she knew it, it would be May and her sisters would return. Juliet found that she missed her sisters. How she wished they were here! If anyone could help her with her issues with Lord parsons and Daniel, they could.

They came to a stop in front of the new cobbler's shop, and Annabel opened the door for Juliet. Robert was leaning against the counter, his white shirt much cleaner than the last time they had seen him, and his trousers appeared new.

"Juliet!" he said in that same dramatic fashion as the first day they had met. "And Miss Annabel. It is a great pleasure to have you in my shop once more."

"Thank you," Juliet said, beaming at the man's exuberance. "It is nice to see you again, as well."

The man grinned as he walked behind the counter and produced a large package wrapped in brown paper. "I finished your riding boots," he said. "I do hope you find them to your liking."

"I am certain I will," Juliet replied as she hobbled up to the counter. Robert unwrapped the box and pulled out a pair of the most exquisite pair of boots she had ever seen. She ran a finger over the soft leather; they were perfect in every way. "Your kindness is much appreciated," she said. "I shall tell every lady of the *ton* of your craftsmanship, for these are the finest boots I have ever seen."

"Thank you," Robert said as he rewrapped the package. "I must admit, I spent some time on them. I hope that my passion for my work shows."

Juliet nodded, and her thoughts turned to Daniel. He had put as much effort into her saddle as Robert had put into the boots, and for the second time that week, Juliet found her mother's words could not have been truer; the best gifts did indeed come from the heart.

"Oh, look," Annabel said. "I see Caroline."

Juliet followed her cousin's gaze until it fell on one Miss Caroline Thrup, a mutual friend, as she peered through the window.

"Go and speak to her," Juliet urged. "Invite her in."

Annabel hurried from the shop, and as Juliet waited, she turned back to the counter. Her heart skipped a beat when she found Robert staring at her, a strange expression on his face. However, as fast as she saw it, it disappeared, and a smile replaced it. Perhaps she had misread that look.

"May I be so bold to ask a question?" he said. Juliet nodded. "In my life, I have seen people suffer from within. You seem to carry a great burden, and if you will allow me, I am a good listener. I promise to keep whatever you tell me in confidence."

Juliet sighed. It would be nice to have someone in whom she could confide. Annabel was well enough, but there simply were things

Juliet could not share with her.

"Forgive me," Robert said. "You are a lady and I am but a simple cobbler. I mean no disrespect."

"Oh, no," Juliet said, thinking of how Daniel would say the same. Her mother was right; these people were humans, and a new ear would lessen her burden significantly. "It is not your work that keeps me from sharing." She glanced at the window where Annabel and Caroline were still speaking. No, she could not share her feelings with a man she barely knew. The fact she had even considered it was enough to make her wish she had stayed home today. However, she could not be rude, either. She could help herself while at the same keeping secret that which had to be kept secret. "It is my cousin. I do not know what to do about her."

"What is wrong?"

"You must understand," Juliet replied, leaning in conspiratorially. "A lady of her station who is as handsome as she must marry a gentleman of society."

"Yes, I understand these things," Robert said. "Is she to be wed to a gentleman?"

"Not yet," Juliet said with a shake to her head. "However, if she continues to allow a particular man to call, I am afraid it will be inevitable."

"But is that not what she wants?"

"You see," she glanced at the window once more, "the man in whom she has an interest is not a man of the *ton*, nor is he of the Landed Gentry."

Robert smiled and nodded. "I think I understand the problem." He rubbed his chin. "If a lady such as Miss Annabel were to even consider courtship with a commoner, she would be left to gossip, shame upon her family, a tragedy unlike the *ton* has ever known."

Juliet nodded. This man did indeed understand, and that brought her a small sense of relief. Perhaps she would gain some advice from him that would help her with her current problem. "If she tells the man she is no longer interested, I would be forced to go with my mother to London for the remainder of the season." She clamped her mouth shut when she realized she had just implicated herself. "That is...I mean to say..."

"Juliet," Robert said, his voice low, "your secret is safe with me. I would not risk speaking of such things, for it would draw your anger. Plus, who would listen to a lowly cobbler, anyway?" He said the last with a laugh, and relief washed over Juliet.

"It is odd," she said, crinkling her eyebrows in thought. "I do not know you well, but I feel I can trust you."

"That is called good instinct," he said with a wink. "It is a rare trait among men, but especially so among women. Once again you have amazed me with your wisdom."

Juliet could not help but beam with pride. This man truly understood her!

"Your problem," he continued, "if I understand correctly, is this. You must continue seeing a man you do not wish to see, for if you do not, you will be forced to go to London. Am I correct thus far?"

Juliet nodded. "Precisely."

"Yet, if you see this man again, it will harm the man you truly wish to see."

"It would hurt him," Juliet agreed. "And me, as well. I do not know what to do. I find myself in a situation from which I have no idea how to pry myself."

Robert laughed and at first, Juliet thought he was mocking her. "Well, I believe I may have a solution for you." He lowered his voice once more. "If I share this plan with you, will you tell me how it went?"

Juliet nodded. "I will tell you immediately."

"Your aunt is ill, an aunt you must go see before her illness takes her life."

Juliet frowned. "But I do not have a sick aunt."

"If you create one, you do. Sadly, for this man...what is his name?"

"Lord Parsons."

Robert gave a single nod. "Yes, Lord Parsons will be sad when you tell him how long you will be away, but he can expect a letter when you will be returning."

Juliet considered the plan for a moment and then smiled. It was brilliant, and she was amazed at how well he had crafted it. "I do not know how to thank you! This will save me much heartache and stop the anxiety with which I have been afflicted."

Robert grabbed the package from the counter as the door opened and Annabel returned. He leaned in and whispered, "I have few friends, but if I dare call you one, your happiness and wellbeing will always be my concern."

Juliet nodded, joy filling her at the man's kindness, a kindness far greater than most of her peers. For all her life, she had looked down on those beneath her, and now she realized her mother's words had been true. Those people were very much like her. "We are friends, and I do believe we may become the best of friends!"

"Juliet," Annabel said, her eyes wide, "we must leave."

"Why ever for?"

"It is..." She paused and looked at Robert for a moment. "I must share something with you about Caroline."

"A lady is in need of your counsel," Robert said. "She should not remain in a shop speaking to an old cobbler like me." He handed the package to Annabel. "But do come and see me again soon."

"I promise," Juliet replied.

She followed Annabel out the door, and once the door was closed and they were away from the shop, Annabel stopped and turned to her. "That man is evil!" she hissed.

"Evil?" Juliet asked in confusion. "I do not believe so."

Her cousin glanced toward the shop. "I will tell you what Caroline told me, but let us be as far away from here as we are able; I cannot have him overhear."

As they moved away from the shop, Juliet found her curiosity deepen. Robert evil? The man was the kindest man she had ever met. However, Annabel had such a frightened expression on her face, Juliet could do nothing but allow the girl to explain. Then she would judge for herself if the information was reliable or not. The fact it came from Caroline gave her the suspicious thought it was not.

***

Once they were a reasonable distance from the cobbler's, Annabel put her hand on Juliet's arm. "Here," she said. "I shall tell you here."

Juliet glanced around. Few people were about, and none were close enough to overhear. "Please, tell me."

"Caroline had a pair of slippers fitted last week," her cousin replied. "The man touched her leg!"

Juliet pursed her lips as she waited for her cousin to continue, but when the girl said nothing more, she said, "That is the worrisome news? The man touched her leg?" She could not help but laugh.

"Do you not think it improper?" Annabel asked. "Surely a man should never touch a lady, and on her leg of all places. What boldness it would take!"

Juliet sighed. "My dear Annabel, how naive you are; so much like Hannah." Seeing the disappointed frown, she continued. "First, if the man is a cobbler, how do you suppose he would support a woman's foot?"

Annabel bit at her lip. "I suppose by holding her leg."

"You are correct." Juliet shook her head. "Although it pains me to say so, Caroline does have a tendency to tell tales, and oftentimes they are great exaggerations."

Annabel laughed but quickly attempted to cover it with a cough. "Pardon," she said, her cheeks now red. "Please, continue with what you were saying."

"Robert is a dear friend of mine. We have grown close over these last two visits to his shop."

"He confides in you?" Annabel asked in shock.

A man walked past them, and Juliet waited for him to be well away before speaking. "Yes, of course he confides in me. He has heard of my wisdom and told me of his woes." She let out a dramatic sigh. "However, I cannot repeat what he told me, for I fear we would both succumb to tears right here in the middle of the footpath."

Annabel gave a sympathetic nod, her hand going to her breast. "Is it that bad?"

"Quite," Juliet replied. "I assure you that I am a good judge of character, and the cobbler is no rogue, nor is he a man who would treat a lady with such disrespect." The more she considered the notion, the more she believed she was right in saying so. She may not know the man well, but he had given her the shoes for free, complimented her, and best of all, had given her expert advice. She had no reason to believe such a man could do something as scandalous as what Caroline Thrup accused.

"If you believe so," Annabel said, "then I trust you."

"Those who trust me always find that I am right," Juliet said. "Take heed of my advice, for when you begin courting, you must be aware of the dubiousness of some men. Come, I would like to finish our shopping."

They crossed the road, giving as much care as they could maneuvering through the ruts that had dried in the streets. In front of a tailor's, Juliet stopped.

"What are we doing here?" Annabel asked. "Are you getting a gift for Nathaniel?"

"No. Someone else."

They entered the shop, and a man wearing a black coat approached them, his graying hair receding significantly. "May I be of assistance?"

"Please," Juliet replied. "I am looking for an overcoat."

"I see. Unfortunately, I am afraid we do not carry any clothing for ladies."

Juliet laughed. "Of course not. I am in search of a man's overcoat. It is to be a surprise, you see."

The man gave her a deep bow. "Ah yes, of course. My apologies." He led her to a catalog not much different from those in a dressmaker's shop. "What does this man look like?"

Juliet swallowed hard and glanced at Annabel, who wore a smile of anticipation. "His hair is dark and he has brown eyes. He is ever so handsome, and has very muscular arms..."

The man's jaw dropped and he quickly clicked it shut. "My apologies. What I meant to ask was what is his height and weight?"

Juliet knew her cheeks had to be a deep crimson. "Perhaps your height, but he has a little more weight about him."

"And are you in search of something formal?"

"Not formal, but something of good quality. Something warm."

The man bowed again. "If you will give me a moment, I shall see if I have something ready-made that meets your approval."

As soon as the man was gone, Annabel asked, "Is this gift for the cobbler? Have you taken an interest in him?" That same worry appeared on her features as when they left Robert's shop.

"No, of course not," Juliet assured her cousin. "I have no interest in the cobbler." She lowered her voice. "The overcoat is for Daniel."

"The stable boy?" Annabel asked in what sounded much like shock, and much louder than Juliet thought appropriate. The covered her mouth so quickly, Juliet thought she may have loosened a tooth.

"Do you wish to go out to the street and shout this news like one of the newsboys?" Juliet admonished.

Annabel shook her head. "No, I am sorry."

Juliet lowered her voice further, to the point Annabel had to lean in closer in order to hear. "I will explain everything later. However, for now, we shall speak no more about it."

Annabel nodded just as the tailor returned. In his hands was a brown wool overcoat that appeared well-made.

"Miss...I am sorry, your name?"

"Juliet."

"Miss Juliet, this is perhaps the finest overcoat we carry. Do you believe this will fit?"

"I do."

"Shall I have it delivered?"

"No!" Juliet blurted in horror. The idea of her mother receiving such a package terrified her. "What I mean to say is that I shall take it home today."

She followed the man to the counter, and after paying for the purchase, the coat was wrapped like Juliet's new boots. Once outside, Juliet sighed with happiness. She could not wait to see what Daniel looked like in the new overcoat, and she was certain it would only increase his handsomeness.

"Juliet?" Annabel asked as they made their way to where the carriage waited. "May I ask you why you bought Daniel a new overcoat? Was it because you ridiculed him?"

"That is partly the reason," Juliet replied. "However, I also purchased it because I wanted to give him a gift. I have learned that the best gifts come from the heart. Do you believe he will realize that this comes from mine?"

"Oh yes, most assuredly," Annabel replied. "You chose it with perfect intention and care. It is finely made, so I imagine he will cherish it."

The thought of Daniel cherishing something she had given him pleased her so much that she told the driver to hurry their journey home.

***

"I can't accept this," Daniel said, much to Juliet's distress. She had gone straight to the stables to present her gift, after spending hours hobbling around the village on crutches, and he was unable to accept it?

"I do not understand," Juliet said, completely baffled by the man's response. "I bought that for you. Do you want a different overcoat?"

Daniel sighed, and his brown eyes were so soft, Juliet considered snuggling against the man. That was silly, of course, but she struggled to keep down the urge to do just that. "Miss Juliet, this coat's for someone like Lord Parsons. What would a stable boy do wearing something so fine? I thank you for your kindness, but I can't accept it." He lifted it toward her, but she took a step back.

"Lord Parsons," Juliet said through clenched teeth, "is no gentleman. I do not care for him, nor is he someone with whom I wish to spend time. That overcoat, much like your gift to me, came from my heart. You deserve it, not because your overcoat is worn, nor because you are one of my servants, but because I wish you to have it. Now, do not make me beg. Please, don it to see if it fits."

Daniel hesitated, but then finally nodded. He removed his old overcoat, and Juliet allowed herself to soak in his broad chest that lay beneath his shirt. When he had donned the new overcoat, he put his arms out at his sides and asked, "Do I look like a gentleman?"

Juliet felt weak, her heart fluttering and her lips unable to bring forth words. In his new overcoat, he was far more handsome than any gentleman she had ever seen. And as he went to do up the buttons, Juliet wished she had water to cool herself, for the muscles pressed against the material with his movements.

"You…" She swallowed in an attempt to bring moisture back into her dry mouth. "You look extremely dashing." As the words left her lips, she found she feared his reaction. Would he laugh? Or would he tell her she was mistaken?

However, he said neither as he took a step forward to stand directly before her, a small smile playing at his lips.

"I'll accept it," he said. "It's the nicest gift anyone's ever given me. I'll cherish it forever, Miss Juliet."

There were many things Juliet had done in her life that could not be considered ladylike. She sneaked brandy from parties. She told stories that were slightly—and sometimes more than slightly—exaggerated. However, despite the fact she recognized those actions were frowned upon in most circles, she had not cared. Now, she did not care that her next action would top the list as the least ladylike.

She lifted up on her toes and placed a small kiss on his cheek.

His skin was smooth against her lips, and a burning sensation washed over her body.

"Miss Juliet," he muttered, "I…Thank you."

She gave him a small smile. "For the kiss or the overcoat?" she asked.

"Both." His cheeks had grown extremely red; even his ears were a bright crimson. "I-I should be getting back to work." He turned to leave, but Juliet grabbed his arm.

"Whether your coat is new or old," she whispered, "it does not matter. You are a good man, defined by your heart as one should be, not by what can be purchased from a shop."

"I'm glad you see it."

"More than ever," she replied.

The sound of footsteps had Daniel take a step back, and Juliet had to fight to keep herself from falling over.

"Juliet," Annabel said as she rounded the corner, "your mother is outside." She shot both of them a wide grin, and Juliet wondered if she had been listening in. But no, she would not have seen her mother if that were the case. That gave Juliet a small sense of relief.

Daniel gave a stiff bow first to Annabel. While his back was to the girl, he winked at Juliet and also gave her a bow. "Enjoy your day." Then, straightening his new overcoat, he went to a wall filled with tools and removed one before heading out of the room.

Juliet and Annabel made their way toward the house. Indeed, her mother waited on the stoop, her face devoid of any clues as to her mood. The lines around her eyes had grown deeper as of late, but she still maintained a relative youthfulness to her looks.

"And what did you purchase today?" her mother asked.

"New boots," Juliet replied as she tapped the top of the package Annabel still carried.

Her mother asked nothing more, and Juliet suspected something was wrong. "Annabel, I shall meet you in the drawing room."

Once her cousin was inside the house, she turned to her mother. "Is something wrong?"

The woman blinked and then sighed. "Isabel sent a letter. Although she is uncertain, she believes Hannah has become interested in a gentleman."

"Hannah?" Juliet asked with shock. "Perhaps the man is mad..." Then she stopped. She should be happy for her sister! "I am sorry. That is good news, but how can that make you sad?"

Her mother looked over the grounds before speaking. "I am not sad," she said after a few moments. "I had hoped she would find love during the season."

"I am certain she will if she has shown an interest. If she had, that is more than any of us could have imagined."

"Since you were little," her mother said, "my dream has been for you to marry, not for money but for love. To be perfectly honest, I rather doubted that Hannah would marry for love, if at all."

Juliet frowned. She could not have agreed more. As a matter of fact, she had made a small wager with Caroline Thrup that Hannah would become a spinster.

Her mother turned toward her and smiled. "Never mind me. Just some ramblings of an old woman." She linked her arm in Juliet's. "So, tell me, are you still finding an interest in Lord Parsons?"

Juliet smiled and nodded. "Every moment," she replied, replacing in her mind an image of Daniel in his new overcoat for that of Lord Parsons. "I look forward to the coming months." As she said this, she thought about the advice she had received from Robert earlier. She would have to work on a plan, and tonight she would seek Annabel's aid.

"That makes me happier than you can ever imagine," her mother said. "He is a pleasant man, and I suspect that with him already sending another card, courtship may soon follow?"

"Another card?" Juliet blurted with shock. Then she pasted on her smile once more. "Oh, that is simply wonderful."

"It is. My sweet Juliet is now a woman, and she will soon be courted by a gentleman." She stroked Juliet's cheek. "I will miss you the day you leave here."

"I do not plan to marry anytime soon," Juliet assured her mother. "I hope you have not devised some sort of plan to push me into a quick marriage."

Her mother laughed and shook her head. "I will not push you, and I fear that, even if I did, you would never allow it." Juliet laughed and her mother hugged her. "I am happy you have found someone, at least for the time being. Now, go inside; I will be in shortly."

Juliet nodded and made her way up the steps. When she reached the door, she looked back at her mother, who stood looking out over the grounds as if this was the last time she would see them. Home had been different over the past year with Isabel remarrying and Hannah now eying a gentleman.

If Hannah were to marry—and the likeliness of that happening was small as far as Juliet was concerned despite the fact she had an interest—it would not be long before talks of Juliet marrying would begin.

Well, she would not allow that to happen if she had anything to do with it! At least not to a self-absorbed buffoon such as Lord Parsons.

Once inside, Forbes helped her out of her coat before handing her the card from Lord Parsons. She thanked him and made her way to the drawing room where she and Annabel would devise a plan to keep the boring baron from calling anytime in the near future. Or beyond if she could make it happen.

Chapter Ten

C andlelight flickered, creating shadows on the walls of Juliet's bedroom as she and Annabel lay on the bed together, the blankets pulled up to their chins to ward off the chill. Tonight, she would share all with her cousin, although she was unsure where to begin.

"I suppose it was last year," Juliet said. "I recall going to the stables to speak to him like I often do, but for the first time I saw him in a different way."

"Do you mean to say that you saw him with interest?"

Juliet nodded. "I noticed how handsome he was." She sighed. "I suppose, looking back on it now, my constant engagement with the man was a sign of how I viewed him. I did not realize it, but somehow Isabel and Mother certainly did." That bristled more than she cared to admit. "And now, I find myself more than interested in him. In fact, I consider him in a romantic sense."

Annabel gasped. "He is but a stable boy. Your mother would never allow it!"

"I know this," Juliet said with a sad sigh. "However, I do wish to explore what I feel for the man. I will have more than enough time in the coming months to do so." She turned and looked at her cousin. "What do you think of this matter?"

It was quiet for a few moments before Annabel replied, "Do you love him?"

"I do not believe so," Juliet said. "Yet, I have never experienced love, so I am unsure I would know if I did."

"That is my concern," Annabel said. "What if one day I fall in love with a man and do not even know it? That would shame not only me but my parents, as well."

Juliet could not help but laugh. "It would be a terrible predicament." She stared back up at the ceiling. "No, I do not love him, but I would like more from him. I may not know what that is just yet, but I will find out soon enough."

"How do you suppose you will go about it?" Annabel asked. Then she turned in the bed and faced Juliet, her head resting on her arm. "I must be honest. Is it worth the trouble you could garner from such a relationship?"

Juliet frowned. "Trouble?"

"Yes. Your mother believes you are interested in Lord Parsons. What do you plan to do about him? And what if your mother finds out about Daniel? Surely, she would be angry, as would Lord Parsons."

The questions were valid, but Juliet did not care about the feelings of Lord Parsons. Yet, she did not wish to hurt her mother. Unfortunately, Daniel, the man with whom she would enjoy spending time, was caught in the middle.

"I will not lie. I must be careful and keep my stories aligned or Mother will become suspicious. As to your question, yes, it is most definitely worth the effort. I care for Daniel." She clamped her mouth shut, those final words surprising her as much as they did Annabel, who let out a squeal.

"I knew it!" she whispered when Juliet gave her a stern glare. "I knew you cared for him!"

"How? I have just come to realize it myself!"

Annabel giggled. "The way you smile at one another," she said. "Or the manner in which he does everything you ask. He risked his position by sneaking away and making that campfire for the four of us last year. In fact, he has done much for you that puts him at risk." She sighed. "It is all so beautiful, what that man has done. He is like a hero in a romantic novel."

Juliet could not help but smile. "He is. And if he has risked much, then it is only right that I take a risk, as well." She pulled herself up into a seated position and leaned her back against the headboard of the bed, and Annabel followed suit. "I will need your help in this. I will say, however, that the consequences of agreeing could be great, and I cannot promise you will escape with anything more than your life. Will you lend me aid?"

Annabel's eyes glinted in the candlelight. "An adventure?" she asked with a wide grin.

"Most definitely. I must rid myself of Lord Parsons."

"You mean to kill him?" Annabel asked with a gasp, her eyes wide in shock.

Juliet laughed. "Of course not. What I mean is this. I will write a letter explaining to him that my aunt—not your mother—has become gravely ill and we shall be gone for some time."

"That is an excellent idea!" Annabel said. "How might I help?"

"I will write a second letter, one that appears that it comes from Lord Parsons. It will be you who just happens to be outside when it is delivered and therefore it makes sense you would give it directly to me."

For some time, Juliet explained her plan, and at the end, both women were smiling.

"You are so intelligent!" Annabel said, and Juliet's pride swelled. "You promised me adventure, and I am pleased to find our first to be very exciting."

"I could not agree with you more," Juliet replied as she removed the blanket and swung her legs over the side of the bed. "It will be one of many, that I promise you. Come, we will write the letters tonight while everyone is abed."

Annabel rushed around the bed and helped Juliet stand. Then they donned their nightdresses and made their way to the door. Before they could leave, however, Annabel placed a hand on Juliet's arm. "Thank you for being my closest friend," she whispered. "And for sharing with me what was on your heart."

Juliet hugged her cousin. "And thank you for being here to listen. Come, we have much work to do."

With Annabel holding the candle, the two made their way to the drawing room—Juliet doing her best at keeping her crutches quiet. All her practice over the weeks was finally paying off.

***

Juliet rose from the chair in the study. She had already written her letter to Lord Parsons, and now they would write the letter meant to be from the man. The plan Robert had devised was brilliant, and Juliet was thankful that they had become friends. Now she would have to create a letter believable enough to allow her to remain at home.

"If I dictate the letter to you," she asked Annabel, "will you write it?"

"But would it not be better if you wrote it yourself?"

Juliet snorted. "If Mother were to ask for the letter, she would immediately recognize my penmanship."

Annabel gasped. "I had not thought of that!" she exclaimed as she reached for the quill. "How is it you are able to perceive so much in comparison to others?"

"It is a burden I must carry," Juliet sighed. "And I tell you, it is unfair. Many nights, I have heard Hannah and Isabel weeping because of my beauty. I believe they are also handsome, but compared to me, they do not believe it is true."

"That is sad," her cousin replied. "For all of you are beautiful. I can see why they would be jealous, however. I understand firsthand." Her face took on a melancholy look.

Juliet arched an eyebrow. "Do not forget yourself. The woman who is so beautiful, her parents hide her away lest every noble man come asking for her hand."

This brought on a wide smile. "You are too kind." Her cheeks were a bright red as she placed the nub of the quill to the parchment. "What would you like me to write?"

Juliet adjusted the crutches and moved back to lean against one of the bookcases. "We must make it convincing; heartfelt to be sure, but above all, believable."

"Yes. We would not wish to make your mother suspicious."

"Exactly. Let us begin thus: 'My Dearest Juliet, the lady above all ladies, It is with a sad heart that I inform you of my sudden departure…'"

For some time, Juliet dictated the letter, and Annabel penned the words. When they finished, Annabel signed the man's name, returned the quill to its holder, and covered the letter with sand to dry the ink.

"Now, you know what to do when it arrives, correct?"

Annabel nodded. "I do. I will say I was outside and a man on horseback arrive with a letter that was to reach you immediately." She rose from the chair. "Do you think the letter will achieve what you wish?"

"What do you mean?"

"It does talk much about your beauty," Annabel said.

"It is meant to be believable," Juliet admonished. "Anything short of a glowing admiration will make Mother doubt its authenticity." She folded the letter and added a drop of wax to seal it before securing both letters away. Then they made their way back to their rooms.

Although she was weary, Juliet was restless as she lay on top of her covers in her shift as she thought of Daniel. Annabel had asked her if she was in love, and her mother had told her she was in the first steps toward just such a predicament. For so long, she had thought Daniel beneath her, but the fact of the matter was, she wanted to be his equal. Yet, what did that mean?

As her eyelids grew heavy, she drifted off to sleep. Later, she stirred during a dream, a dream where he was in her room, whispering how beautiful she was. Then he kissed her forehead.

Not only had the dream seemed real, it felt wonderful in her heart. A feeling that she would certainly explore over the months to come.

Chapter Eleven

Time has a strange way of changing one's outlook on life. Just five weeks prior, Juliet's sisters had left for London for the season, the season of which she had dreamed since she was a young girl. However, those dreams had changed, and now she found she wanted nothing more than to spend time in Daniel's presence.

It had been a week since she had gifted him the overcoat, and Juliet had spoken to him only once for a brief time since. Fear was not what kept her from dropping by the stables, but instead Juliet remained in the house and spoke of Lord Parsons—in a positive light, of course—in order to convince her mother that she did, indeed, have an interest in the man.

Her mother, as was expected, was delighted and spent a goodly amount of time asking questions whilst Juliet and Annabel worked on their embroidery or sat with a cup of tea in hand.

Today, Doctor Comerford had arrived to look at Juliet's foot, and her mother sat in a chair to observe. Juliet gave a tiny nod to Annabel, and the girl stood.

"Forgive me," her cousin said. "I feel slightly warm and need a bit of air." Earlier, Juliet had asked one of the footmen to see that the fire was well built up as a way to play into the excuse.

"You are not coming down with something, are you?" Juliet's mother asked.

"Oh, no, not at all," Annabel replied. "I should not have sat so close to the fire is all." Another step they had taken beforehand.

93

She left the room, and Juliet looked down at the balding head of the doctor as he studied her foot.

"This seems to be healing quite nicely," he said. "The bruising and swelling are gone. Miss Juliet, would you please attempt to stand on it?"

"Yes, Doctor," Juliet said. She pulled herself up from the couch with the aid of one of her crutches—she was getting quite good at using them!—and gingerly placed her injured foot on the floor. She slowly added more weight to it. "There is only a slight pain, but nothing overly so."

"Excellent," Doctor Comerford replied. "Now, see if you can walk without the aid of the sticks. I will hold them for you in case you are unable to maintain your weight on that foot, so do not worry you will fall."

Juliet laughed. The doctor continued to refer to the crutches as sticks, and she found it quite humorous. She took a step forward, her injured foot first, and put her weight on it without difficulty. She took another step and grinned. Her foot throbbed a bit, but otherwise she had little trouble moving about.

"You can walk again," her mother said. "Doctor, will she now be able to walk without the crutches?"

The man nodded. "I believe so. I would suggest two things, however. One, there is to be no activities that might injure the foot again, at least not for some time. You must be gentle with your foot."

"Yes, Doctor," Juliet replied, pleased she would once again be able to walk unaided. Now she would be able to go out exploring once again, and thoughts of sneaking out of the house at night came to mind.

"My second suggestion is to keep the sticks with you if you travel. If your leg grows weary, you may need them."

"Thank you, Doctor," her mother said. "It is good to see her up and walking again."

"You are most welcome, Lady Lambert," the man said with a bow to his head. "Send word if you need anything more."

"I shall," her mother replied. "Allow me to walk you to the door."

Juliet moved across the room once more, unable to believe that she was finally free of the 'sticks'. She had never realized how fortunate she was to have such an ability.

When her mother returned, the woman smiled. "You must be happy."

"I am," Juliet replied with all honesty. "Now I will be able to move about freely and perhaps not be a burden on Lord Parsons when he calls over next time."

"You are not a burden to him, I assure you," her mother said with a click of her tongue. "In fact, I can see in his eyes that he is as enamored with you as you are with him. Your eyes have never been brighter."

"You have seen a change in me?"

"I have," her mother replied. "I have never seen you more cheerful, and you have a kindness about you. Even the manner in which you address the servants has vastly improved."

"It is because of you," Juliet said, and that was the truth. It had been her mother who had, for so long, attempted to get Juliet to look at those around her with compassion. She had done so with Daniel, and even some of the other servants, and she found it somehow rewarding. "Thank you."

The sound of the front door opening and closing made Juliet brace herself for the lines she and Annabel had rehearsed several times. The door to the drawing room opened, and Annabel entered, the letter in her hand. "Juliet," she said, "I took a short stroll and a man on horseback delivered this letter to you."

"For me?" Juliet asked in feigned surprise. "I am expecting no letter. Are you certain it is for me?"

"It is from Lord Parsons," Annabel said. Juliet gasped dramatically. "The rider said it was urgent and that you are to read it at once."

"Do you believe he no longer wishes to call on me?" Juliet asked with a glance at her mother. "Have I not been a proper lady? Perhaps it is my injured foot that has offended him."

"Calm yourself," her mother admonished. "Read the letter before you make yourself ill with worry."

Juliet nodded as she walked over to the fireplace and broke the seal on the letter. "I shall read it for all to hear, for then you will know from where my heartache comes."

"You do not have to," her mother said. "It is a personal matter, after all."

"No, I must, no matter how great the shame." She counted to five and then read.

My Dearest Juliet, the Lady above all Ladies,

It is with a sad heart that I inform you of my sudden departure. My aunt, a woman who is strong, as you are, has fallen ill, and I fear her days are short. It is this woman who taught me that women such as you, those who possess great beauty and wisdom, are to be cherished.

I do not know for how long I shall be gone, but know that, as I attend to her, I shall think on your beauty in order to guide my broken heart. And when I no longer have strength to carry on, and the temptation to give up becomes too strong, I shall reflect on your strength for inspiration.

I will send word immediately upon my return, but know I shall think of you every moment that I am away.

With my greatest apologies,
Lord Hugh Parsons

Throughout her life, Juliet had crafted tales that few doubted, and this by far was her best work yet. However, the letter was only part of it, for the tears she conjured would be needed to make the plan complete.

"Oh, Mother," she said, allowing the tears to flow down her cheeks. "How will I live without seeing him?"

"Now, now," her mother said, hurrying to her side and pulling her into an embrace. "You will be fine in his absence. Just you wait and see. All will be well."

Juliet grinned over her mother's shoulder and winked at Annabel, who grinned as she clasped her hands together in front of her.

"I do hope so," Juliet said, wiping her eyes as the embrace broke.

Her mother pursed her lips and then glanced at the letter. "May I read it?"

"Yes, of course," Juliet said, her heart pounding in her chest. "Do you doubt his words?"

"I find them odd," her mother replied. "The man was quite forward with his admiration of you."

Her eyes scanned the letter, and Juliet began to worry that perhaps she had overdone it like Annabel had suggested. However, her worry left her when her mother returned the letter to her.

"I can no longer ask you to stop speaking so highly of yourself when a gentleman does, as well."

"I do try to be humble, Mother," Juliet said. "Perhaps I will reflect on that whilst the man is away." She sighed as she took one more look at the letter before throwing into the fireplace, allowing the flames to quickly take it away. "What shall I do now? I am afraid I will be lonely and suffer."

"We could work on embroidery," Annabel offered. "Perhaps you can make the man something for his return."

"Yes, that is true," Juliet replied, although they both knew she never would. "What does a lady do in such times?"

Her mother walked over and took a seat in the chair across from them. "Perhaps you should consider doing something for charity. There are many people suffering in the world these days."

"What a marvelous idea!" Juliet said. "I suppose I could make a handkerchief."

"What about the stable boy?" Annabel piped in. The words hung in the air, and Juliet felt her breath taken from her. Had her dear Annabel, her most prized pupil, betrayed her?

Her mother leaned forward, and Juliet found she could not speak. "What about him?"

"He cannot read," Annabel replied. "Perhaps we could teach him. That would be very kind, and is that not what charity is about? Furthermore, we do not need to go far to do it. What is it the Good

Book says? 'But if any provide not for his own, and specially for those of his own house, he hath denied the faith, and is worse than an infidel.'"

Juliet found her breath and wished to throw her arms around her cousin. "Oh, Annabel!" she exclaimed. "That is an excellent idea!" She turned to her mother. "Do you not agree?"

Her mother gave them a dubious look. "I do not know..." She shook her head. "It is not unusual for those of us in position of authority to teach the lesser, I suppose."

Juliet found herself holding her breath, and she had to force herself to breathe so her mother did not become suspicious.

"You are the one who has shown me that class is not what matters in this world. This boy, a simple stable hand, like others, has dreams. Can we not teach him how to read so those dreams might become a reality?" Her mother pursed her lips as if in thought, and Juliet knew she had to choose her words carefully. "Perhaps I am wrong." She hung her head. "These things are to be said but not actually done. I was mistaken."

"No," her mother replied with a sigh. "You are correct; they are to be done. Very well. I will allow it under a few conditions."

Juliet and Annabel both nodded their agreement.

"You shall give the instruction after the other servants have retired for the evening. Neither of you will go alone, and you will not share a word of this to anyone. It is a noble idea to be sure, and one worthy of one's time; however, it will remain between us three...or rather four when we include Daniel. Is that understood?"

"Yes, Mother," Juliet replied.

And as the conversation turned to other matters, Juliet could not help but think on Daniel and the months ahead. She would have no concern for Lord Parsons or the season. In fact, she had nothing of which to cause her worry at all.

***

The following day, Juliet found herself in the cobbler's shop with Annabel. Her mother had accompanied them into the village, a rare treat, for the woman left the house only when she had business to conduct, which she was off doing at this very moment.

Annabel browsed the various shoes on display as Juliet stood beside Robert. "Therefore," she said after having explained all that had transpired since she had last visited the shop, "with Lord Parsons now out of the way, Annabel will aid me in teaching Daniel how to read, which in turn allows me to be near the man without fear of scrutiny."

"It seems your plan went swimmingly!" Robert replied with a wide grin. "Even better than you expected. And with your foot now healed, your spirits seem high."

"Oh, yes, they most certainly are," Juliet said. "Although, I must admit that it was your plan that had been so brilliant. I must thank you again for giving me the idea."

Robert smiled and pushed away a wave of dark hair that had fallen over his brow. "It is not the plan that was brilliant, but rather the brilliance of the woman who implemented it. I had no doubt you would see success."

"Is that true?" Juliet asked, unable to contain her pride at his words.

"Oh, yes," he replied. "You are very wise, and that is why I wanted..." He stopped and shook his head. "Forgive me. I am a fool. Forget I said anything."

"No. Do tell. I will not tell anyone if what you have to say is to be kept secret."

The man placed his hands on the counter and looked past her for a moment. "You will not laugh at my request?"

Juliet glanced over her shoulder to see if anyone was nearby as memories of Caroline's warning came to mind. Was Robert going to ask to see her? Would he wish to touch her leg?

However, when she turned back and saw the kindness in the cobbler's face, she knew she was allowing her imagination to get the better of her. "I will not laugh, I promise."

He cleared his throat. "Well, you see, I am looking for investors for my business, or rather someone who is willing to buy a piece of it.

With your wisdom and knowledge of fashion, I thought that perhaps you would be that partner."

Juliet could not help but stand taller and her head had to be twice its size. "I am truly honored," she said. "However, I must admit that I know nothing of business."

"I understand," Robert replied with a sigh. "It was nice to believe it would happen, even if it was only for a moment."

"The fact is, women rarely have anything to do with business," Juliet said. "Furthermore, Mother would never allow it. If word got out to anyone, the results would be disastrous."

"I agree wholeheartedly. That is why you would remain a shadow partner."

Juliet frowned. "A what? What is a 'shadow partner'?"

"That is simply a partner who is unknown to anyone but those involved and who remains in the shadows. Of course, you collect your share of the profits and never speak a word of it." He tapped his knuckles on the counter. "Again, I am sorry for asking. A lady of your station partnering with a man of mine..." He said the last with a laugh. "You cannot fault a man for dreaming."

The last words struck at Juliet's heart. The man had a dream of improving his business, and he had turned to her, a lady of beauty and wisdom, for aid. Her mother had spoken of others' dreams, and if Juliet could help this man who had been such a wonderful friend, there would be no harm. Especially since her mother would never learn of it.

"I will do it," Juliet said with finality. "With my fashion knowledge, and my money, I can be a shadow partner." She liked the sound of that phrase, and she allowed it to lay on her tongue like a sweet.

"Excellent!" Robert said. He lowered his voice and added, "We must not tell a single soul, for I do not want anyone to learn of our arrangement and you to be shamed. Now, what is your allowance?"

For a moment, Juliet considered not telling the man. However, it did make sense that he should know how much she would be able to contribute, and therefore she told him. After some discussion, they came up with an agreement.

"Every month, you will bring the money to me," he said. "Then, you can collect your profits from the previous month at that time. Or, if you prefer, we can wait and let the profits build until we are able to open a second shop, which will, in turn, earn you more profits."

Juliet nodded. The idea of having her own shops intrigued her. "Yes, let us wait on the profits. We must have more shops."

He gave her a proud smile. "I knew you would see the wisdom in that." He went to say more, but the door to the shop opened and Juliet's mother entered.

"Oh, Mother," Juliet said, hurrying to meet the woman at the door, "I would like to introduce the most wonderful man, who is not only my cobbler, but my friend, as well."

"Juliet," her mother said in a harsh whisper, "conduct yourself as a lady."

Juliet turned as Robert approached, his smile most becoming. "You have a most fascinating daughter," he said with a deep bow.

Juliet grinned at her mother but then frowned. The woman was not smiling. In fact, she had blanched significantly.

"Mother?"

"Mr. Mullens," her mother said in a choked voice, "I do believe we have taken enough of your time for today. Good day to you."

Juliet went to speak, but her mother gave her a fierce glare.

"We must leave immediately."

"Do you not…"

"At once, Juliet," her mother snapped. "Annabel, you as well."

Juliet sighed and nodded, turning only long enough to wave a farewell at Robert before following her mother and Annabel out the door.

"Mother, I must ask…"

"You will remain quiet until we are inside the carriage," her mother said without looking at her.

Juliet shot Annabel a glance, who simply shrugged, and a few minutes later, they were sitting in the carriage.

"How long have you been speaking with that man?" her mother asked. Her tone still held the same anger it had when they left the shop. "Tell me now!"

"A little over a month," Juliet replied. "Mother, he is kind. My new riding boots? He gave those to me as a gift. And he knows my knowledge of…"

"You know nothing," her mother snapped. "You know nothing of this man! And receiving gifts from him?" She clicked her tongue at this.

Then Juliet realized her mother must have believed that she, Juliet, had fallen in love with Robert! "I do not care for him in some romantic sense," she said with a laugh. "I can assure you of that, as can Annabel. The man has been nothing but kind."

Annabel nodded her agreement. "He is a nice man."

"I do not doubt you are telling the truth," her mother said. "Nevertheless, the man is a cobbler, and you will no longer frequent his shop. If you are to see him in the street, you are to walk the other way. Is that understood?"

Juliet could not understand her mother's anger. Robert was a friend, and now he was her business partner. Although she could not tell her mother about the latter.

"Did he offend you in some way?"

Her mother pursed her lips and turned a glare on her. "I will not ask again. Defy me in this, and I shall send you off to London immediately."

Juliet sighed. "Yes, Mother," she whispered, although she wished only to shout at the woman. Her mother had spoken of being kind to those of the lower class, yet this man gives her a pair of riding boots, and Juliet is to never speak to him again?

None of what had transpired made sense, but one thing Juliet knew for certain. She did not wish to go to London, and therefore, she kept her angry retorts to herself.

Chapter Twelve

E very Tuesday for as long as Juliet could recall, her mother would send her children outside, or have them leave the home to call on friends for the majority of the day. The servants, including Forbes, would leave for the village to take care of errands or to see to their own business as well as do the weekly shopping for the house, thus leaving her mother alone in the house for whatever reason Juliet never knew. It was such a common occurrence, it never came to Juliet's mind there had to be a reason.

That was how now, on the Tuesday following the debacle at the cobbler's, Juliet found herself, with Annabel at her side, in the home of Miss Caroline Thrup.

For the past ten minutes, Caroline had been speaking of the etiquette of courting, the girl's mother chiming in from time to time, and Juliet soon found herself bored. Her mind kept returning to the events of the previous day, and she could not help but wonder why her mother had been so angered. Although she was unsure, she did have a suspicion. Jealousy.

Even older women were prone to bouts of jealousy of their younger counterparts, and with Juliet making a new friend and receiving riding boots at no charge, word must have spread throughout the village. Although it angered Juliet that her mother would forbid her to see the man because of envy, she also felt sad that it had driven her mother to such lengths.

Juliet would continue to converse with Robert; after all, they were in business together. She did not wish to defy her mother, but in this instance, it was necessary.

"Juliet?" Caroline said. "Is it true?"

Juliet turned her attention to the woman. "Forgive me. Could you please repeat the question? I am afraid my thoughts wandered."

"Caroline mentioned that Lord Parsons is courting you," Lady Thrup said. "He is a fine gentleman. Your mother must be very pleased."

"Indeed," Juliet replied. "However, we are not courting as of yet, but he has called a few times." She turned and gave Caroline a smug smile. There were many gossips in Rumsbury, including Caroline Thrup, and Juliet was curious how the girl had learned of she and Lord Parsons. "However, as you said, my mother is pleased."

Lady Thrup rose, her yellow skirts crinkling with her movement. "It is difficult to believe that you three were once so little and now you have grown into women." She sighed. "I believe I will rest for a while. Please enjoy each other's company in my absence."

"We shall try," Juliet said, and Annabel giggled and covered it with a polite cough.

Once the woman was gone, Juliet rounded on Caroline. "How did you learn about Lord Parsons and me?" she demanded.

"Stephen," she replied of her brother as if Juliet's tone was as conversational as it had been before. "He spoke to Lord Parsons while he was in the village last week, and your name came up. He told me, and I told Mother." She said the last with a firm nod, and Juliet clenched her fist. Caroline and her mother could not keep a thing to themselves, and soon everyone would know about Juliet and Lord Parsons.

"Well, I will assure you, we are not courting," Juliet snapped. "Such rumors are silly."

Caroline gave a coy smile over the rim of her teacup. "Annabel, you told Juliet what I told you about the cobbler, did you not?"

Annabel nodded. "I did. I relayed everything you told me to her."

"The man is a rogue," Caroline said firmly. "I am not the only lady he has touched in an inappropriate manner thus far."

"Oh?" Juliet asked, knowing full well the woman was lying. "It is true, then?"

Caroline gave her a haughty look. "I would not lie," she said as she placed the cup on the table with such force the liquid sloshed over the side. "Betty experienced the same as I."

Juliet pursed her lips. Although Miss Betty Chancellor was many things, an exaggerator of stories was not one of them. Regardless, Juliet suspected both women were taking it all too far. "Surely a cobbler would be expected to touch a woman's leg as much as a tailor must touch an arm. How else will he help a lady with her shoes?"

Caroline laughed. "You are so stubborn!" she said. "It is not merely a simple touch. When he touched my leg, the look of lust in his eyes was unmistakable. I fear that if I had not hurried myself from his shop, the man would have made an attempt to kidnap me."

"Why ever would he do that?" Annabel asked, and Juliet nodded her agreement.

"It is simple," Caroline replied as she jutted her chin, "A beast such as he preys upon women." She sighed and moved back a strand of her blond hair. "Many of the shopkeepers look at me with desire. It is crude, but it is a fact."

Juliet could not help but roll her eyes at the woman's arrogance. Although Caroline was pretty, she did not receive the number of compliments Juliet did. Sadly, like Juliet's mother, it was another case of jealousy brought about by Juliet's handsomeness.

For a majority of her life, Juliet had considered her beauty a blessing, but it was becoming more and more prevalent that it was to become a curse. As she grew older, she would only become more beautiful, and men would fight just for a chance to gaze upon her. She imagined them calling one another to duels or sharing in fisticuffs over her. From the crowd would emerge Daniel, and although his face would be bruised, he would stand tall and take Juliet into his arms...

"Do not fear," he would whisper as the other men hung their head in shame as they walked past, "I am here to take care of you."

Juliet would sigh and place her head on his chest as she had when he carried her into the house after her fall, his strong arms holding her tightly to him. Once alone, he would ask for a kiss, and Juliet, proud of the bravery he had shown on her behalf, would grant him one.

"Juliet," Annabel said, breaking her from her thoughts and causing her cheeks to heat, "are you going to return to the shop?" It was clear from her tone that it was not the first time the question had been asked.

Juliet had to stop and consider this question. She would have to return in order to conduct business, but how could she do so without wagging tongues informing her mother? Then an idea came to her. "I do not doubt your story," Juliet said to Caroline, although she knew it to be an outright lie. "I shall return to the shop to learn more about this man, even if I must risk my life to do so."

Caroline gasped. "You would put yourself in danger?"

Juliet nodded. "If it means I am able to save the women of the *ton*, then I shall do so without concern for my wellbeing."

"It is like the highwayman," Annabel said and quickly covered her mouth with her hand.

Juliet suppressed a smile. She had taught Annabel how to reveal a secret and make it appear an accident, and she performed the task as if she had been doing it all her life.

"What highwayman?" Caroline asked in clear interest.

Annabel looked at Juliet, who gave her a nod. "The night was full of thunder and lightning," Annabel began in theatrical tones that were close to matching those of Juliet. "A rider came to the door, drenched from the rain to inform us of a highwayman who was being sought after."

"Is this true?" Caroline asked with a gasp.

"It is," Annabel replied. "It was that night, as lightning flashed, that Juliet and I spotted the highwayman in the stables of Scarlett Hall."

As Annabel continued the story, Juliet studied Caroline. She sorted the information she had received about Robert, what little she had, but no matter which way she organized what she knew, none of it made sense.

The fact of the matter was Caroline was desperate for attention and had resorted to telling tales. It was sad that a woman would go to such lengths, but Juliet knew the story was not believable. If any man were to look upon any woman with lust, it would have been she, Juliet, who would have been on the receiving end of that look, not someone like Caroline Thrup. Yet, Robert had not done so even once, and therefore he could not have done so to Caroline.

Yet, she did have her mother's concerns with which to contend. Although she did feel her mother might be struggling with jealousy, she sensed there was more there than the obvious. Therefore, she decided to speak to her mother once more to see what more she could glean from the woman about the cobbler.

Pleased to have worked out a plan, Juliet turned her attention to Annabel's story. The girl was quite convincing, evident by how Caroline listened with wide eyes, and although the story was not completely true, it was entertaining, nonetheless.

***

Tuesdays had proven to be Eleanor's favorite day of the week. The house was empty and she was given time alone without any distractions, a tradition she had begun years before as a way to work through any issues with which she might be struggling at any given time.

The house was quiet, and although it might be considered silly, at times, Eleanor found herself whispering to the thick walls whatever might be on her heart. In doing so, she released secrets and burdens and Scarlett Hall absorbed them all.

Today, her concern was great, and she feared she would no longer be able to handle it as she had in times past. There was her worry over Hannah, for one. Her middle daughter, by all accounts, had taken an interest in Laurence's cousin John, for which Eleanor felt a great relief. However, there was still the chance the woman would wish to leave London and throw herself into the arms of a sheep farmer of all people.

Then there was her sweet Juliet, the one over which Eleanor always worried. Now, however, her worries had become significantly worse with the girl's newfound friendship with that cobbler, Robert Mullens.

The rumors concerning the man had already reached Eleanor, and upon hearing the man's name, she had hurried to the shop with quick steps. When she entered, her fears were confirmed, and she wanted nothing more than to get Juliet as far away from the man as she could.

One question plagued her above all. Did the man know?

Eleanor could not answer that question. Perhaps it was merely coincidence the man had returned to Rumsbury, but regardless, Eleanor would do what she could to keep Juliet, as well as Annabel, away from him. She poured herself a glass of wine and sat beside the fire in the drawing room. Perhaps she should send Juliet to London in order to avoid the possibility of trouble.

A knock at the door made her start, and she wondered who would be calling in the middle of the day without sending a card first. Her skirts rustled as she glided through the foyer. She took a deep breath to calm her pounding heart; it would do no good to answer the door with a look of fright on her face.

When she opened the door, however, her heart jumped into her throat when she saw Robert Mullens standing on the stoop.

"Lady Lambert," he said, although his tone was more mocking than diffident, "how wonderful to see you again."

"What do you want?" she demanded, attempting to keep her voice from choking. "And what are you doing at my home?"

The man laughed, an evil sound to her ears, as he adjusted the lapels of his coat. Eleanor looked past him, but no one else was there. Had the man walked all the way from the village?

"I came to speak to you of matters that concern us all," he said. "May I come in?"

Eleanor shook her head. "You are not welcome in my house, nor on my property. If you will excuse me, I have matters to which I must attend." She moved to close the door, but Robert pushed against it, and she took a step back, her fear so great, she thought she might faint.

"Ah, Eleanor," he murmured with a shake to his head, "I know your secret; did you know that? And what a secret it is! Perhaps the most damning secret one could have."

"I have no idea what you are speaking about," Eleanor said with a shaky voice that belied her attempt to appear unshaken. "In fact, I believe…"

Robert's laughed made her cringe in fright. "You know of what I speak," he said in a low hiss. "A secret that came to my ears not even a year ago."

Eleanor took another step back, tears threatening to spill over her lashes as Robert stepped through the door. "Now, will you invite your former servant into your home, or shall I leave and tell everyone what I know?"

"No!" Eleanor cried. "Do not do it. It would cause…"

"Shame?" he asked with a laugh. "Yes, it most certainly would add a stain on your good name. And your poor children! If they were to know…" His eyes narrowed, and Eleanor knew she was at his mercy. "Now, invite me inside."

"You may enter," she said, knowing she had no other choice.

He glared down at her. "Invite me as a man of substance, not as a servant," he growled.

Eleanor took a deep breath to calm her pounding heart. "Mr. Mullens, would you like to come in?"

"Thank you," he said as he stepped into the foyer and closed the door behind him. "I believe I would."

The former servant stood before her, and he did nothing to hide his appraisal of her. "Your beauty is still to be admired. How many times did I look upon you with awe?"

"What do you want?" she asked, pushing aside her fear with as much effort as she could muster.

"I would like to sit," he said, removing his coat and hanging it over his arm. "I do not wish to speak of business in the foyer like some peasant."

Eleanor did not want this man in her home, let alone the drawing room. However, as he stared down at her in expectation, she relented. "Follow me." She led him down the hall to the drawing room, and he sat on the couch as she took one of the chairs, assuring that he could not sit beside her. "Mr. Mullens..."

"I'd like a drink," he said as he threw his coat over the back of the couch. He eyed the heavily laden liquor cart. "The finest brandy you have, of course."

Eleanor nodded and poured the man a glass of brandy as she fought back tears. She would not allow this man to see her weep! He was nothing, a pauper who thought himself a cobbler, and she would deign to giving him the pleasure.

When she turned, the man's gaze made her tremble, and she regretted allowing herself to be alone with him.

"Well?" he demanded. "Are you not going to bring me my drink?"

She handed him the glass, and to her mortification, he took a hefty gulp and smacked his lips afterward. "Very good," he said.

"What is it you want?" she asked. She moved to return to the chair, but he reached out and grabbed her wrist.

"Sit beside me," he said.

Fear shook her to her bones as she lowered herself to the couch. If she had attempted to stand for any longer, she would have fallen, for her legs trembled so.

"Now," he said as he eyed the brandy, "what is it that I want?" He sighed and took another sip, this time without the dramatics he had used earlier. "I would like to enjoy some of the finer things in life just like you."

"I do not have much money," Eleanor replied. "However, I shall give you..."

"I don't want just money!" he snarled. "But *you* I want."

"Me?" Eleanor asked in astonishment. "Whatever do you mean?"

"You don't know the hours I spent wishing you were my wife. The dresses you wore, the jewels. Our positions separated us, but now, I think that no longer matters. We can come to an arrangement."

She stared at him. "What arrangement?"

"One of business, of course. It is quite simple, really. I plan to open more shops in the future, and your monetary contribution to my enterprise would be most welcome. Say, twenty-five pounds a week to start?"

"That is blackmail!" she said incredulously.

The man laughed. "It is business," he replied. "It is the cost you must pay for what you have done!"

Eleanor's heart stung. "My finances are not what they were even five years ago. We have struggled to maintain…"

Robert snorted. "I don't believe you, and even if it were true, I don't care. Do whatever you have to in order to see I receive my funds."

With no choice, Eleanor nodded. "And you will keep what we know, this secret, between us?"

"There are a few other expectations, as well. The way you spoke to me in front of Juliet and Annabel, for example." He gave her a look of scorn. "That was quite rude. I'll assume you told them to stay away from me?"

"I did," she whispered as a single tear escaped her eye.

He reached up and wiped it away, and she felt her stomach roil in disgust. "You will tell them they are to return to me," he said. "In fact, encourage it, and tell them you regret your behavior."

Eleanor shook her head. She would not allow either of the girls to be in his company! He was dangerous, and the possibilities of what might happen terrified her.

"Then you have decided," Robert said as he stood. "In that case, I cannot make any promises to keep what I know hidden."

"Wait!" Eleanor had to fight down the bile as she rose to face the man. "You will not hurt them?"

"I am not a cruel man," he said with a smile that made the hairs on the nape of her neck stand on end. "I am merely a man of business. Now, for my final request."

He wants more? Eleanor thought, the agony consuming her. "What is it?" she asked.

He placed a hand on her arm, and she could not keep from trembling beneath his touch. "You have not changed in all these years. Your beauty, the way in which you hold yourself, it is all the same. I wondered to myself, 'Will she still send everyone away on Tuesdays as she did when I was worked here?' And here I am inside Scarlett Hall. Not as a servant, but as your equal."

If the man wanted recognition, then Eleanor would give it to him. "You are my equal," she managed to say, hoping the words would appease him and thus make him leave.

He gave her a wide grin. "Now that it is confirmed, every Tuesday, I will call over, and we will spend time together." He moved his hand down her arm. "A few drinks, a bit of conversation, and I will then collect my payment."

Eleanor clutched her skirts to keep her hands from reaching out to grab the man by the throat. "And word of what you know?"

"Never leaves my lips." He leaned in and placed his mouth to her ear and whispered, "Do not disappoint me again, Eleanor. Next time, I want a warmer welcome."

Eleanor closed her eyes, her heart racing. When he moved away, she opened them again.

"I will leave now to allow you time to think about what we have discussed."

She followed him to the door, and as he stepped through, he stopped and turned back to her, "Do not forget to send the girls back to me," he said with a tiny smile. "And do not forget about my money."

Without another word, he turned and walked away, and Eleanor had to fight back the urge to slam the door behind him. Once the door was closed, the tears poured from her eyes. What the man knew would bring shame upon her family, and worse, her children. How he learned what he knew, she did not know, but it did not matter. The fact was he knew.

As she returned to the drawing room, she felt numb. Yet another attack on her family, and the stress of it caused her steps to slow. Falling against the wall, she whispered her heart into the walls of the house in hopes of finding some semblance of peace.

However, as the final words left her lips, she rested her head against the wall, for the weight of this new burden weighed heavily on her shoulders, and it was far worse than anything she had endured before.

For years, Eleanor had enjoyed the solitude of Tuesdays in Scarlett Hall, for that was when she could speak from the heart and the walls would hide away her secrets. Now, however, with her ear pressed against the stone, she could hear the voices of shadows past returning to haunt her.

Chapter Thirteen

The last remaining rays of the sun peeked over the horizon as Juliet made her way to the stables, Annabel at her side. The pain in her foot had subsided even more today, and she enjoyed the freedom of not being forced to rely on the crutches to get about. Clutching a book in her arm, they walked past the stalls and into the workroom at the back of the stables.

Daniel bowed when they entered, and Juliet could not help but stop and take in the man. With his new overcoat and his usual smile, he looked even more handsome than he ever had, and she had to force herself to take the final steps to stand beside him.

"Miss Juliet. Miss Annabel," he said formally as he indicated one of the tables that held several candles with two stools beneath it.

"Are you ready for your first lesson, Daniel?" Juliet asked. Simply saying the man's name made her knees grow weak.

He nodded. "I have an extra seat for Miss Annabel, too. I'll sit on the floor."

Annabel turned to Juliet. "If you do not mind, I would like to go admire the horses for a while." She wore a sly smile, and Juliet could not have been prouder of the woman. She was putting to good use all that Juliet had taught her, and without prompting!

"I believe that will be fine," Juliet replied as if the request meant nothing to her.

As soon as Annabel disappeared around the corner, Juliet turned her attention back to Daniel. She still could not believe her luck at being able to spend time with the man without fear of being chastised by her mother; to finally be able to learn what she truly felt for him.

The past few weeks had not been easy. For so long, she had become accustomed to spending time with Daniel whenever she pleased, if only to have someone who would listen to her without rebuke. How strange it was to see him as perhaps something more than a friend.

She walked over to one of the stools, which he pulled out for her as if he were seating her at a lavish dinner party—that surprised her, for she would not have expected a man of his station to know the proper conduct for formalities—and he sat on the other stool. She was disappointed that he sat across from her rather than beside her, but she would have to make due for the moment.

"Miss Juliet," he said, "I wanted to thank you for doing this for me. It's kind, and I know I don't deserve it."

"Why would you say such a thing?" she asked in shock.

"I'm nineteen of age," he replied with a shrug. "I'm just a stable boy who can only read a few words. I know you're taking a risk by teaching me." His words caused her heart to ache, for Juliet knew it was she who had commented on more than one occasion that his position was lowly.

"You are more than just a simple stable boy," she replied. "You are a brave and strong man. And you are my friend. Now, there will be no more talk of your position in such a disparaging manner, for I hold it in very high regard."

Daniel's cheeks went red. "Thank you."

Juliet looked at the book on the table, glanced up at Daniel, and a thought came to her. "Bring your stool beside me so you can see the book with ease."

He nodded and did as she bade. As he sat, his knee bumped hers, and her breath caught.

"I'm sorry," he said.

"No need to apologize," she replied, although her heart raced. Her hands trembled as she reached for the book and opened it to the first page. It was a book she had used when she was a child just learning to read. "These are the letters of the alphabet. Do you know any of them?"

Daniel bit at his lip and leaned over, placing his arm on the table beside hers. Although it was a cold winter's night and the barn was chilled, Juliet's body felt like it was a summer afternoon.

"This one," he said, pointing. "That's the letter J. J is for Juliet." As he said this, he looked at her, and Juliet wished at that very moment that he would kiss her. She would not resist. In fact, she would welcome it. And she did not feel a bit embarrassed for thinking it.

"That is very good," she said, glad her voice was not shaking. "Do you know this letter?" She pointed to the 'H', and he shook his head. "H is for horse." He nodded and her finger moved to the 'K'. "K is for kiss."

Her heart thumped in her chest. Why had she said that? She cleared her throat and moved to the beginning of the list as quickly as she could. "Do you know this letter?"

"That's an A," he replied, beaming.

"And this?" she pointed to the 'B' and he stared at it as if it were some unknown species of animal. "That is a B."

They continued on with the remainder of the alphabet in order for Juliet to gain an understanding of which letters Daniel already knew and which he did not. She quickly learned he knew far fewer than she would have expected, so they went through the letters again, this time with her naming each and him repeating, until they arrived at the end once again.

"How was my first lesson?" he asked.

"You did well," Juliet replied as she closed the book. "You have remembered much from your childhood lessons." His smile widened and she felt proud of him. Although he had not remembered immediately, he was a quick learner. "Now, do you remember the first three letters of the alphabet?"

He nodded. "A, B and C," he replied. "I do remember that."

Juliet pointed to the letters. "Every day look at this when you have time. Say the name of each letter as you move your finger over them like this." She traced over first one letter and then another, as if she was writing them. When she finished, she found that his eyes were on her rather than on the book.

"Thank you." He then turned his attention to the instruction once more.

116

She closed the book and set it before him. "Now that we have finished your reading lesson, I would like to ask you a few questions." He nodded and she continued. "What do you think of me?"

The man fidgeted on his seat. "I think you're kind."

"No. I mean as a woman."

"You're kind," he repeated. "You're kind to me."

Juliet could not help but smile at his naivety. She glanced toward the door to assure herself that Annabel was not close enough to overhear and leaned in closer. "What I mean to say is...you said I was beautiful." He nodded, his redness moving to his ears. "Well, I think you are handsome."

His eyes went wide. "Miss Juliet," he said, his voice panicked, "I can't have you saying things like that about me."

He moved to stand, and she grabbed his hand. It was rough and heavily calloused, but the feeling it provided very much resembled how she felt being in his arms.

"Why can I not say that?" she asked.

The man sighed. "You are beautiful, more beautiful than any man may realize. I won't lie; I've thought so for a long time."

"Then why did it take you so long to tell me?" she demanded. "I was forced to attempt to make you jealous in order to get you to say so."

To her surprise he laughed. "You mean you weren't offered money for a kiss?"

Her cheeks burned from his words, but they heated all the more when he gave her hand a gentle squeeze.

"I'm honored you'd think of me as someone you could make jealous," he said in his soft voice. "I have to admit that I was."

Juliet had never heard sweeter words in all her life, and she took a deep breath to calm her racing heart. However, the elation she felt was struck down by the words that followed.

"But only a fool would believe that."

"It is not foolish," she said with a small smile. "You see, I have a great interest in you." She swallowed hard in an attempt to add moisture to her suddenly dry mouth. "I do not know what exactly I feel for you, but it is something I wish to explore further."

He pulled back his hand and stood. "You mustn't speak like that," he said in a firm tone. "Never again can you do that."

"I do not understand," she said. "What is it about me that is so wrong that you cannot tell me that I am beautiful nor want me to learn more about you?"

He shook his head but gave no answer.

"Is it my stories?" she asked. "I know I exaggerate a bit, but I will stop if that is what you need." Her heart hurt when he did not respond again. "I know that, in times past, I have treated you horribly, but I did not mean to harm you."

He sighed. "I know this. I understand why you treated me like you did and said what you said." He took a step closer to her. "It's because you feel the same about me as I do about you."

"Then what is wrong? I am lost in understanding your explanation."

"I'm just a stable boy," he replied. "Don't you see?" Juliet shook her head. "You're to marry a rich man, a man who can provide you with dresses and beautiful things. To attend parties and be with others like you. You deserve all that and more."

Juliet did nothing to stop the hot tear that rolled down her cheek for the horrible words he said, even if they were the truth.

"I'll never be able to do those things for you. Your mother wouldn't allow it, and your friends would be revolted."

"I do not wish to marry you," Juliet said, wiping at her eye. "I only wish to explore our feelings for one another. What is the harm in that?"

"It's because I care about you that I refuse," he whispered. "And though it pains me to say it, I can't let it happen."

A rush of anger washed over her, and she clenched her fist and jaw at the same time. "There is nothing wrong with speaking to one another," she said. "And, if anything were to come from it, Mother would approve, for she has never denied me anything." As Daniel gazed down at her, she wanted nothing more than to reach out and take his hand again. "Please. All I ask is that we continued to speak to one another as we have. Nothing more, I promise."

"I don't know if that'd be wise," he said. "I'm afraid it'll only cause trouble. If your mother found out the truth, it won't end well for either of us."

"She will not learn of it, I promise," Juliet said, not caring if she sounded as if she were pleading. "Do not hurt me."

Daniel peered down at her with such kindness in his eyes, she trembled. "I would never hurt you," he said. He motioned at the stools. "I suppose there's no harm in talking."

Juliet retook her seat, and he did the same. "Now, answer my question," she said with a smile.

The candles flickered on the table as Daniel wrung his hands. "I remember how I thought you were beautiful the day you came to ask me for help with Miss Isabel."

Juliet listened with interest as Daniel spoke about the past summer before Isabel married Laurence. It was then that Juliet asked him to build a campfire at a particular location away from the house and to bring a bottle of wine. The man had done so at the risk of losing his position, and Juliet cherished him for doing so; even more so now as he spoke of it.

"When I watched you with your sisters, and seeing the smiles you created, that was the moment I realized how beautiful you truly are."

"Because I made them smile?" Juliet asked in amazement.

He nodded. "Yes. You were worried about Isabel and wanted everyone to be happy. That's what is beautiful about you. It's not only the outside but also what's on the inside. I saw it that night." He rubbed his overcoat. "And when you gave me this."

"It did come from my heart," she whispered. "Much like what you did with my saddle. I told you then, as I do now, it is the greatest gift I have ever received." They sat smiling at one another, and then Juliet said, "I would like to tell you something more."

"Please," he replied. "I'd like to hear what you have to say."

Juliet grinned. With the sun long set, she knew her mother would be waiting for her to return soon to the house, but she wished to use the time she had as best she could. "Over the past year, I found myself intrigued by you, more so than before. You must understand, I realize now that you caught my eye some time ago, this stable boy to whom I would tell what some would consider slightly untrue stories. I found myself unable to keep myself away from you."

"You mean stories of highwaymen in the loft?" he asked with a chuckle. "And the fool of a man unable to catch you?"

Juliet's cheeks burned. "Well, yes," she said with a giggle. "I must admit now that it was foolish of me to say such things, and I realize now that I must put those ways behind me."

She smoothed out her skirts to give her hands something to do. From where had this mature version of herself come? She almost did not recognize herself, and yet, it was a person she enjoyed being. Especially when she was speaking to Daniel.

"That night I invited you to the loft with me? I understand now why you declined. I imagine it is because you respect me."

He nodded. "That's exactly why I said no."

"When you carried me to the house, the manner in which you looked at me…" She looked down at the ground in order to keep her courage to say the words. "I find I wish to see that look again."

A horse whinnied, and Juliet knew poor Annabel more than likely had grown bored long ago.

"I admit I enjoyed that look, and now I find myself giving you the same."

Daniel cleared his throat. "I suppose I liked that look myself," he said.

Suddenly, they were grinning at one another like two mischievous children, and Juliet wanted this moment to never end. Or if it did, it was with her in his arms. However, she kept her distance; neither of them was quite ready for that step.

"I have been wishing to ask you something else," she said as she searched his eyes. "What are your dreams in life?"

He did not hesitate in replying. "I'd like to own my own cottage. I want to keep working at a place like this, but it'd be nice to return to my own home at night. It's a simple dream, but that's it."

"I think it is a beautiful dream," Juliet said with a sigh. "And one I am certain you will realize one day." She paused. "What did you mean, 'a place like this'? Could you not do that here?"

He looked down at the ground once more, and Juliet's heart skipped a beat. "In the North, there are homes and land able to be bought for much less than here. With the number of villages sprouting in that area, I've decided to leave Scarlett Hall and move up there."

Juliet thought she would fall over at his words. "Leave?" she asked in a panic. "When?"

"I'm thinking May at the latest, when travel is easier."

The idea of this man leaving frightened Juliet, but May was a long way off. She decided to push it aside for now.

"May I ask you a question?" Daniel said.

"Please, do."

"You asked me about what I want."

She smiled. "And it is a beautiful dream."

"But I want to know, what do you want? What is your dream?"

The words seemed to echo off the walls, and she sat uncertain how to reply. Her idea of happiness had changed much in the past month, and now she was, for the first time in her life, without any idea of what she desired.

"I'm sorry for asking," Daniel whispered. "Forgive me for being bold."

Juliet laughed. "Not at all. It is a fine question and one I am glad to answer." She looked at him and wanted nothing more than to tell him everything that was on her heart at that moment. What was the harm in doing so? "I am seeing things as I have never seen them before. You see, since I was young, those things you spoke of before, about when I was married—fine dresses and beautiful things? Those were part of those dreams I once had. I believed that, as long as I had those things, I would be happy in life."

"There's nothing wrong with wanting the best things in life. If I had them, I'm sure I'd be happy, and you deserve them a lot more than I do."

"But do you not see? That is now my dilemma. Lord Parsons gave me a gold bracelet, and I know many men of the *ton* who would buy me anything I desired in exchange for my hand in marriage. Although I believe I could have the finest dresses and attend the grandest of balls, in the end, I would have nothing. For those things do not bring me the joy they once did." She took a deep breath and released it in order to calm her rattled nerves. Never before in her life had she ever been so frank with anyone, even Annabel. "I will not lie, a woman will always desire beautiful things, but perhaps there is more to life than that."

Daniel smiled and rose from his stool. "It's a lesson I've learned all my life," he said. "I used to envy your family for what they could buy, but I came to realize that those fine things your father had weren't meant for me." He put his arms out. "Especially now since I got a nice overcoat. And friends like you. A friend I can listen to or maybe tell what I'm thinking." He sat back down on the stool. "I believe the best things in life can't be purchased in a shop."

"No, they cannot," Juliet whispered. "I am seeing that now more than ever. Thank you for your friendship and the manner in which you have endured my presence in the past."

"Miss Juliet," Daniel said, "I think we have a very good friendship, and I'm the one who'll treasure it. No matter what may come of our lives, I hope to always remain your friend."

"And I yours," Juliet said. Then she put her arms around him, not to feel his muscles or to give him the opportunity to whisper to her how beautiful he believed she was, but to relish in the hold of a friend she adored.

"You probably should return to the house before Lady Lambert worries," he said. "Will you come to teach me tomorrow?"

She nodded. "Yes. If you will have me."

Daniel laughed. "Tomorrow, it is."

When Juliet found Annabel, the poor girl was stifling a yawn. "How was the lesson?" Juliet could not see the smile, but she heard it in the girl's tone. "Were you able to teach him?"

Juliet laughed. "It was I who learned," she replied. "I realize now that he has taught me more than I could ever teach him."

A young child had left the house earlier that evening, but a new woman returned to take her place, and Juliet found she liked her very much.

Chapter Fourteen

The house was warm compared to the stables, and Juliet handed her cloak to Forbes as she looked down the hallway toward the study, curious as to what her mother was doing. Juliet had seen little of the woman over the past two days, and after the night's events, she needed advice that only a mother could give.

"I wish to speak to Mother," she told Annabel. "Shall we meet in the drawing room?"

Annabel nodded. "I will see you there."

Juliet made her way down the darkened hallway until she came to the study. The door was ajar, and she inched it open. Inside, candles glowed, highlighting her mother, who sat at the desk once belonging to her father. The woman had no book or quill in her hand, but instead sat with her elbows on the desk and her head buried in her hands.

"Mother?" Juliet whispered, hoping not to startle the woman. Her mother looked up as Juliet closed the door. "What are you doing?"

Her mother chuckled, but it sounded forced. "I was merely thinking," she replied. "How was the lesson with Daniel?"

"It went well," Juliet replied, taking a seat in one of the two chairs in front of the desk. "He already recognizes a few letters from memory, but I am hoping that, in a few months, he will be reading."

"That is good," her mother replied, placing her hands together on the desk. "However, you must remember that it will take some time. You will need to be patient with him."

Juliet nodded. "I will. I must admit, he is as eager to learn as I am to teach."

"No more than three nights a week," her mother admonished, and Juliet's heart sank. "You have no reason to conduct that many lessons, as it will only hinder his learning."

In times past, Juliet would have argued; however, this time, she did not. Her mother was correct, and she did not wish to place an added burden on Daniel.

"I understand," she replied. She studied her mother's face. "You appear tired, Mother. Are you well?"

"Oh, yes," her mother replied with a sigh. "I am tired, but well. It is the daily running of the household that fatigues me. I suppose I am not as spry as I once was." She said the last with a light chuckle.

Juliet was certain the woman was not telling the complete truth, but she did tend to be stubborn and would never reveal what was bothering her. There were things Juliet wished to ask concerning Daniel, but she knew she could not do so outright.

"And what is on your mind?" her mother asked, her eyes narrowed. "Is something wrong?"

"Nothing is wrong," Juliet said as a story began to form in her mind. "It is just that, when I was at Caroline's, she told me a story, but I doubt its probity."

Her mother laughed. "Caroline is quite the storyteller," she said. "What story has she told you this time?"

"She claims that her cousin's cousin," she waved her hand dismissively, "was to be wed to a baron. However, she has fallen in love with one of the gardeners. I thought such a thing would never be allowed, but Caroline says that the woman's parents allowed it."

Her mother pursed her lips for a moment. "I suppose they could; although, it is very rare. In the end, it would not benefit either person, for the woman would be shunned by her peers, and the man would never be accepted by the *ton* regardless of how sophisticated he became."

"He owns property," Juliet added. "Or rather, he has plans to buy several parcels. Would he not then become a part of the Landed Gentry by doing so?"

Much to Juliet's disappointment, her mother shook her head. "The amount of land he would have to own would be vast, and then he would have to petition..." She paused and looked at Juliet. "Why does this story interest you so?"

Juliet's heart raced. Did her mother suspect her true intentions? However, she had one more question to ask. Biting back a retort she preferred to speak, and choosing her words carefully, she said, "We have spoken of love recently, and Caroline said it was due to the love the couple share that the parents allowed it. What do you believe you would do if such a situation arose?"

Her mother's eyes seemed to bore right through Juliet, and it took everything in her to keep from breaking down and admitting her feelings for Daniel. "This has nothing to do with the cobbler, does it?" her mother asked. "Or you or Annabel?"

"Robert?" Juliet replied with a relieved laugh. "Of course not. I can assure you of that fact. I was simply curious what you thought, is all."

Her mother leaned back in the chair and sighed. "Forgive my question, but as to yours, I would do everything I could to stop it from happening."

"Even if Hannah or I were in love?"

A few moments of silence followed. What could the woman be thinking?

"Hannah has an interest in a gentleman, and you have Lord Parsons. I believe this conversation has no merit and therefore no longer worthy of our time."

Frustrated, Juliet rose when her mother did the same. "Well, thank you for listening. I believe I will join Annabel in the drawing room. Would you care to join us?"

"I do not believe so," her mother replied. "I must speak to you a moment before you go concerning the cobbler."

"What of him?" Juliet asked. Her mother had warned her once, and now she meant to do so again?

"Perhaps I was a bit rude in the shop," her mother said, much to Juliet's surprise. "It seems that you and Annabel enjoy going there?"

Juliet nodded. "We do."

"I must ask...has the man..." She paused. "Is he kind to the two of you?"

"Yes, he is," Juliet said. "He has been nothing but a gentleman. Why do you ask?"

Her mother sighed. "I see no reason why you would wish to return there often, but if you choose to, I will not stop you."

Juliet was confused. "But you were angry and told me never to return. Now you are allowing me to go?"

"I am. However, promise me you will always take Annabel with you." Juliet nodded her agreement, and her mother added, "I have one more request of you. There are things which are said by others that are not always true. Whether it be something from this man or someone else, be careful with what you might hear."

Juliet almost asked her mother why, but then a realization came over her. With the story she had just shared with the woman, it was no wonder her mother was concerned.

"Most of what people discuss are simply tales," Juliet replied with a sniff. "Do not worry; I will not return to his shop often, and when I do, I will always take Annabel, and I will keep my ears guarded."

Her mother walked around the desk and embraced Juliet. "You are my sweet Juliet," she whispered in her ear. "So precious to my heart." She said this as if she were saying goodbye, and it left a stone in Juliet's stomach. "You know I Love you, do you not?"

"Yes," Juliet replied, confused at her mother's tone. "And I love you. It has always been that way and shall always remain so."

Her mother smiled. "A woman of fire," she said. "Now, go to Annabel and talk about things that women your age discuss."

Juliet laughed and walked to the door. She opened it and glance back at her mother, who had returned to the chair behind the desk. She gave the woman a smile and closed the door behind her, replaying the conversation in her mind. There was something about the cobbler that worried her mother, but Juliet could not reason it out. And to now change her mind about returning to the shop made little sense.

Well, there was little she could do about it now. She shrugged and made her way to the drawing room to see what Annabel thought of the situation.

Chapter Fifteen

The sun had set some time ago as Juliet sat beside Daniel at the worktable. Annabel was off doing whatever she had become accustomed to doing during the lessons, more than likely off talking with the horses as she was wont to do.

It had been nearly two weeks since Juliet had given her first lesson, and she found herself enjoying Daniel's company all the more with each session. These more intimate moments were the only opportunities she and Daniel had to sit close beside one another so they could review the books she brought with her. With each letter he uttered, Juliet had never been so proud, for the man was making great strides.

"E," Daniel said with his easy smile. "Elephant or enjoy."

"Very good," Juliet said before pointing to the next page. "What is this letter? Do you remember?" She despised sounding like a tutor with a child, but she knew of no other way to instruct. When Nathaniel, her brother and the youngest in the family, was small, she shared in part of the responsibility of teaching him, but Isabel had held the reins of the lessons, so a majority of the time Juliet was left to sit quietly and watch. Not that she did much watching either, not when there were so many other interests on which to focus.

Daniel studied the page for a moment and frowned. "K?"

"It is an F," Juliet said.

The man groaned and stood up so quickly his stool fell over.

"Daniel?"

"It's no use," he said, waving his hand at the book. "I'll never learn to read! Even if I do, what good will it do me? A stable hand doesn't need to know how to read to do his job!" He walked over to the bench, and Juliet rose from her stool.

"You are doing well," she said as she came up behind him. "And you are allowed to make mistakes. It is a natural part of learning."

He turned and she could see the frustration clouding his face. "You're a fine teacher, and I appreciate the lessons, but I'm not an educated man and I'll never be. This is just a waste of your time."

Juliet was unsure as to what to say, and the more she thought on his words, the more frustrated she became. Then an idea came to her. "A letter came for you today," she said with a smile. "A very important letter."

"A letter?" he asked in clear shock. "A letter for me? Who'd be writing to me?"

Juliet smiled as she turned and walked away from him, taking the smallest of steps. "It is a letter of great importance. I know I should not have read it, but I did. I must say, you are a very fortunate man."

Daniel hurried to her side. "Can you tell me what it said?" he asked, much like a small child receiving a gift who is unable to wait to open it to learn its contents.

She put away her grin and gave a dramatic sigh before turning to look at him. "I will make a deal with you," she said. She waited for him to nod his agreement before continuing. "I will bring the letter tomorrow, and you may do with it as you wish."

"But I can't read!" he exclaimed in frustration.

She raised a single eyebrow. "Then perhaps you should not throw a fit like a child and return to your stool so we are able to continue your lesson."

Daniel's eyes widened and then he laughed. "You're a very good teacher," he said before returning to the table. He sat back down and looked up at her from his low perch. "Thank you."

She pretended to give a haughty sniff. "You are most welcome," she replied as she also retook her seat. "Next time if you act as such, there shall be no sweets for you for a week!" She pointed her finger as she said this, which made them both laugh. The sound of his laughter was so sweet it made her heart happy, and she wished to hear it again.

She did not have to wait long. "I'll write a letter to my parents and tell them how mean the headmistress is," he said, which made them both laugh once more. He shook his head. "I'm only teasing. I could never speak an ill word against you."

"And nor could I you," Juliet said. In times past, she would have used this time to speak about her life or perhaps tell a tale. However, now she realized that the joy in helping Daniel was far better than those things. "Now, back to this letter. F."

"F," he repeated.

As the candle burned lower, Juliet continued her lesson, repeating the same words over and over again. Soon, enough time had passed and she did not want to overwhelm the man. "You are learning far faster than I ever did," she said. "I am very proud of you. My guess is that, by summer, you shall be reading."

"That would be wonderful," Daniel said as if she had told him he would be moving into the great house where he would be a part of the family. "Knowing how to read'll be helpful when I leave for the North." He set a few tools on the table he had removed for their lesson. He stopped and looked down. "I'll miss you, Miss Juliet," he whispered.

"And I will miss you," she said, fighting back tears. "Might I make a request?"

He looked up at her with an earnest eye. "Anything."

"Address me as simply Juliet."

He cocked his head to the side and stared at her for a moment, and she found herself wishing to shift in his gaze. "I'll do that only because you requested it. And only when we're doing our lessons. I don't want Lady Lambert to be angry with me."

She gave a relieved sigh. When had she begun to hold her breath? "And we shall not speak of you leaving," she added. "You never know; perhaps you will wish to remain here by the time May comes around." The thought of visiting the stables and finding Daniel gone made her heart clench.

"Maybe. It doesn't matter, really. It's still a long time away and I mightn't have enough money." He shrugged.

"If funds are an issue," Juliet said, "then I shall ask Mother to dock your wages so you will never leave."

Daniel laughed. "You'd do that?" he asked in mock consternation.

Juliet nodded. "In fact, I mean to tell her tonight. Right now!" She turned as if to leave, but he grabbed her by the waist and pulled her into him. Her heart beat faster than it ever had in her life, and she knew he was going to kiss her. Juliet closed her eyes in expectation, parted her lips just so, and whispered. "It is all right."

"Juliet!"

Annabel's harried voice had Juliet and Daniel both taking several steps back from one another.

"Juliet, your mother is coming!"

If her heart had been pounding before, it struck her sternum so hard she worried it would jump out of her chest. They scrambled to their stools, Daniel shoving the tools he had set out to the side, and looked over the book they had been studying before.

Annabel joined them, leaning over with her elbows on the table as if she had been watching them all along, and when Juliet heard her mother's footsteps, she said, "Very good." She closed the book. "That is enough for this evening. You are doing well, and I believe that, if you keep studying, you will continue to improve."

"Thank you, Miss Juliet," Daniel replied. "I'll practice as you've suggested."

Juliet gave him a nod and then turned to see her mother standing in the doorway. "Mother," Juliet said as if she had been startled by the woman's sudden appearance, "I did not realize you were there."

Her mother gave her a smile. "I only just arrived." She waited for Juliet and Annabel to join her, and the trio began the long trek through the main corridor. "How go the lessons?"

"They are going well," Juliet said. They stepped outside where the stars shone in the dark cloudless sky and the moon cast its glow upon the walls of Scarlett hall. "He is learning quickly, and Annabel and I are enjoying tutoring the man."

When they reached the steps to the front door, her mother stopped and asked, "Have you made arrangements to call on Caroline on Tuesday next?"

Juliet worried her lower lip. "She will not be home," she said, although, with her mind on her lessons with Daniel, the truth was she had forgotten to send a card. Then an idea came to her. "Annabel and I shall go riding."

Her mother nodded. "Have Cook pack you a basket and make it a day of adventure and fun."

Juliet studied her mother. What had brought on this sudden urgency to have them gone? It had been tradition for so long, with few Tuesdays gone unchanged, but now her mother was insistent in her request. "If you wish to be rid of us, might I suggest sending us to Paris?" She and Annabel giggled, but her mother did not.

"Goodnight, girls," she said.

Annabel glanced at Juliet before they followed Juliet's mother into the house. "Your mother," Annabel whispered, "I worry about her. I have seen her change over the last year, and although I may be mistaken, it seems to have worsened as of late."

Juliet nodded. "I fear the same," she replied as she watched her mother continue to the drawing room. "First, we are to stay away from the cobbler, and then we are told to return to him. Then she makes a fuss over something to which I have been accustomed for as long as I can remember." She shook her head.

When they arrived at Juliet's room, Annabel asked, "What are we to do now? I am not ready to go to bed."

"We are not old women," Juliet replied with a wide grin. She walked over to the large trunk at the foot of her bed and opened the lid, from which she produced a bottle of brandy. "We are young and therefore going to celebrate."

"Celebrate what?" Annabel asked, her grin as wide as Juliet's.

That Daniel wishes to kiss me."

***

Early in the afternoon on Monday, Juliet and Annabel headed to Rumsbury. Although Juliet had promised her mother she would keep Annabel at her side whenever she went to see Robert, she knew when she made that promise that the chances of her keeping it were unlikely. Furthermore, Annabel wished to visit the millinery, and Juliet had no interest in looking at new hats, not with so much to tell Robert.

The bell over the door tinkled lightly as Juliet entered the shop. She paused after closing the door behind her when she saw Miss Teresa Finch speaking with Robert at the back counter. The woman was much older than Juliet and unmarried, although as Juliet looked at her unflattering yellow dress, it was no wonder. The color made the woman's skin look jaundiced and did little to brighten her dull gray eyes.

Robert and Miss Finch were in a quiet conversation, and Robert was whispering in the woman's ear when he looked at Juliet and winked. This relieved the bit of jealousy that threatened to overtake Juliet, for the man was her friend and certainly not that of Miss Finch! The woman was an arrogant and nosy gossip who always intruded in everyone else's business. Why the *ton* allowed the woman the dignity of invitations was beyond Juliet's understanding, but for some reason she received just as many as Juliet did.

Clearing her throat, Juliet approached the counter, and the two broke their secret gathering.

Miss Finch turned and gave Juliet a bright smile. "Miss Lambert," the woman said in her nasally voice that always grated on Juliet's nerves, "I see that your foot has healed. Your mother told me that you fell?" The way the woman asked was as if Juliet's suffering brought her great delight.

"I did fall," Juliet replied. "The doctor believed I would never be able to walk again, and yet, here I am defying the best scientific thought."

Miss Finch covered a snort with a light cough, and Robert walked around the counter to join them. He wore a well-fitted coat that was most definitely new, which told Juliet that business was going well.

"Ah, Miss Juliet," he said with a bow. "It is an honor to have you in my shop once again."

The frown that Miss Finch wore pleased Juliet greatly.

"Thank you, Robert," Juliet replied. "I was hoping to speak to you, but I can always return later when you and Miss Finch have completed whatever business you are conducting."

"There is no reason to leave," Miss Finch said. "Robert, I shall speak with you soon." She gave Juliet an overly-sweet smile before leaving, and Juliet stared at the door that closed behind the woman.

Why had she addressed Juliet's friend by his Christian name? And about what could the woman possibly wish to speak to Robert that she could not discuss in Juliet's presence? It was not as if purchasing a new pair of shoes was a private matter.

"She is trouble," Juliet warned Robert. "You would be best to keep your distance from her. Her gossip and tales are an embarrassment to her family and friends."

Robert laughed. "She may be those things, but I have wonderful news to share with you." The man's face lit up, and Juliet could not help but smile. "Miss Finch is also investing in the shop. Her family is quite wealthy, and she receives a hefty allowance."

Juliet's smile faded. "Oh, that is wonderful," she said, attempting to keep her disappointment from her voice. Reaching into her reticule, she produced a single note. "I was able to get extra funds this week. I am able to procure more if need be. I do not want Miss Finch to own more than I."

Robert smiled as he took the note and slipped it into his coat pocket. "Do not worry about her," he said. "No matter how much she invests, it is you who is my top partner."

"You are not lying to me, are you?" she asked.

The man frowned, and she regretted the words. "Never," he replied. "The money I am receiving from Miss Finch will not only give us more funds in order to buy the necessary supplies, but it also allows for me to search far and wide for more shops to open." He took a step toward Juliet. "It is my hope that my business partner and I own three shops by the end of the year. In five years, we shall have shops in London."

Juliet grinned thinking of all the shops and the money they would bring. Then her mind turned to Daniel. What did her future hold if he was not there to share it with her?

"You look upset," Robert said.

Juliet sighed and glanced around the shop. She had not noticed how empty it still was, but she was not the expert in running a shop. Plus, how much room did one need to simply display a few shoes? It was not as if he had a batch of ready-made shoes like some of the cobblers were offering. Robert had said on more than one occasion that shoes had to be designed to fit a particular foot, and that could not happen when shoes were produced in quantity.

"Do you remember when I mentioned the stable boy and how I wish to be near him?"

Robert nodded and leaned against the counter. "I do."

"I asked Mother about marrying a person outside of her station—through the presentation of a fictitious situation, of course. I am unsure as to what to do, for she will never allow Daniel and me to be together."

"You want to marry this man?" Robert asked.

"As of right now, although I can see the possibility, I only wish to further our friendship and see where it may lead. What are your thoughts?"

Robert rubbed his chin. "I believe your mother is right," he replied, much to her irritation. "What you wish for cannot be allowed for a woman of your standing."

Juliet sighed in frustration. So, Robert took her mother's side?

"However," he added, "if you are an established businesswoman, you may do whatever your heart desires."

This was not a perspective she had considered before. "I suppose you are right," she said. Yet, as much as she wished to be with Daniel, she also did not wish to upset her mother. If the woman ever learned about her feelings for Daniel, it would crush her.

As if hearing her thoughts, Robert said, "A day may come where you might hurt your mother. Such is the risk one must take. If that day comes, which I hope it does not, you and Daniel are welcome in my home as a place of refuge. It is not what you are accustomed to, but you may have all that I have."

Juliet was overcome by the man's offer, and tears filled her eyes at his gentle spirit. She had seen so much kindness as of late, and it was a joy to be a recipient of it. "Thank you," she said as she wrapped her arms around the man. "I will keep that offer in mind."

Robert returned to his place behind the counter. "As I said when we first met, your strength is great, and many will be jealous of it."

"That is very true," Juliet replied with a smile as she wiped away the few tears that had fallen over her lashes.

"Much like your mother."

A bolt of anger replaced the tranquility that had taken hold of Juliet. She did not appreciate the man speaking ill of her mother, and it was her duty to say so. "My mother..." she began, but the man interrupted her.

"Came into my shop looking for you a fortnight ago, and upon seeing her daughter conversing with a cobbler, became jealous. That is the short of it."

"Jealous?" Juliet asked. The man was mad! "Of me speaking to you?"

"Indeed," Robert replied. "She saw that we were conducting business together. You cannot deny she became angry."

Juliet frowned. "No, I suppose I cannot."

"Tell me. Did she not demand that you keep away from me?" Juliet nodded. "And what does one do when they make a mistake?"

"Apologize," Juliet replied. "One says they are sorry."

"Either you are here because you have defied your mother's wishes, or the woman realized her envy of her own daughter and was overcome with guilt."

Had Juliet not made this conclusion herself at some point? However, even then, she had pushed the idea aside, for there was little evidence that her mother was jealous.

"No, I cannot believe it," she said, although the truth of the words dawned on her as bright as the morning sun at mid-summer. "My own mother jealous of me? I have always known my sisters were, and of course other women of the *ton*, but my mother?"

"Your mother is a great woman," he said. "Forgive me for being the bearer of bad news, but as I have told you before, you are far wiser than most women I have known. And therefore, more women will seek to hurt you." He leaned forward and lowered his voice although they were alone. "I may be a simple cobbler, but I am your friend. I am the one you must trust, not only in business but in life. Do you trust me?"

Juliet did not have to think of her answer, for she did trust this man. He was wise and had seen far more into situations than she possibly could. "Yes, I do trust you."

"Excellent," he said standing upright. "Then we must continue to invest in our business together and find those who can, as well. Tell me, would you ask Miss Annabel to join us on our business venture?"

"I do not know if she would wish to," Juliet said doubtfully. "But I can ask." Then a thought came to mind. "With Miss Finch, and then Annabel and myself, would that not be too many investors?"

Robert laughed. "Not at all," he replied. "The more, the better. The others will only own a small percentage, as you, my friend, will by far take the larger cut. As well as Annabel, of course."

"Of course," Juliet said. "I will ask her when we return home. And since Miss Finch has decided to invest, as well, I have a tidy sum I have hidden away. I would like to invest that, as well."

"Excellent," he said. "I believe this meeting has gone well."

"Meeting? This was a meeting?"

He laughed again. "But of course. We spoke of business, did we not? It was our first official business meeting, and I must say you did quite well. I am impressed."

The compliment made Juliet grin like a fool, but she could not help herself. She was a businesswoman! What she did not know about business, Robert did, which balanced it all out rather nicely.

"Trust has increased this day," he said. "Trust that is going to serve us both well. Do you agree?"

"I do," Juliet said, unable to keep the silly smile from her lips. "Thank you for everything you have done for me."

"You are too kind," Robert replied. "But the truth is, it is you who has done everything for me."

Juliet could not help but beam all the more.

***

That evening, Juliet could not keep from thinking about her friendship with Robert and her mother's envy at that friendship. Juliet found it difficult to believe she had been correct in her earlier assessment, but the facts thus far seemed to confirm it as true. Her mother was jealous.

Juliet sighed as she twisted the quill in her fingers. She was in the study alone with her thoughts while the house was filled with the dreams of all those who slept. Perhaps her mother would one day marry again; that would deplete whatever jealousy the woman had for Juliet, or so she hoped. As she thought back, she realized her mother had become sullen after her father's death, and Juliet could not blame the woman—she missed her father terribly, so she could not imagine how her mother felt.

Her thoughts turned to Daniel and she could not help but smile. They held no lesson tonight, but after she and Annabel returned from their ride the following day, they would continue then. The thought of the final lesson they would have come May stilled her heart as memories of their shared laughter came to mind. However, when he had grabbed her and pulled her against him, a warm sensation had invaded her body and heart like never before. She had given the man permission to kiss her.

What had she been thinking? If news of that kiss, or rather attempted kiss, had gotten out, she and her entire family would have been shamed! Yet, the way he had held her, the possessiveness of his hands, had brought about sensations about which she had only read. It had been a perfect moment, one worthy of a scene in Hannah's novel.

Oh, why had they been interrupted!

She sighed. It was not the kiss that brought her to the study at this hour, and although it was difficult, she pushed the memory away. Daniel's frustration at his lessons was on what she needed to focus. She told him he had received a letter, and tonight she would write it. It would be a letter sharing her heart, which one day he would be able to read.

However, what did a lady tell a man for whom she cared but did not love? Juliet was not as well-read as Hannah or even Isabel, and she wanted to be certain the words were perfect.

Shaking her head, she put the pen to parchment and began to write.

My Dearest Daniel,

If you are reading this letter, then you have done well. You are not simply a stable boy as I once said; you are an educated man. Although, even if you could not read, it would not matter, for I care for the man you are now. The man who is kind and listens to every word I speak and asks the most thoughtful of questions.

You spoke of leaving one day, perhaps this summer. As I have thought on that possibility, I must admit that it breaks my heart.

Juliet took a deep breath and let it out slowly. She could not allow the man to leave, not without him knowing her true feelings for him. Therefore, she returned to the letter, and this time the words poured from her heart to the pen. She wrote of past dreams as well as new ones, and she concluded with the fact that he was an important part of them, as well.

Chapter Sixteen

Every Tuesday morning, the servants left for the village, and on many of those days Daniel joined them. He would purchase any personal items he might need or spend the day speaking with what few friends he had made over the years. Today, however, he delayed his journey in order to prepare the horses Juliet and Annabel would need in order to go riding.

Assuring the strap on Miss Annabel's saddle was tight, Daniel thought back to when Juliet was in his arms. His heart had raced so forcefully, he thought it would bound out of his chest and run away. His body had burned with a desire he had never known existed, and he felt a mixture of pleasure and shame course through him. If anyone had seen them, he was certain he would have been relieved of his position and Juliet would have been in trouble with her mother.

However, something had come over him, a beast of sorts that he could not control, and he had come so close to kissing her, he could feel their breath mingle. He had so wanted to show her what he felt for her, and she had even given him permission to do so. He would have honored that request if they had not been interrupted just in the nick of time.

He let out a small laugh as he returned to the worktable to retrieve Juliet's saddle. For so long he had listened to her many tales, many of which he did not believe, for they were much too far-fetched to be true. However, he enjoyed them all the same.

Running his hand over the letters that spelled out her name, he smiled. It was the only word he could read on sight, and that alone brought him great pleasure. The lessons had gone well, but he was a far cry from reading. Yet, the fact she took the time to instruct him gave him a sense of being worthy of an education, something he had never considered before, especially after years of ridicule from the other servants. And Juliet, as well.

He shook his head. She had apologized for her behavior; there was no sense bringing it to mind any longer. The truth was the woman had changed for the better since her fall from the loft. By all accounts, she was beautiful with her raven dark hair and matching eyes. Her skin was flawless, her smile contagious, but it was the kind heart to which he had been attracted, and to see it become so pronounced was wonderful. Was she mischievous? Indeed, she was. However, that only added to her allure.

For a moment he allowed his imagination to take over as he thought of what it would be like to have her as his wife. He would work day and night if there was even the slightest chance to have that happen, and their love for one another would be great. His cheeks burned as he considered that word: love. He cared for her, yes, but did he love her? As a man who had never experienced such an emotion, he was unsure, but he was willing to guess that he came close, and had for a long time. But he knew he had no right to love her, not a stable boy, and so he was happy to love her as a friend, for it was better than no love at all.

Not only would he never be allowed, he could not have her enduring the whispers that were bound to come no matter how far they lived.

Why is this woman of the ton *with such a simple man who cannot read?* they would ask. Men would scoff at him and ladies would shake their heads at Juliet for marrying a man unworthy of her.

Daniel sighed. It was nice to dream, but he needed to find the courage to tell Juliet that what they shared was just that—a dream and nothing more. It would hurt her as much as it would him, but it had to be said. He should have never allowed their talks to go so far, for it as cruel to give her hope for something that could not be. For if she were to agree to marry him, it would not take her long to realize her mistake, and by then it would be too late.

His thoughts were interrupted when Juliet and Miss Annabel

walked in, Miss Annabel carrying a large basket on her arm. Juliet was as beautiful, if not more so, as ever in a dark blue riding dress beneath a matching coat, her hair pulled back in a way he had never seen before. It had been put into a thick braid that she pulled over her shoulder, covered by a hat with dark blue lace and ribbon falling down her back. How could a woman be so beautiful?

"Your horses are ready," he said with a smile. "I've also rolled up two blankets and tied them behind the saddles as you requested. Is there anything else I can do?"

"Thank you," Juliet replied, that tiny smile playing at the corner of her lips. Her eyes sparkled as she reached into her pocket, produced a letter, and handed it to him. "This is for you. Please, keep it safe."

He looked at the writing on the outside, recognizing a few of the letters but not knowing what they said. "I'll hold it close," he said, folding it and placing it in the inside pocket of his overcoat. "Your hair looks very nice."

Juliet grinned in response. "Thank you."

Not wanting to forget the girl's cousin, he turned to her and added, "As does yours, Miss Annabel."

Annabel laughed. "You are always so kind," she said. "And if you are going to use Juliet's name, I do not see why you should be so formal with me. I am Annabel, if you do not mind."

"Only in private, as I told Juliet," he said with a bow. He turned back to Juliet. "I hope you enjoy your outing. Be careful; there are storm clouds off in the distance."

Juliet sighed and turned to Annabel. "I am afraid of storms and the trouble they bring."

"As am I," Annabel replied. Why were they grinning at one another? "What are we to do if trouble comes? What if the storm is severe and we become lost?"

Juliet tapped her lips with a gloved finger and then her eyes lit up. "Perhaps Daniel will accompany us. Will you do so?"

Daniel's heart skipped a beat. The idea was entertaining, but Daniel knew he had to draw a line, and the sooner the better. Things had already gone further than they should have, which was only going to make the truth that much more difficult, but he had no choice. If Lady

Lambert were to learn he had left with them, he would have no work and no home. He doubted the woman would ever strike him, but he would not blame her if she did.

"I can't go," he said. "I'm sorry, but it's not proper for ladies to be alone with…"

"I have a chaperon," Juliet said with a pout. "Annabel will watch out for me."

The last thing Daniel wanted was to hurt Juliet's feelings, but he would not put her at risk. "I'm honored you want to invite me, but your mother wouldn't be much pleased, and I doubt it would end well."

"My mother is locked away in her study as always," Juliet stated as she took a step toward him. "She will never learn of it. Although, even if she did, I cannot help that you were worried about the storm and came searching for us…"

Daniel was unsure if it was her smile, her beauty, or her heart that made him unable to argue, but in the end, he could do nothing more than simply nod.

"I'll follow after you leave," he said with a sigh. "I'll never understand how you get me to do these things"

But how he wished he did!

***

There was a chill to the air, although it was not overly cold, and the winter sky was a dark blackish-gray as Juliet rode Penelope beside Annabel's Rose Petal. The storm of which Daniel spoke was still on the horizon, and she predicted they would have more than enough time to reach the place where they would stop and eat what Cook had packed for them in the basket.

Glancing over her shoulder at the top of a hill, she was pleased to see Daniel riding up behind them.

"Do you love him?" Annabel asked.

The question was so unexpected that Juliet nearly fell from her saddle. "I do not believe so," she replied. She turned to look at her cousin. Although she wore a hat much like the one Juliet wore, the girl had left her blond hair unbound so it flowed behind her. "What are your thoughts?"

Annabel puckered her lips in thought. "I am uncertain," she replied. "I do not know what love is, but the manner in which the two of you look at one another—the shared smiles and fleeting glances—these tell me that you are in love."

Juliet glanced back at the approaching stable boy and sighed. "It is a beautiful smile he has," she said. "He is handsome, is he not?"

Annabel giggled and nodded. "I believe so."

Juliet barely heard her cousin respond as she continued. "Strong muscles, a heart that exudes kindness." She sighed again. "He is everything a man should be, and I do care for him."

"I believe it is love," Annabel said firmly. "Perhaps when you kiss him, you will experience it. Hannah told me that is what happens."

Juliet snorted. "My dear Annabel, Hannah knows noth..." She clamped her mouth shut. Her old ways of belittling her sisters was one thing she did not wish to resurrect, and she took a moment to push away the retort. "Many women our age, as well as that of my sister, have yet to experience love and therefore cannot make rational judgments about it."

"Do tell me the moment you know," Annabel said. "I do not wish to attend the season next year without knowing for certain."

"I will be sure to do that," Juliet replied before clicking her tongue and tapping her heel on the horse's flank to send her in a slow amble. They had yet to leave her family's property, for what they owned was vast. She had spent many hours as a child playing in these fields with her sisters and brother, and thoughts of blind man's bluff and shuttlecock—a challenge on windy days—played in her mind.

However, those days were well behind her. She was now a woman, one involved in a business and interested in a man, her stable boy, with whom she wished she could spend more time. Life was perfect. Who would have thought that injuring her ankle would be the best thing to happen to her?

"I could've left an hour later and still caught up with you," Daniel said as he rode up to them. "Maybe even two."

"Is that right?" Juliet asked with mock haughtiness. Then she gave him a small smile as he brushed away a wave of dark hair from his brow. Just that simple action made her breath catch and she had to force moisture into her dry mouth. "Are you saying that you are a more skilled rider than I?"

He laughed. "I wouldn't call myself skilled necessarily, but compared to most women, I'm a far better rider than they are."

"That might be true," Juliet replied smugly. "However, you have forgotten one simple thing."

"Oh? And what's that?"

"I am not like most women." She took a tight hold of the reins and winked before shouting, "Ha!" Penelope snorted, ducked her head, and shot forward, her powerful legs creating a significant distance between Juliet and Daniel in a very short amount of time.

"Wait! You can't do this!" Daniel yelled.

"Oh, but I can," Juliet shouted back. "And I will." Joy rang through her soul, and she placed a hand on her hat before it blew away, laughing all the while.

Daniel's horse was faster, however, and soon he was riding alongside her. "Juliet, I must insist you slow down," he begged, but Juliet took his words to be a challenge.

Lowering herself, she whispered into Penelope's ear, urging her to go faster as she dug her heel into the horse's side. Penelope shot forward and Juliet laughed when Daniel groaned as the distance grew between them.

Soon after, she slowed the horse as she approached an outcropping of trees, their limbs bare in the winter air. She turned as she brought Penelope to a stop and Daniel joined her.

She expected him to be angry, but he was not, for he wore a wide grin. "I've learned an important lesson," he said as he dismounted and walked the horse toward where she had stopped beneath one of the trees.

"And what was that, pray tell?"

"You, Juliet, are not like most women. In fact, I believe you're far better in everything you do."

"You are learning more than I had hoped to teach you," she said with a laugh. "Now, let us see if this time you do not allow me to fall." Her heart thumped and her head felt light as he helped her from the horse, his hands wrapped around her waist.

"I won't let you fall," he said, a huskiness to his voice that she found enthralling. "Never again."

Juliet looked past Daniel to see Annabel still some ways off. With the density of brush beneath the trees, she was certain her cousin could not see them. "I believe myself safe in your arms," she whispered. "It is a feeling I enjoy."

Daniel closed his eyes for a moment. "I have that feeling, too, but we can't…"

Juliet could not wait a moment longer, and she lifted herself onto the tips of her toes, wrapped her arms around him, and pressed her lips to his. It was as if she weighed nothing in his arms; her heart soared to places she did not know existed. And his lips! They were gentle and soft, and she was pleased to realize they were a perfect match to hers.

She now understood that Daniel meant everything to her, and what Hannah had told her was correct—she would know love when she found it. For she did love Daniel, and it was the most wonderful feeling, one she wished to never lose.

Suddenly, Daniel pushed her away. "I'm sorry," he said as he took a step back. "I shouldn't have…"

"You did nothing, so you have nothing for which to apologize. I felt something beautiful in that kiss."

He glanced at the ground. "I did, too."

"Then do not look so sorrowful," she said with a teasing smile as she leaned over to look at his turned down face. "You should be happy, for I know I am."

Daniel looked up at her, a smile on his face. "I should fix up the blankets or Annabel will become suspicious."

Juliet nodded, and Daniel turned to walk away just as Annabel arrived, her smile telling Juliet she knew what had taken place.

"I believe she is already suspicious," Juliet said with a light laugh.

Chapter Seventeen

Juliet sat on the blanket Daniel had spread in a clearing at the edge of the tree line, the bank of trees and underbrush blocking the light breeze at their backs. Annabel had made a feeble excuse of wishing to catch up on some light reading and had moved to lean against one of the trees some twenty paces behind them, a blanket both beneath and wrapped around her shoulders. Juliet was thankful for the girl's willingness to being discreet when it was necessary and allowing Juliet and Daniel time alone—or relatively alone as it were—demonstrated the girl's good nature.

Although the weather was far from perfect—the storm that had been on the horizon was drawing near—simply being with Daniel made everything right.

Sitting beside the man she had kissed not ten minutes earlier left Juliet without words, and with Daniel's already quiet demeanor, they sat in silence, the only sounds the rustle of the empty branches and the light whistle of the breeze through the trees.

"Do you realize the risk I took by being here?" Daniel asked with a mischievous grin. "I keep expecting Lady Lambert to come riding over that hill."

Juliet laughed. "Mother always remains inside the house to do whatever it is she does on Tuesdays, so there is no need to worry." He gave a nod and wrung his hands. "If you are concerned that I mean to kiss you again, I assure you there is no need. I will not do it."

He chuckled. "No, it's not that. I thought that was wonderful."

"Then, what worries you?"

He glanced around for a moment before turning his attention back to her and saying, "I worry about us, if I'm honest. The time we spend together..."

"I told you my mother is not going to see us," Juliet interrupted. She reached over and took his hand. "You need not worry about that." She glanced down and noticed how his large calloused hand completely engulfed hers, and she felt protected by it.

"Not just today," Daniel said. "I said before; you're a lady and I'm just a stable boy."

Juliet jutted her chin defiantly. "And I told you, I do not care."

He shook his head. "My dream is to own a bit of land one day. Finding the money'll be challenging. I also want to have my own business so I'm keeping the money that's being made. That's not going to be easy, either. Your mother has her own dreams for you, and I'm sure they don't include me."

"This is not about what my mother wants," Juliet said in frustration. "It is about what I want."

"And what do you want?"

The question was honest and forthcoming, and Juliet knew the answer immediately. "To be with you."

"That's nice of you to say, and I'd like nothing more than for you to be with me. But this path we're taking will end up hurting us both in the end."

Juliet placed a hand on his stubbled cheek. "Do not worry. You must trust that I will make it all work. Do you trust me?"

The way he looked into her eyes made her heat, but she waited with as much patience as she could for him to respond. "I do, I suppose."

"Good," she replied. "For I am already investing in a business."

Daniel raised his brows in surprise. "Who with?"

"The new cobbler in Rumsbury," Juliet replied. She explained how the arrangement came to be, and Daniel listened, giving nods as she spoke. "Do you not see? In time, I will own my own shops and be able to secure my own income."

What she had expected was Daniel to congratulate her on her business prowess, but instead, he asked, "How long have you known this man?"

"A couple of months," she replied. "However, he is kind, like you."

Daniel did not look pleased. "Be careful," he said. "Those who seek money from you may not have the best intentions."

Juliet snorted. "You are kind to be concerned," she said as if speaking to a child. The man was clearly jealous! "However, I am much too intelligent to be fooled by the likes of him." She reached into the basket and removed the glasses and a bottle of brandy. "Now, let us have a drink in celebration."

"What are we celebrating?" Daniel asked. "This business you're in?"

"No." She handed him one of the glasses and poured her own. "We are celebrating you and I courting."

"Courting?" Daniel asked in surprise. "Courting is for gentlemen and ladies. You might be a lady, but I'm definitely no gentleman. What do I know about courting?"

Juliet giggled at his naivety. "It is simple, really," she replied. "You ask if I would like to court, and I give you my answer."

Daniel smiled. "I suppose I can do that," he said. He sat up a bit straighter. "Juliet, I'd like to court you. Will you say yes?"

She sighed with a slow shake of her head. "A lady must be told how important she is, or she will refuse the offer. In such a situation, I would reject you outright, but for you I shall make an exception." She said the last with a wink, which only broadened his smile.

"I see." He raised his brows. "Maybe I don't want to ask."

For a moment, her breath caught in her throat. Had she gone too far? She had worked too hard to bring them together to lose now!

Just as she made to apologize, however, he winked at her. "I was only teasing," he said.

Juliet playfully slapped his arm. "You!" she said with a laugh. Inside she sighed with relief. This was why she enjoyed their time together.

"Forgive me," he said. "I'll try again."

She smoothed her skirts. "Thank you."

"Miss Juliet, there are many things in life I've wished for, and many of them have come true. But to be able to court a lady such as yourself would be the greatest wish ever granted. So, will you allow me to court you?"

Juliet felt as weightless as a leaf floating on a current of air. "Yes," she whispered. "I would like that very much."

He lifted his glass. "To us, then," he said.

Juliet raised hers, as well, and then took a sip of the brandy. A thought struck her—she was officially being courted! And by a simple stable boy, no less. No, there was nothing simple about Daniel, and she thought herself the luckiest woman in the world.

For several minutes, they sat in silence, both looking at the ground between them; although, she caught him sneaking glances at her when she attempted to sneak a glance at him. Then, her thoughts went to him leaving.

"When you mean to leave," she said, "if I were to wish to join you, how would you respond?"

He ran a finger around the rim of his glass. "I'd like that," he said, but his tone did not match his words. "But I fear..."

She had no desire to hear his doubts. "My mother, the *ton*, and everything I have been raised to know have nothing to do with what is on my heart. No one will stop that which I desire."

"If that's true," he said, "I'd want you with me. But you must understand that the life you have led? I can't provide those things." He looked down as if shamed by his words, and once again Juliet reached out and slipped her hand in his. Before she could respond, however, he continued. "The dresses, the servants; you've lived such a wonderful life of leisure. All of it would be gone. I'm worried you'd miss what you once had."

"Daniel," she whispered, and he looked up at her. "I no longer care for those things; I only care for you. I once thought that the importance of a gentleman was what he could buy for me or the recognition I would receive." She sighed. "Those days are past. I realize now that love is when a man loves a woman and provides her with what she needs for her heart as she does the same for him."

Daniel smiled. "For years, I cherished every moment I saw you. I was afraid every moment would be my last, because I knew a gentleman would take you away. Now, I want to be that man who cares for you." He paused. "I do worry what your mother'll say. I don't want to see you hurt."

"I worry at times, as well," she replied truthfully. "However, I believe she will understand. Come May, with or without her consent, we will leave Scarlett Hall and start a new life. Together." Although he nodded, she did not miss the look of doubt etched in his features. "Remember, I am not like most women," she added with a wide grin.

He laughed and the doubtful look disappeared. "No, you're not," he said. "I should stop doubting you."

"That is very wise," Juliet said with another wide grin just as the first sprinkles of rain fell upon them. She glanced up at the sky. "We had best leave."

She went to stand, but Daniel hurried to his feet and stretched out a hand to her. "I won't have a lady I'm courting stand by herself."

Juliet smiled and allowed him to help her rise. "That is good," she said. "You are learning quickly, but there are other rules you must learn, as well."

"Oh?" he asked. "What other rules?"

"Stop your worrying," she chastised. "I will tell you all of them in time."

***

Rain pelted against the drawing room window as Eleanor stood gazing out into the beginnings of a storm. Although the fireplace roared, she felt anything but warm. She replayed the events that led to this moment in time and wondered what had gone wrong.

"The finest brandy," Mr. Robert Mullens said from behind her as he smacked his lips together. "I am glad you have decided not to hold back by serving me anything less."

Eleanor nodded but did not reply. It was the third time the man had come to her home, and she wished she knew a way to make it the last. Unfortunately, she had yet to devise a plan that did not leave her and her family open to ridicule and shame.

"Do you believe yourself so much better than I that you will not respond?" he whispered in her ear.

She choked down a gasp but could do little to stop herself from spinning around in surprise at his sneaking up behind her without her knowledge. Now she was trapped between him and the window, and she could do nothing to ease her pounding heart.

"My apologies," she said, although she felt no sorrow for her actions. "I tend to let my mind wander, and..." Her words were cut off when he took her hand. Her stomach rolled at his touch, and it took every ounce of strength she could muster to not pull it back.

"Come and pour me another drink," he said, guiding her toward the cart that held the liquor decanters. Once there, he set down his glass, and she took the decanter and poured. "More," he commanded when she poured him only a measure that was appropriate for a gentleman.

She had to get this man out of her house. "It is raining," she said. "I am worried the girls will return home early. They cannot see us together."

The laugh Robert produced sent a shiver down her spine. "That is what worries you?" he asked. "Being seen with me?" He shook his head and abruptly stopped his chuckling. "Pour me more. I do not care what they see."

Eleanor did as the man bade and then handed him the glass. He wasted no time in taking a large gulp.

"That is much better," he said with an appeased sigh.

Eleanor cringed as Robert's eyes looked her up and down. "How beautiful you are, Eleanor," he murmured as the back of his hand touched her face. "To think that a lady such as you and a simple man such as I share such an..." He paused as if attempting to find the right words, "intimate secret."

Repulsed, Eleanor took a small step back, and although her back touched the cold window, it allowed her even the tiniest amount of space between her and Robert. "I shall get your money," she said, slipping past him and walking over to the small ornate box above the fireplace. She removed the required amount and handed it to Robert, who had returned to his place on the couch.

He took it with quick hands, shoved it into his coat pocket, and sighed. He grabbed her hand, and she sat beside him, for she already knew he would demand it of her.

"My new coat?" he said, sitting up straighter in his seat. "Do you like it?"

"It is a nice coat," she said. Why did this man insist on remaining where he was not wanted?

"I worry, however, about its cost and what it has done to my funds. I am afraid that the next time I call, I will require more money."

Eleanor bit back a gasp. "How much more?"

"Double."

This time she did gasp. "I cannot pay that much," she said with shock. "I realize that you do not believe me, but I assure you that the funds we have are low and will remain so until my new investments produce more income. This will still take some time."

Robert scowled and finished off the remainder of his drink. "Then we will find another way for you to pay me," he said as he set his glass on the table. His gaze returned to her face. "I assume you have jewelry?"

She shook her head although she had plenty. Yet, how would he know?"

"Oh, very well," he said with a heavy sigh. "I will make a note of the payments owed. You can pay me in full when the funds arrive in the future."

Worry and anger coursed through her. "How long do you require payment?" She attempted to keep the demand from her tone. "Another year?"

"Oh, Eleanor," he said as if speaking to a child for whom he was disappointed, "do you believe I would be so cruel?" He stood and walked over to the fireplace, put his hands out as if to warm them, his back to her. "I will stop asking once you have given me what I want."

Her heart pounded in her chest. "What is it you seek?" she asked, fearing what his answer would be. "I told you the funds I have..."

"Do not exist," he finished for her with a sigh. "Yes, I know this." He turned and walked toward her so quickly, she feared he would knock her over in the process. "What I want is what I have desired for years. It is what I dreamed of while working at this home."

Eleanor attempted to look away, but he grabbed her chin and forced her to face him. "Your children are grown and are now leaving. This home is much too large for you to be alone in it."

"I will not marry you," she said, her anger rising. "You have your money, now leave!" She reached up to pull his hand away, but he removed it before she could.

"You forget," he said in a low, threatening tone, "I know a secret, and unless you want me to reveal it, I suggest you start thinking of the future."

"You are mad!" she whispered as he reached up and brushed a thumb to her cheek. "You think that, by marrying me, I would..."

"It does not matter what you believe I think," he interrupted. "All that matters is what I want. And you as my wife is what I have always desired. Now I have the means to see it happen." He leaned in and Eleanor quickly turned her face, his lips grazing her cheek. When she turned back to him, his face was red with anger.

A noise in the hallway caught her attention. "The girls have returned," she said, although it was more than likely the house settling. "Please, leave."

"Do not do that again," he said with a hiss. He turned and headed to the door. "I want my money, Eleanor, and I want a life that I never had. You can give this to me and at the same time keep your secret hidden." He then turned back to her. "I will be gone for nearly a month on business. When I return, have my money and your answer ready."

The moment he was gone, Eleanor clenched her fists. What was she to do?

However, before she was able to give it thought, the front door closed, and she let out a sigh of relief. The man was most definitely mad. How dare he ask to marry her, for it was something to which she would never agree!

Yet, he held knowledge of a secret so great, it would destroy her family.

Her mind played over the possibilities of what she could do. Soon, payment of money would not be enough to appease the man, and her stomach twisted at what more he would demand. She had to find a way to stop him! Yet, how? Her eyes fell on the flames that roared in the fireplace, her mind going to her children. Robert was evil, and unless stopped, he would ruin them all.

Unsure as to what to do, she made her way to the front door and stepped out onto the covered stoop just as Annabel and Juliet hurried toward her, laughing as the rain fell on them.

Not only was Eleanor in danger, but these two were, as well, and she would do anything to protect them!

Anything.

***

Juliet shook the rain from her overcoat before pushing the front door open, glad to have escaped the rain. She went to ask Annabel a question when she heard the voice of a man coming from the drawing room. Holding a finger to her lips, she crept down the hallway, Annabel following behind just as quietly.

Had a servant returned due to the inclement weather? The voice did not sound like that of Forbes, yet it did sound familiar, although Juliet could not place it.

Placing an ear to the door, she waved for Annabel to do the same and strained to hear every word.

"All that matters is what I want. And you as my wife is what I have always desired. Now I have the means to see it happen."

Juliet pulled back from the door, anger boiling inside her. Nodding toward the front door, she and Annabel hurried to it and outside, easing the door closed until she heard the familiar *click*.

"That was Robert!" she declared as they huddled under the covering over the stoop. "Did you hear what he said?"

Annabel nodded. "I did!"

Juliet clenched her teeth. "I cannot believe that woman! The man kissed her; he must have! Come with me."

They hurried through the rain to the stables, where Juliet stopped and turned to glare at the front of the house.

"Why would she wish to see the cobbler," Annabel asked.

Juliet shook her head, still amazed at her mother. "I cannot believe what a hypocrite that woman is!" She gave a derisive sniff. "Robert was right about her!"

"What do you mean?"

"He told me she was jealous of me, and although I suspected it, I did not wish to believe it." She gave her cousin a beseeching look. "Do you not see? Mother kept us away from him because she wants him for herself! She then had him come here where she could seduce him!"

"Perhaps," Annabel said with a shake to her head.

Then a thought occurred to Juliet. "It all makes sense," she whispered. "Robert had a position here at Scarlett Hall years ago. I wonder if this is the reason Mother has everyone leave the house on Tuesdays; she had been seeing Robert all those years ago."

"But why would she keep her Tuesday routine after the man left?"

"Maybe there has been more than one man," Juliet replied with a shrug. "And to think she has attempted to deter me from seeing Daniel! She told me that, because of his class, we could never have a future together, and yet, there she is in the drawing room alone with a cobbler sharing kisses! I would have never thought her capable of such a thing."

"Neither would have I," Annabel said. "What will we do?"

Juliet sighed and peeked out the opening of the door to the stables. Her friend and business partner walked away from their home, the man too poor to afford a horse or to rent a carriage. She was angry he had not informed her of the lurid affair he was having with her mother…

Yet, had he not done so? Had he not been the one who had spoken of her mother's jealousy of her? Perhaps he had not wished to hurt her. Furthermore, if her mother had lured the man into their home with promises of kisses, it was likely he was not in his right mind.

"We will return to the house and act as if nothing has happened," Juliet replied in response to the question Annabel had asked. "If Mother wishes to pursue this man, then she has every right to do so. However, she had best not make any comment when I tell her of Daniel and my plans."

"What plans?"

Juliet opened the stable doors and glanced over her shoulder. "We are to be married one day and leave this home full of jealousy and lies."

Chapter Eighteen

More people made their way down the footpaths than a month earlier as Juliet stood outside the cobbler's shop, the warmish air more than likely calling people from their homes. It had been nearly a week since Juliet had overheard the cobbler and her mother speaking, and thus far she had made no mention of it to her mother. However, the growing curiosity as to the relationship had her wanting to make inquiries, and she had the perfect excuse to explain her sudden appearance at his shop.

"Now remember," Juliet said. "You will remain a shadow partner, and you cannot ever speak of our business with Robert to anyone."

"I understand," Annabel whispered. "Thank you for allowing me to do this."

Juliet smiled. "If I am to make my own wealth, I will not allow my cousin and best friend to go without."

Annabel smiled, and the two women headed inside the shop. Robert, as usual, stood rubbing his chin as he leaned against the back counter as if deep in thought.

When he saw them, he straightened and said, "What joy it is to have two fine ladies in my shop." He bowed and Juliet and Annabel giggled. "Tell me, what brings you here today?"

Juliet nodded to Annabel, who reached into reticule and produced several notes. "Juliet informed me of your need for investors," she said. "I would like to be involved, if I may."

Robert smiled and came to stand before her. "Juliet is a woman I trust. And if she trusts you, who am I to deny you this opportunity?" He took the notes and put them into his coat pocket. "Do you know business like Juliet?"

Annabel shook her head. "I do not," she replied. "I have watched my father work in his business ledgers at times, but he never allowed me to help."

"Such a shame," Robert said shaking his head. "Very well, you may help with mine. I can teach you when I return from Oxford."

"Oxford?" Juliet asked in surprise. "What will you be doing there?"

Robert looked past them both and then grinned. "Word has come to me of new business opportunities." He leaned in and lowered his voice conspiratorially. "If what I hear is true, I will take your investments and open another shop in that grand city."

Juliet and Annabel both gasped.

"That is wonderful!" Annabel said. "You are so kind to allow us this opportunity."

For a moment, Robert smiled at Juliet's cousin. Did his eyes spend too much time on her? Then she recalled his interest in her mother. No, if her mother caught his eye, he did not have time for the likes of Annabel.

"It is your kindness that I must applaud," he said with a grin. "Investing in the business will be greatly rewarded." He returned to the counter and leaned against it once more. "Juliet will be the woman others look to for the latest fashion in shoes." Then he turned to Annabel. "And you, my dear, will be the one who make sure the ledgers are complete and everyone is paid fairly."

Annabel gasped. "I cannot do that!" she insisted, but her smile belied her denial. "This is all so exciting!"

"These are exciting times," Robert agreed. "And you will be at the forefront of it all. However, I must make one request." He walked over and took each of their hands in his. "When the wealth comes to us, do not leave for Paris or somewhere more exotic with all that money you will earn!"

This brought on a bout of laughter, and Annabel turned to Juliet. "I must speak to a friend of mine." Juliet had asked her to say this in order to make an excuse to leave Juliet alone with Robert. "Thank you again for allowing me to partake in this wonderful opportunity."

"No," he said as he kissed her knuckles. "Thank you."

Once Annabel was gone, Juliet turned to Robert. "I must ask a question, if you please. And I would like an honest answer."

The smile faded. "And what do you wish to ask?"

"Tuesday last, I overheard you speaking to my mother."

The man pursed his lips. "And what did you hear?"

She started at the sternness of his voice, but she had to know the truth. "That you have wanted her. Then, I assume you kissed her. I realize it is none of my business, and I left immediately thereafter, but I wish to know if it is true."

"Forgive me," he said. "I grew angry, for I feared you would be upset with me."

"I am not upset; I am simply confused. How long have you been seeing my mother?"

Robert sighed. "One moment, please," he said before reaching under the counter and pulling out a bottle of brandy and two glasses. "Such a story deserves a drink."

"Only a little," Juliet said, and the man nodded as he poured a small measure into one of the glasses.

He handed her the glass and poured his own. "I told you your mother is jealous of you. And although you agreed, you did not believe me, did you?"

"I admit that I did not, at least entirely," Juliet replied, her cheeks heating.

Robert shrugged. "It is understandable. I am but a mere shopkeeper and your mother is a lady. However, she is envious of you, your cousin...of everyone, in fact, if I am to be honest."

"I still cannot believe it," Juliet replied with a shake to her head. "However, if you are courting, why should she be jealous of me? That makes no sense."

"I do not know, but I do desire to be near her, and she feels the same. It is why I go to your home on Tuesdays. As to her jealousy over you, it has subsided, at least concerning our friendship."

"What else could there be?" Juliet asked. "Have you told her of my investments?"

He gave her a smile. "No, I would never do such a thing. She is jealous of you because you are young, beautiful, and wise. I am trying my best to get her to appreciate that she is also a beautiful woman and to not allow her jealousy to consume her."

"You are kind to show her that. She has not been herself for some time now, and I do not wish to see her driven to madness."

"You do not care that I call on her?"

"No," Juliet said, her eyes misted with tears. "I believe it is fine. And do not worry; I shall say nothing of this matter or our conversation today."

Although the man had explained, she still did not understand. How could her mother still be jealous of Juliet and yet wish to be with a cobbler? Yet, it did explain a few things, such as why her mother had withdrawn and why the woman insisted Juliet and Annabel keep away from Robert.

"I take it you have not asked your mother about me?"

Juliet shook her head.

"You were wise to come to me first in this matter."

"I am glad I did," Juliet said with a smile. "Although it pains me to say so, my mother is a hypocrite. She feared I had feelings for Daniel, all the while having an interest in you."

Robert placed a hand on her arm. "Your mother is a good woman who is overcome by many issues. You mustn't be angry with her; try to be patient."

Juliet nodded. "I will be patient. Thank you."

"We will keep this between us," Robert said with a friendly smile. "And if she mentions anything about me, I would like you to inform me at once."

Juliet frowned. "I do not see why she would."

"We know of her jealousy, and her hiding away. She is improving, but she may regress and lash out again. You must come to me no matter what she says or does. I may be the only person able to help her."

His steady gaze eased her mind. "I will, I promise. Thank you again." She hugged the man, thankful for his friendship and kind words. She might not have known him long, but she felt as if they had known one another for years. Then her thoughts returned to her mother, and fear gripped her. "You do not believe Mother is going mad, do you?"

"Not at all," Robert replied dismissively. "Now, I must prepare for my journey to Oxford, but I will return in three weeks."

Juliet nodded as he returned the glasses and the decanter to their place behind the counter.

"Remember, Juliet," he said as she turned to leave, "I can only help you if you help me. Do you trust me?"

Juliet gave him a wide smile. "I do trust you," she said. "More than anyone else. Is there anything else?"

He pursed his lips. "As a matter of fact, there is one more thing," he replied. "Find more money and more investors. Oxford is just the beginning! Dover will soon follow. At this rate, within a year, we will have dozens of shops. And then, you can help provide for you and Daniel."

Juliet beamed, and the sadness over her mother vanished. "Annabel and I know many women who would love the opportunity to be a part of such a proposal. However, I will not ask those who are fools. I will only contact those I trust."

"I have no concerns about you," Robert said with that smile that always made her feel as if she were the most important person in his life. "You are wise, and I trust you with everything."

"And I trust you," Juliet replied firmly. "I shall talk to you upon your return."

As she stepped out of the shop, she took a long deep breath. Her mother had grown so envious that she had resorted to seeing a cobbler of all people. Although at first it had made Juliet angry, she now laughed. If her mother was happy with a common man, informing her about Daniel would only be that much easier.

***

It had been five days since Juliet had spoken to Robert, and although she had promised not to mention their discussion to her mother, Juliet could not stop the thoughts of her mother's secret from nagging at the back of her mind. It was that nagging that had prompted the conversation she and Annabel were currently having in the drawing room.

"My only thought is that your mother did not inform you about the cobbler because of his station," Annabel whispered as she sat beside Juliet on the couch. "The shame it would bring her would be great. She is too well-respected to have anyone in the *ton* learn of it." She sighed. "If word got out, it would ruin not only her name, but that of your sisters and brother."

Juliet shook her head. "Daniel says the same about the situation, as well; although, he does not know Robert personally, I get the feeling he does not like him."

"Could he be jealous of him?" Annabel asked. "I have heard that men can be very possessive of their women."

Juliet could not help but giggle, but Annabel frowned. "I am sorry," Juliet said. "It was the way you said 'their women', as if I am some sort of prize."

"If he cares for you, then you are," Annabel said.

It was a good point, and Juliet thought about the lesson the night before. Daniel had been working ever so hard and was now able to write several simple words such as 'cat' and 'dog'.

"You are thinking about him again," Annabel snickered. "I know when you are."

"You know no such thing," Juliet replied in admonishment. "To think you know my thoughts!" She laughed. "Oh, all right, I was. How did you know?"

"It is the faraway look as if you are in a dream. It is the same look Isabel gives His Grace."

Juliet considered this for a moment. "You are right," she said in astonishment. "Where has the year gone? We were children and now we are women bound to marry and lead new lives."

"It will be my birthday soon," Annabel said. "Eighteen." She sighed. "I recall when you were but nine and I eight. Do you remember when we were children and you told me that you found an old map of Scarlett Hall and that the walls were filled with gold?"

Juliet nodded, her cheeks burning. It was one of the many stories she told as a child. Now, as she looked back on it, she realized her stories never stopped.

"Your father was so angry when we made a hole in the wall!"

Juliet laughed. "He was!" She gave a heavy sigh. "I do miss him. He worked so hard to provide the life we have lived."

"He did," Annabel said.

The door opened, and Juliet's mother entered the room. For a woman sneaking kisses, she did not smile much.

"I told you I would be leaving for London in a few days, did I not?" her mother asked.

Juliet and Annabel nodded.

"Your chaperon will arrive tomorrow evening. I expect you to treat her with dignity and respect."

"Yes, Mother," Juliet replied, although the idea of having what was essentially a governess in the guise of a chaperon irritated her.

"The lessons with Daniel will stop while I am away. You may resume them upon my return."

Juliet had to fight down the anger that rose in her. This hypocrisy had no end! It was not as if Annabel did not attend the lessons—or so her mother believed. Rather than voicing her annoyance, she bit her tongue.

"Annabel, your mother sent a letter, as well. Your parents are returning from their trip and shall be here in a fortnight to collect you."

"Thank you," Annabel said, although the sadness in her tone was unmistakable.

Juliet reached over and took her hand. "Will she be able to return again soon?"

"I know nothing of their plans," her mother replied. "However, you know you are always welcome here anytime you wish."

"I do, thank you." Annabel rose and embraced Juliet's mother. "I have always felt as if this were more my home than my own."

Juliet's heart hurt seeing her cousin in such pain. In truth, her parents sickened Juliet. They might be her uncle and aunt, but the manner in which they treated Annabel was disgraceful. Yet, if the next few years were anything like the previous, Annabel would return within the month.

Although glad Annabel found comfort in her mother's arms, Juliet could not help but feel a bit of envy, for her mother had her eyes closed, and Juliet wished it was she being held and loved rather than Annabel.

That was just silly! Her mother loved her, and she had no right to be jealous over her cousin, a girl who received little or no love from her own parents.

When the embrace broke, her mother looked at Annabel. "Soon, it will be your birthday, the most special of them all. I may bring you something from London in celebration, even if it is in the fall."

"Thank you," Annabel said with a weak smile. "But I do not deserve it."

Her mother looked first at Annabel and then at Juliet. "You are both good girls," she said, and Juliet felt relief in being included. "I am proud of you both."

Juliet's heart went out to the woman, and as her mother turned to leave, she rose from the couch.

"Mother," she said.

Her mother stopped and turned around. "Yes?"

Juliet wished to tell her mother that it was fine about Robert. That she, Juliet, had been selfish in times past. However, that no longer mattered. What did matter was that, although she was angry at the woman, she was still her mother. "I love you."

"And I love you," she said. "Both of you."

After her mother left, Juliet took both of Annabel's hands in hers. "And I love you, Cousin."

Annabel threw her arms around Juliet. "As do I."

"Now," Juliet said, taking Annabel's hand once again, "Mother is to leave us for a week with a chaperon, which means..." She allowed the words to hang in the air.

"We must behave as the ladies we are?" Annabel asked.

Juliet laughed. "Of course not! It means we must plan a grand adventure!"

This made Annabel laugh as well. "And what do you have in mind?"

"A campfire and brandy," Juliet replied. "Would you like that?"

Annabel nodded so quickly, Juliet worried the girl's head would fly off.

"Good. Then we must begin planning right away!"

Juliet had no idea where their adventure would take them, but she knew it would be better than staying inside the house with a chaperon doing the terribly boring activities she was certain the chaperon would insist upon. Embroidery? Not if she could help it!

Chapter Nineteen

Sitting beside Annabel in the drawing room, Juliet understood she had to give her best impression to the chaperon, who was due to arrive soon. They sat rigid of posture with hands neatly folded in their laps as if practicing good behavior beforehand.

"I do hope she is not cruel," Annabel whispered. "Caroline told me of a chaperon she had who made her do the servants' work."

Juliet snorted and rolled her eyes. "My dear, Caroline is nothing short of a bald-faced liar. Do not worry; this woman will not control what we do, and certainly not to that extent."

Annabel looked down at the floor. "She also told me that I am rather plain," she whispered with a sad sigh. "And that my parents wish to leave me behind because of the embarrassment they would otherwise be forced to endure because of it." A tear rolled down her cheek, and anger rose in Juliet.

"When did she say this?" she demanded, ready to rush over to the other girl's house and gouge out her eyes.

"Oh, it was some time ago," Annabel said wiping at her eye. "I know I should not listen to her, but a woman with so many friends does make one think."

Juliet leaned over and hugged her cousin. "I did not want to do this, but I am afraid I must."

"What?" Annabel asked, her innocent eyes wide.

"I have told you not to listen to that girl, have I not?" Annabel nodded. "And I have told you how beautiful you are, yet you

166

continue to not believe me. You leave me no more choice. I am sorry."

Annabel's eyes went wide. "I do not understand," she said, her voice filled with worry.

"Tonight, I shall write to every eligible man of the *ton* and inform them that the highest bidder shall have your hand in marriage."

Annabel made an attempt at gasping, but her giggles won out over it.

"When you see the amount of wealth I acquire as they fight over you," Juliet continued, "perhaps then you will finally believe me."

Annabel was outright laughing by this time. "I do believe you," she said between gasps. When their laughter died down, she added a quick "Thank you."

"And do not worry about Caroline," Juliet said. "No one speaks ill of you without me getting revenge."

Annabel smiled, and Juliet turned as the door opened. Her mother and another woman, perhaps of the same age as her mother, with a severe blue dress that reminded Juliet of the headmistress at Mrs. Down's School for Young Girls and a smile that curdled Juliet's insides. Annabel jumped to her feet, and Juliet was not far behind.

"Girls," her mother said, using her formal tone that indicated her expectations of both of them, "this is Mrs. Helen Jarvis."

Juliet gave the woman a deep curtsy, Annabel doing the same, each also giving a polite greeting.

"Mrs. Jarvis has already been shown her room. Please make her feel welcome in our home."

"I am certain they will," Mrs. Jarvis said in a gravelly voice. "You look a bit tired, Lady Lambert. If you wish, I can speak with the girls alone and you may retire for the evening."

"I do feel a bit weary," Juliet's mother said. Juliet wished the woman would remain; she was uncertain what she thought of this new chaperon in whose care she had been placed. "I will see you early in the morning before we leave." The woman left the room.

As soon as the door closed, Mrs. Jarvis eyed Juliet and Annabel as if she could determine who they were by a simple gaze. "Will you not invite me to sit?" Her request was more a demand than a question.

"Oh, yes, please," Annabel said. She indicated one chair, but Mrs. Jarvis took the other, and Annabel shot a quick glance at Juliet.

Juliet fixed her smile on her face and took the seat beside Annabel on the couch, never taking her eyes off the older woman.

"Are either of you ladies being courted by a gentleman at the moment?" Mrs. Jarvis asked.

What an odd question, Juliet thought, but then she thought of Daniel. *Yes, I am being courted by a stable boy.* She had to stifle a giggle at how the good Mrs. Jarvis would react to such a statement. Instead, she replied, "I soon will be courted by Lord Parsons. However, the man is away for some time and not due back until summer."

"Wonderful!" the woman said with a crooked grin. "I will not have any gentleman in the house while your mother is away. Instead, we shall enjoy doing embroidery and any other activities permissible to ladies such as yourself."

Juliet wished to ask what the woman meant, but she was unable to.

"There is too much risk going into the village, and your mother has already told me to be certain the two of you stay within the confines of the house."

"We cannot stroll around the property?" Juliet asked in surprise, not liking the idea of being a prisoner in her own home. "Not even the gardens?"

The older woman narrowed her eyes at Juliet. "You will see that I am strict but not unfair. We may schedule an outing in the gardens if you wish to visit them."

"Schedule?" Annabel asked, sounding as every bit as shocked as Juliet. "Are we to schedule our day in advance?"

Mrs. Jarvis chuckled, not a pleasant sound. "Indeed, Miss Annabel," the woman said as she rose from her seat. "Part of what is expected of me is that I see that you are kept busy." She walked over to the liquor cart. "No alcohol, either," she snapped. "A drunken woman is a foolish woman." Despite her words, her fingers traced over the stopper of one of the decanters as if in longing.

Juliet shot a glance at Annabel, and both of them shook their heads in wonderment. When Mrs. Jarvis turned back around, they straightened once again.

"It is late, and a lady needs her rest. I shall see you both in the morning."

Juliet wanted to argue but instead she stood, an idea forming in her mind. "Thank you, Mrs. Jarvis. I look forward to the week ahead, as does my cousin."

Annabel shot a look of confusion, which Juliet returned with a stern stare. As they walked toward the door, Juliet looked over to see Mrs. Jarvis gazing once again at the liquor cart.

Once outside the drawing room door, Juliet indicated the stairway, and Annabel nodded. "She is a monster!" her cousin whispered when they were at the bottom of the stairs. "We cannot survive an entire week beneath her watch!"

"I agree," Juliet replied. "However, we must find a weakness in the woman; one we can exploit. I refuse to spend an entire week sewing handkerchiefs."

They both giggled before heading toward their rooms. When Juliet arrived at hers, she walked over to the window and gazed out at the night sky. The week had presented a perfect opportunity to spend time with Daniel, and she would see that it happened. Somehow.

***

The following morning, after bidding her mother and Forbes farewell, Juliet found herself along with Annabel in the parlor as they leaned over their embroidery. It was a task she loathed, and by the look of agony Annabel attempted to hide, the girl felt the same.

However, it was more than the act of sewing which bothered Juliet. It was the manner in which Mrs. Jarvis spoke without succession, as if her entire life story was in need of sharing. Twice, Juliet had to stifle a yawn as the woman rambled.

"It was then that I told Harold I could not marry him," the old woman said, her hands clasped tightly at her breast as if she were an actor on a stage. "I did love him as a friend, but it was Lord Collins who held my heart." She gave a dramatic sigh and took up her needle once more. "Sadly, I came to learn that Lord Collins had an interest in another woman." She said this with a light shake to her head, although she sounded bitter. "Notice that I did not say 'lady', for she certainly was not." She gave a look of disdain before her eyes grew wide. "Forgive me for raising my voice. It is unbecoming of me."

Juliet's curiosity was piqued, and she chewed her lower lip, her mind piecing together what Mrs. Jarvis had said thus far, much like piecing together a jigsaw puzzle. She was quite good at piecing together jigsaw puzzles.

"It appears that this woman," she emphasized the word for Mrs. Jarvis' sake, "was a horrible person. And as to this Lord Collins," she gave a sniff that outdid that which Mrs. Jarvis gave, "it seems he somehow fell under her spell. At least that is what I have gathered from what you have told us."

"Yes!" Mrs. Jarvis said, placing her embroidery in her lap. "It was quite unfair of him. Honestly, it was as if I had disappeared from existence when he laid eyes on her."

Juliet rose and poured a glass of sherry as Mrs. Jarvis continued speaking. If the woman were to accept it, perhaps they could get her to drink more. The hope was to get her into a state that she fell asleep.

"And here you are," Juliet said with a click of her tongue, "a woman of great wisdom, and this woman, she is with him living in love."

Mrs. Jarvis gave a sad nod. "It is exactly as you say."

Juliet offered the woman a comforting smile. "I would suspect that the mere thought of this woman makes you both angry and sad at the same time."

"Indeed, it does," Mrs. Jarvis replied. "I was the perfect bride for him, and it was certainly not she."

Juliet walked over and offered the older woman the glass of sherry. "Here, this should help you cope."

The woman eyed the glass for a moment. "Oh, I cannot drink while watching over the two of you."

Juliet squatted beside Mrs. Jarvis. "The pain you feel? I see it in your eyes. Do not drink for me, nor for Annabel. Drink for the hurt this other woman has caused. And most importantly, for Lord Collins."

Voices of Shadows Past

Mrs. Jarvis eyed the glass once more, but then she accepted it with a firm nod. "Yes. A sip and nothing more."

"Of course," Juliet replied with a small smile. "Just a few sips." She winked at Annabel as she retook her seat.

"If you were married to Lord Collins," Annabel said, "what would his life be like? Would it be far better than the life he currently leads with this other woman?" Juliet suppressed a grin, proud of Annabel's questioning.

The older woman pursed her lips. "The woman, who does not deserve to be called by name, was promiscuous and known to be most inappropriate with many men."

Juliet gasped, feigning surprise. "No! This cannot be. Such women certainly do not exist, do they?"

"It is true," Mrs. Jarvis replied. "Such debauchery does take place. It is why I keep such a strict eye on those I look after."

Juliet gave the woman a warm smile. "I admire your strength," she said.

Mrs. Jarvis took another drink of her sherry, this time much more than a sip. "This has a wonderful flavor," she said as she swirled the liquid in the glass.

"Oh, yes, it does," Juliet replied. "Mother says three quick drinks makes the flavor all the better. Although, I have never had such drinks pass my lips."

"Hm," Mrs. Jarvis murmured. "If Lady Lambert deems it worthy, then so shall I." She took three quick drinks before pursing her lips as if in thought. "She is right. It does have a much bolder taste." She gave the glass a disappointed look—it was now empty—and then turned her attention back to Juliet and Annabel. "Where was I?"

"Your life with Lord Collins," Annabel replied.

"Oh, yes. At first, the man would never..." As she spoke, Juliet took the glass from the older woman's hand, refilled it, and returned it. Mrs. Jarvis barely took notice as she continued with her story.

Soon, her words began to slur, and Juliet knew her plan had been successful thus far.

171

"I believe we will nap this afternoon," Juliet said with a forced yawn, which caused Mrs. Jarvis to yawn, as well. Annabel nodded her agreement.

"I believe I will do the same," Mrs. Jarvis said, frowning at her empty glass. When she stood, she wobbled a bit on her legs. "I believe I may have caught a slight fever."

Juliet and Annabel rose, and Juliet rushed over to place her hand on the woman's forehead. "I could have dinner sent to your room, if you would rather."

"That will not be necessary," Mrs. Jarvis replied. "However, it is kind of you to suggest it."

"Perhaps this will quell the illness," Juliet said, taking the decanter of sherry and handing it to Mrs. Jarvis, whose eyes widened with anticipation. "Mother says a lady may drink without worry when she is feeling ill."

The woman gave no hesitation as she took the decanter from Juliet. "Are you certain you girls will be all right alone for a few hours?"

"Oh, most definitely," Annabel said. "After our nap, I wish to begin a new embroidery pattern. If that is acceptable, of course."

Mrs. Jarvis patted her hand. "Do not be silly. That is more than acceptable. I shall see you when I have woken from my nap." She swayed out of the room, the decanter clutched against her chest.

Once she was gone, Juliet turned to Annabel. "That was successful this time, but I do not believe it will work again."

"What are we to do?" Annabel asked. "Endure the days with her?"

"Not at all." Juliet took her cousin by the hand. "We will find something else to distract her. Each day will be a testament of our wisdom."

Annabel grinned. "I like that."

"However, tonight is our night," Juliet said with a grin. "Tonight, we will sneak out under the cover of darkness and go on an adventure."

Chapter Twenty

D aniel knew the one thing he cherished in life could also be his undoing, and that was Juliet. She and Annabel stood before him, bundled in their overcoats and muffs as he attempted once again to dissuade them from their plan.

"I don't think it's wise," he said. "If your chaperon caught us, I'd be hanged by the rafters. What about highwaymen?" He hoped this would frighten them enough to convince them, and when Annabel gasped, he knew he was halfway there.

Unfortunately, Juliet simply laughed. "Have you forgotten that I chased a highwayman into this very stable?" she demanded. "It was I, fearing for the safety of my sisters and not having a care for my own life, who went in search of him and fell and was hurt for my troubles."

Daniel gave her a worried glance. "I don't think it's a good idea," he repeated for the third time since the two women had come to him with their plan of leaving the grounds.

Juliet's shoulders slumped and she tilted her head. "Perhaps you are right," she said with a sigh.

She glanced up at him, her fluttering lashes causing his heart to hurt. How could he say no to her? However, he had to make the right choice for them. The safe choice.

She sighed again. "I never thought you were one to break a promise."

With her best interests in mind, he went to speak, but as her lower lip pouted, he could no longer deny her wishes. "I won't argue," he said, although he wished he could have clamped his mouth shut instead. "If you want to go..."

She threw her arms around him. "It will be great fun," she said.

How he loved holding her, smelling her natural fragrance, and how he wished they could remain in each other's arms forever.

"And do not worry about Mrs. Jarvis," she added. "The lady has a weakness for the drink." She giggled at this and pulled away from the embrace.

"And you?" he asked Annabel. "You're all right with this?"

Annabel, who was generally quiet and reserved, surprised him by placing a hand on her hip and replying, "Juliet is not the only one who enjoys an adventure. I do, as well. It is something we share as family."

Daniel laughed. "I'll finish saddling the horses. Where're we going at such a late hour?"

"It is a surprise," Juliet said, and both she and Annabel giggled.

Daniel could not help but shake his head as he saddled a horse for himself. What was he getting himself into? His concern was not only for the fact they were leaving for the night. He had no idea where his own feelings for Juliet would lead him.

***

If it was not for the full moon that lit the landscape, Daniel doubted the group would have gotten far. They had been on the road for close to an hour, and he guessed it was nearly midnight when Juliet steered them down a well-worn path. To his left was an endless row of fields and to his right thick clumps of trees and bushes.

Although he worried as he often did where Juliet was concerned, he could not help but admire the woman's boldness. Unlike her sisters, she was outspoken, determined, and, if he were to be honest, stubborn. What Juliet wanted, she always received, a fact he had witnessed many times. Whether it be a new dress, a new pair of shoes, or sneaking her sisters out of the house for a midnight journey, she concocted plans that nearly always resulted in her getting what she wanted. It was that determination he had admired for so long.

He had to admit that it was because of her tenacity that had him practicing his letters every night, even when she was confined to the house. His confidence continued to grow as he now recognized smaller words, and he hoped he would soon be able to read the letter she had given him.

In all that, he still worried about what he could provide for her if they were ever to begin a life together. Juliet had never struggled in life, and he did not want to be the one to introduce her to such ways.

"Here," Juliet said with a firm nod. "Let us dismount here." They had arrived at a small cluster of trees where they tied their horses to low-hanging branches. "Annabel, we will return in a few moments. You will not be frightened, will you?"

"No," Annabel replied, although her laugh sounded a bit nervous. "I am safe here." Her eyes darted to and fro, but she smiled, nonetheless.

"Come with me," Juliet commanded, and Daniel nodded, curious as to where she would be leading him. "Unless you wish me to stumble and witness me hurting my foot, I suggest you take my hand."

"If that's what you want," he said, although he, too, wanted nothing more than to hold her hand. Her skin was as soft as he remembered, and he felt as if he was protecting her. How he would protect her by simply holding her hand, he did not know, but it was a wonderful excuse.

The walk was short, and they stepped out into a clearing where a large house stood. Behind it sat several smaller cottages. "What is this place?" he asked.

"It is the home of Caroline Thrup," she replied. Her tone was as if she had bitten into a lemon. "She is someone Annabel and I know."

"Why are we here?"

"Do you see how grand her house is?"

Daniel studied the house for a moment. "Yes. It's grand enough, but it's not Scarlett Hall. But then, nothing can compare to Scarlett Hall."

Juliet nodded. "Those cottages over there? Do you see them?"

"Yes. Three of them. I assume that's where the servants live."

"You are correct. However, if you look closely, you will realize that those homes are close together, yet the people who live in them are far apart."

Daniel frowned. "I don't understand."

"Caroline and her family will never enter the cottages, and the servants will never enter her home, at least not as guests."

"That's the way it's always been and always will be," Daniel said, still not understanding the point the woman wanted to make. "Is this Caroline going to join us?"

Juliet shook her head. "No. She will never join us. I brought us here to demonstrate how different we are from others in our stations. We have crossed into one another's lives in a way none of those people will."

He stared off into the distance for several moments but said nothing. What could he say?

"I always wished to be in a grand house with cottages like those for the servants," Juliet continued in a whisper. "Now, however, I have come to realize that, if we live in a cottage like one of those, I will be happy."

Hearing those words pierced him as deftly as a sword and he turned to her. "Juliet…"

"You worry about what type of life you can provide me. Am I correct in saying so?"

He nodded as he looked down at the ground. She knew him so well.

"And I am telling you that, after years of having what I want, it has never been enough. I could receive everything the world has to offer, and it still would not be enough, for I simply want to be with you. No better gift could I ever receive than that of your heart, for you already have mine."

All worry and concern he had left him as he pulled her into his arms. The moon casted its light on their embrace. "It's what I want, too," he whispered into her hair, hair that smelled of lavender. "I won't lie; I do worry about you. What can I provide for you? And what would your mother do?"

She looked up, her dark eyes searching his. "None of that matters as long as we are together."

He studied her face, the beautiful lines, her perfect nose, eyes that reminded him of a crafty fox, and he knew he could never be without her. "I see that, although the distance between us once was great, it's no longer so. Come May, we'll leave for the North. Together."

"Then you will not leave without me?" Juliet asked excitedly.

"You will come with me, and we'll begin a life together as one."

She rose to her toes and placed a small kiss on his lips. His body stirred, and he fought back the urge to kiss her back. He would protect her from anything, including himself.

"All I want is to be with you," she whispered.

"As do I," he said.

For several moments, they stood wrapped in each other's arms as they stared out over the darkened property before them.

"What's the plan now?" Daniel asked.

"I promised Annabel we would scare Caroline. The woman deserves it for the tales she has told."

Daniel laughed. "You're terrible," he said. "Why would you do such a thing to this poor woman?"

Juliet gave a sniff. "She was rude to my cousin. Annabel is like my sister, and no one upsets the ones I love."

As she said this, her hand squeezed his, and Daniel's heart raced. Was Juliet telling him that she loved him? He had loved her for so long, it hurt, but as he attempted to find the right way to tell her, they rejoined Annabel and the moment was lost.

***

Daniel followed behind Juliet and Annabel as they edged the property belonging to Caroline. A thick hedge ran along the front of the house just below the large windows, most dark except one with the soft glow of candlelight.

What could Juliet be planning? he wondered. Knowing her, it would be either marvelous or disastrous, but either would be exciting.

"Are you sure this Caroline's even home?" he asked.

Juliet gave a derisive sniff. "Oh, yes, she is home. Caroline never leaves the house, for she is far too hideous to be seen either day or night." Annabel snickered at this but said nothing. "It is her candle that glows."

They found an opening in the hedges that allowed them just enough room to move between the hedges and the house if they walked sideways. Stopping at the lit window, located a reasonable distance from the front door, Juliet squatted and placed a finger to her lips, motioning to Daniel and Annabel to do the same.

"There are rumors about Caroline that I wish to verify," Juliet whispered. Daniel went to respond, but Juliet held up a hand and shook her head. She rose to peek into the window. Her eyes went wide and she covered her mouth with a hand before returning to her squatted position.

"What did you see?" Annabel asked.

"Look," Juliet replied, switching places with her cousin.

Annabel peeked through the window as Juliet had, and she, too, covered her mouth. Although Daniel had never spied on anyone, he could not help but feel curious what the women saw.

"Is it appropriate if I look?" he asked, suddenly remembering that he would be looking into the window of a lady. It was bad enough he was caught up in one of Juliet's mischievous plans and quite another to be caught looking in on a lady in her nightdress!

"Yes," Juliet replied. "Have a look."

With a racing heart, Daniel moved past the two women and lifted himself just enough to peek into the window. The room was large, but it was the woman on whom his eyes fell and remained. She wore a blue nightdress and her hands held a pillow in front of her, and by what he was able to make out, she was talking to it.

He went to ask Juliet if the woman was perhaps mad, but before he could, he saw the most humorous thing he had ever seen.

Caroline shook her head and then pulled the pillow to her face and began kissing it!

His reaction was faster than his hands could stop it, and his laugh far louder than he anticipated. Terrified, he dropped to his knees, his hand covering his mouth and tears of laughter rolling down his face. Juliet and Annabel crouched down, as well, but then they all froze when the window slid open above them.

"Is anyone out there?" Caroline whispered. "Reuben? Is that you?"

Daniel had to bite down on his finger to keep silent when Juliet replied in a gruff voice, "It is I, my love. Come out in your shift and run away with me."

He shook his head, uncertain how much longer he could hold in his laughter. Then Juliet rose and walked into the weak light.

"Juliet!" Caroline whispered. "What are you doing here?"

Annabel joined Juliet, and Daniel waited several moments before deciding to rise, as well.

Caroline pulled her arms around herself. "Who is this man?" she gasped. Then she raised her chin arrogantly. "So unbecoming of a lady to be out alone with a man!"

"Perhaps," Juliet replied. "Yet, I wonder what others will believe when they learn you kiss pillows, or that you were mean to my Annabel."

"I...you saw...?" Her words trailed off and she stared at them, clearly horrified.

"An apology to Annabel for your rudeness will keep your secret from others," Juliet said haughtily.

"Whatever for?" the young woman demanded.

"For saying that Annabel is plain. You know as well as I that it is not the truth."

Caroline sighed. "My apologies, Annabel. It was not my intention to be rude to you. You are very beautiful, and I shall never say a mean word against you ever again."

"I forgive you," Annabel replied.

Do all women act this way? Daniel wondered. If they did, he found it all very strange.

"Why are you out this late at night?" Caroline asked. "It is not safe to be about when the moon is full."

"You forget that no highwayman or beast would dare attack me," Juliet said with a huff. "And although I would love to chat with you, we must be on our way."

"Goodnight," Caroline whispered as they moved back toward the opening in the hedges. The light sliding of the window came soon after, and by the time they reached the edge of the property, the light in the window was gone.

As they made their way to wear the horses were tethered to the tree branches, Daniel could not help but chuckle.

"What is so funny?" Juliet demanded.

"You. Everything about you makes me happy. You're truly nothing like any other woman I've ever met."

Juliet sniffed. "Of course I am not." Then she gave him a small smile. "I hope you do not think ill of me. I had to have some fun tonight, even if it was unladylike."

Daniel stopped before his horse. "It's better than ladylike," he said with a wide grin. "It's Juliet-like, and that's what I love."

Chapter Twenty-One

The week passed quickly with Mrs. Jarvis partaking in a glass—or two—of wine or sherry each day in order to hold off her 'illness', allowing Juliet more time with Daniel. Although some days she remained inside the house, at night, she and Annabel headed to the stables in order to continue with his lessons in secret. Daniel was improving greatly in his reading, and Juliet was confident that he would be reading on his own very soon.

Juliet was sad when Annabel left with her parents earlier in the day, but her uncle and aunt rarely remained at home for long, and even more rarely did they take their only daughter with them. Therefore, Annabel would be back soon. Juliet wished it was sooner than soon, for adventuring was no fun when she was left to go on her own.

During those afternoons while working on her needlework or reading a book by the fire with only Mrs. Jarvis for company, she imagined herself revealing her love to Daniel. Each time she had found the opportunity in the past, either Annabel arrived or the words Juliet wished to speak caught in her throat.

Despite her happiness in the fact that she would be leaving Scarlett Hall in a little more than a month's time, Juliet fretted over how much she would miss her siblings and her cousin.

As she sat in the drawing room with Mrs. Jarvis contemplating her future, a voice resounded in the hallway, and Juliet was pleased to see her mother enter the room. She looked weary from her travels, as did Forbes, who came in after her.

"Mother!" Juliet said as she set aside her embroidery and ran to her mother. "You have returned. It is so good to see you."

Her mother held her in an embrace that lasted longer than usual. "It is good to be home," she said before releasing Juliet.

Mrs. Jarvis gave a small curtsy. "You will be pleased to know that the week passed without incident, and Miss Juliet and Miss Annabel were perfect ladies."

Her mother smiled. "Thank you, Mrs. Jarvis. Forbes will help you collect your things and see you out."

Mrs. Jarvis stopped before Juliet. "I am thankful for the time we spent together." Then she turned to Juliet's mother. "If you have need of me again, please send me a letter."

"I shall," Juliet's mother said.

Once Mrs. Jarvis and Forbes had gone, Juliet's mother closed the door and turned back to Juliet. "Have you been to the village?"

Juliet shook her head. "I remained at home with Annabel all week. She left not an hour ago with Uncle Silas and Aunt Joanna."

Her mother's smile faded. "I had hoped to see her before she left." With a sigh, she took Juliet by the hand and led her to the couch.

Juliet studied her mother's face; the lines around her eyes had grown deeper in the short time she was away. "You look worried. I did not go into the village, nor did I cause any trouble; I promise."

Her mother gave a light chuckle. "I believe you," she said. "I have wonderful news. Hannah is engaged to be married."

Juliet's jaw dropped. "Engaged? Hannah? I thought she wanted to be a spinster."

"It seems she has changed her mind."

"And who will she marry?"

Her mother smiled. "He is a wonderful gentleman, a cousin to Laurence. When you see the two of them together, you will be surprised at the love they share."

Juliet could not have been happier for her sister. The idea that Hannah would marry still left her in a state of shock, but it also made her wish to tell her mother about Daniel and her love for him. Yet, no. It would be best to wait. Her mother was much too weary to be told such news.

"I am so pleased for her," Juliet said. "And Isabel? Did she mention how she missed me?"

Her mother laughed. "She did. In fact, everyone made mention of you and their longing to see you. Have you had word from Lord Parsons?"

Juliet's heart skipped a beat. Did her mother plan to send her to London after all? "I have not," she replied carefully. "I have a feeling I shall hear from him soon, though."

Her mother nodded and patted her hand. "That is wonderful, dear," she said. The woman felt distant, even as she sat beside Juliet. "Soon he will ask to court you and then you, too, will be married. Annabel will soon follow." Her voice had a sad tinge to it, and Juliet felt a tightening in her chest. "All of you are now women and soon will be gone. Even Nathaniel is growing so quickly."

"We will always be nearby," Juliet said, giving the woman a hug. "Perhaps you shall find a gentlemen to keep you company."

"You should not say such things," her mother said with light admonishment. "I have no desire for such a life any longer."

Juliet nodded but wondered how her mother could outright lie. Was she not seeing the cobbler? Perhaps, like Juliet, the woman could not bring herself to say the words aloud.

"It was just a thought," Juliet said. "I am glad you are home. The house is not the same when you are not here."

Her mother smiled and kissed her cheek. "I must go and rest. The week's activities were tiring."

Juliet stood when her mother did, but rather than leaving, her mother looked at her for several moments before pushing a strand of hair behind Juliet's ear with a sigh. "You have no idea how much joy you bring me, but I can assure you that, although at times you may not believe it, you hold a special place in my heart."

Overcome with emotion, Juliet grinned. "I know in the past I have not been like my sisters, but I am changing for the better and making wiser decisions."

Her mother chuckled. "I know this," she said. "You are becoming a woman of heart and mind, one guided by love, and that is what I have always wanted for each of you."

They embraced once more before her mother left the room, leaving Juliet alone to ponder. She had to inform her mother about the plans she and Daniel had made. There was no doubt the woman would be angry at first, but once Juliet explained how much she loved Daniel, her mother would be happy. Was that not what the woman had just said she wanted for her daughters; for them to be happy?

Well, Juliet would make her mother proud by fulfilling all of her wishes.

***

Much to Juliet's frustration, her mother stayed awake late every night the following week, and Juliet feared being caught if she attempted to sneak out of the house. She had managed to see Daniel once for a few brief minutes when her mother went to her room to rest a few days earlier, but she could not wait any longer. She had to see him again. Her plan was simple. She was already in her night dress, but she had a simple day dress ready to don over it when she was ready to climb out the window.

A knock at the door had her turn as her mother entered the room. "Annabel has returned," the woman said, "and she is waiting in the drawing room for you."

Juliet gaped. "It has not been a week! Are her parents leaving on another journey so soon?"

Her mother shook her head. "No. However, I must ask a favor."

Juliet nodded, noting the concern in her mother's voice. "Of course. Anything."

"Annabel is quite upset, and rightly so. I ask you to be there for her; give her strength."

"Why? What is wrong? Has she been hurt?"

"She is safe," her mother replied. "But I will allow her to explain."

Juliet drew on her dressing gown and slippers. "I have never said anything disparaging about my uncle and aunt, but I will say something now, and only this once. Her parents are horrible people." Juliet waited for her mother's rebuke and would gladly endure it, but she was surprised when the woman only gave a nod.

"Comfort her," she said. "She needs it."

Juliet followed her mother down the stairs. The house was always eerily dark, but for some reason, it felt darker than usual. Hurrying to the drawing room, she could hear Annabel's sobs, which caused her heart to clench. When she entered the room, she hurried over to her cousin and pulled her into her arms.

"Oh, Annabel," she whispered. "What has happened? Have you been hurt? Was it your parents?"

Annabel nodded as she wiped away tears from her cheeks. "They are angry with me for failing them. It is why I have been returned here."

Juliet shook her head angrily. "Come. Sit down here and tell me what happened."

"Two days ago was my birthday," she said. "And they told me they had a special surprise."

"Was it a gift?" Juliet asked, wondering how a surprise could upset Annabel so.

Her cousin shook her head. "No. It was far worse. I waited with Mother in our parlor for this surprise and was told to look my absolute best. So, I wore my blue dress, the one I love."

Juliet nodded. "You look beautiful in it."

Annabel sniffled. "Then Father joined us, but he was not alone. He was with Lord Agar."

She began to sob, and Juliet held her, understanding what was to come. Lord Agar was a baron, widowed several years now, who was nearly fifty years of age.

"What was the purpose for Lord Agar's sudden appearance?" Juliet asked carefully.

"To court me." Annabel gave her a beseeching look. "I do not like the man, and he is nowhere near handsome. So, when he asked, I refused him. He left in anger, and Father told me that I was nothing more than a disappointment." The sobs came once more, and Juliet felt a surge of anger at the man. He might be her father's brother, but that did not make him immune to her displeasure!

"That is not the worst of it," Annabel said when she was able to speak once more. "It was Mother's words that hurt the most."

"What did she say?" Juliet asked, wiping tears from her own eyes.

"That if I do not allow him to court me, I must find someone else soon, for I have become a burden to them."

Juliet's heart ripped in two. "No!"

Annabel nodded. "I asked her if seeing me marry Lord Agar would make her happy, and she replied that it would, and that it would be the first time I have ever made them happy!"

The poor woman continued to sob, and Juliet held her once more, her ire building for what her cousin had been forced to endure. "Your parents are cruel," she whispered. "But you have nothing to fear."

Annabel pulled away. "I am afraid you are wrong. They mean to marry me off as soon as possible, and I do not know what to do!"

Juliet peered into her cousin's eyes. "First, you are here with me in Scarlett Hall, so no one will hurt you. Lord Agar will never be allowed to enter if I have anything to do with it." This brought a faint smile from Annabel. "Second, and the most important, is this. When Daniel and I leave in May, you will come with us."

"Do you mean it?"

"I do," Juliet said with a firm nod. "I know Daniel will agree, and I will need help keeping the house in order, for I have not the slightest idea how."

Annabel laughed. "I do not know, either."

"Then we shall learn together." She grasped her cousin by the hands. "What do you think? Will you join us?"

Annabel nodded. "I will." She wrapped her arms around Juliet. "Thank you! I do love you so."

"And I love you," Juliet replied, returning the embrace with as much enthusiasm as her cousin. "Now that we no longer have that worry, I have good news to share."

"Oh?" Annabel asked as she wiped the last of her tears with a handkerchief. "Do tell!"

"I have sent out letters to some of my most trusted friends," Juliet replied. "We are to meet at the cobbler's at noon tomorrow. They are going to invest in our business!"

Annabel grinned. "Once the business has grown enough, we will be able to afford a servant to keep house for us," she said with a laugh.

"My thoughts exactly," Juliet said. "We cannot allow Daniel to learn we wish to employ a servant; he must believe we are doing our part, as well."

She gave Annabel a wink, to which Annabel giggled. It was nice to hear her cousin laughing again, and as they talked, Juliet thought of the months ahead. Preparations had to be made to leave, and with Daniel's savings and her investment in the cobbler's business, not only their future would be secured, but that of Annabel's, as well.

Chapter Twenty-Two

Juliet and Annabel had returned to Caroline's house the day after Annabel's return. The woman was by far nicer this time than she had been on previous visits, and Juliet knew that if word of the woman kissing her pillow were to be escape, she would be humiliated for years to come. Juliet had no doubt that the young woman would act as if Juliet and her cousin were her best friends.

However, that was yesterday. Today, she and Annabel were at the cobbler's, and they were more than ready to begin business proceedings. The shop was closed to customers in order to keep the meeting secret—if any of the young women's parents learned their daughters were considering investing money into any business, they would have been dragged kicking and screaming from the shop before anyone could release a single breath.

Juliet opened the door just wide enough to allow Miss Lucy Bowers to enter before closing and locking it behind her.

Robert had returned a few days earlier, sending a message the day he arrived, and now eight women besides Juliet and Annabel stood with heads together speaking excited whispers to one another. Having arrived an hour earlier, Juliet had explained her plan to Robert, who in turn had praised her brilliance. Juliet could not have been prouder.

The women who had arrived were those to whom Juliet had written informing them to bring whatever money they had with them. Of course, she did not mention the investment to Caroline, for the woman could not be trusted, even if Juliet had information about her that would otherwise keep her quiet. Furthermore, Caroline had already spread malicious rumors about Robert, so there was no reason to speak to her regardless.

Annabel stood beside Robert, a quill in her hand and an ink bottle beside several pieces of parchment on the counter. She nodded to Juliet, and Juliet turned to address the group.

"Ladies, I am pleased to see you here, and I promise that your time here will not be in vain." She shot a glance at Robert, who smiled, and her pride increased. "I am certain you are all wondering why I called you here to this shop." All the women nodded in unison. "And more importantly why I requested you bring every farthing you had."

"I am curious," said Miss Bowers, her blond curls bouncing with her head nodding. "You said you promised great wealth if we attended today."

"I did, and you will attain much wealth if you are willing to invest."

"Invest?" Miss Margaret Shilling asked, her dark hair a deep contrast to that of Miss Bowers. "In what are you asking us to invest? I know nothing of such things."

Juliet attempted to keep the mocking from her laughter. "That is why I am here. Now, listen carefully. This shop is own by Mr. Robert Mullens, a dear friend of the Lambert family." She stopped for dramatic effect. "And by myself and my cousin Annabel."

Several women gasped, but one sniffed derisively. "You cannot own a business," Miss Sally Thompson said, her already upturned nose rising further. "Women, especially ladies, do not do such things, do they?"

"In times past, they could not," Juliet explained. "However, we are no longer in those times. Mr. Mullens has secured a second location in Oxford, which Annabel and I will also be part owners. Soon, we will have shops all over England."

"Then, what you are asking is that we be part of these businesses, as well?" Miss Bowers asked. "How will we be able to do this without our parents learning of it? You know what my father would do if he learned I had given my allowance away in a business agreement."

Several other women nodded their agreement, but Juliet had anticipated such reactions.

"It is simple, really," Juliet replied. "We will be called 'shadow partners'. We will remain hidden, and we will not be braggarts about what we are doing. If we adhere to this, no one will know unless you tell them, or if you are caught boasting of the wealth you will acquire. Just think! We will not be required to rely on men for what we have. Rather we will rely on ourselves!"

The women smiled and nodded their heads enthusiastically.

"Annabel is waiting to collect your funds and make note of them. You will receive a receipt for the amount you paid. Imagine having your own money to purchase whatever you wish without being forced to beg your parents—or your husbands when you marry."

Miss Bowers took a step forward and lifted a fist full of notes in the air. "Well, I wish to invest!" she said. "I have brought ten pounds. It has taken me some time to save it, but if I can have it back at a later point, then that is fine by me."

"You will get quite a bit back," Robert interjected. "In fact, the more money invested, the more shops we are able to open and thus the larger the return for everyone."

Juliet went to say more, but the women were hurrying over to the counter, their money already in hand. As each signed the entry book, Annabel handed out the receipts, and Robert joined Juliet.

"You have done well," he said with a wide grin. "Once again, I am elated to have a lady of wisdom in my shop."

Juliet knew she was beaming. "Thank you. Look at their faces; they are excited."

"As they should be," Robert replied. "You have brought them an opportunity they will never have again."

Her pride deepened, and when her eyes fell on Annabel, she sighed. "Annabel is smiling again, and that makes me very happy."

"Has she not been happy?" Robert asked, his voice filled with concern.

"No." She glanced to ascertain no one else was nearby before lowering her voice. "It is her parents. They are horrible people." She explained the situation, and Robert shook his head in response. When she finished, only two women remained to sign the ledger, the others sharing in excited whispers amongst themselves.

"We will look after Annabel," Robert promised. "If I have to pay her from my own share for her to keep the books, it does not matter."

"You are a kind man," Juliet said. However, a twinge of guilt pierced her, and she turned to the man. "Do you plan to court Mother?"

Robert smiled. "We are working on that together," he replied. "When the time comes, I will tell you. Let us worry about increasing the number of shops and focus on our profits, not on my business with her."

Juliet gave him a sideways glance. His words had been said as if he was angry, and she had not meant to upset him. Perhaps she was being nosy. "You are right. I am sorry."

"No need to apologize," he said. "She allows you to come here to see me, and Annabel is happy. Nothing else matters."

Annabel walked up to them. "I have it all accounted for."

Robert smiled. "Then I will deposit the funds after I go over the numbers. If you can find more friends to invest, it will serve us all."

"I will find more," Juliet said firmly. "Dozens, perhaps."

This made Robert laugh. "Very good!" He glanced at the other women. "You will see them out?"

Juliet nodded, and Robert walked away. Although she did not know what he said, he whispered in Annabel's ear, causing her smile to broaden. Then he disappeared through the white door.

Juliet turned to the women. "It is time to leave. If you have any friends you deem trustworthy, ask them to speak with me if they would like to join us. However, I cannot say this firmly enough. They must be trustworthy, for we are all in this together."

When everyone was gone and Juliet and Annabel were alone, Juliet turned to Annabel. "You seem happy. Are you feeling better?" She locked the door behind her, and they crossed the street together.

"I am. Robert said he has never seen neither man nor woman keep a ledger as well as I. He truly is a kind man, is he not?"

Juliet could not agree with her cousin more. "He is. And we are lucky to know him."

***

Eleanor Lambert gazed at the old oak tree through the large window of the drawing room, thinking of times past. She could picture her children sitting under the tree, their laughs so beautiful they would carry through the thick walls of their home. She smiled as she remembered Nathaniel running up to them, excited to show them a small creature he had found. Although Isabel and Hannah would be aghast in horror, Juliet would laugh and take it from him.

How Eleanor missed those days, and she wished their laughter would once again fill the house. However, on this Tuesday, the only sounds besides her own came from Mr. Robert Mullens, a person from her past of whom she wished to be rid.

"I believe we have reached the courting stage," Robert said, breaking Eleanor from her beautiful thoughts. "I do not expect you wish to make any official announcements, but it is something I want. You will not deny me this, will you?" The last words came as a whisper in her ear as he rested his hands on her shoulders.

Since her return from London, the man had called twice, and each time his actions grew bolder. When he had attempted to kiss her, however, she had pulled away, which in turn angered the man. Balancing the safety of her family and the happiness of the wretched man was far more difficult than she would have ever imagined.

"No," she said in a whispered reply. "I will not deny you that." Saying the words curdled her stomach, but as he caressed her arms, she forced a cough in order to pull away. "Forgive me. I have been weary as of late."

"Illness?" he said with a laugh. "Oh, you are good." He raised his glass and finished off the remained of his brandy.

Eleanor collected the glass from him; not to serve the man but to give an excuse to broaden the distance between them.

"We must discuss marriage."

Eleanor felt her blood congeal, and she swallowed hard. "Marriage?"

"Yes." He sighed heavily. "I have spoken of this before. Do you believe I will be content with just the payments you make?

Her heart raced, and she made every attempt to devise a plan to stall the man. Then an idea came to her. "If we were to marry," she said, offering a small smile, "it would benefit neither of us. In fact, it would cause those associated with my former husband's estate to look elsewhere. Then there would be no money." She handed him the refilled glass.

The man narrowed his eyes as he looked into the glass. "There may be some truth to that."

Relief washed over her. "I have a cottage that is never used. Perhaps I can arrange for you to take possession of it in exchange for payment."

The words had no more than left her lips when the man threw his glass against the wall, the tinkling shards falling to the floor, an amber trail flowing down the wallpaper. "Have you not learned yet?" he shouted as he grabbed her by the arms. "It is not about the money! Do you not see? It is you I want!"

"I-I know you do not want money," Eleanor stammered. "However, you must understand. I do not have the wealth you believe I do." She glanced at his hands. "You are hurting me."

He released her, but his voice was low and harsh. "I desire you, this home, everything in it. That is the payment you owe me. I am sick of these games between us. Come to a decision soon, or I will tell everyone what I know."

"No," Eleanor said, a shake to her head. "You cannot do that. You know the…"

"Enough with your excuses! Consider what I have said." He walked over to the door and stopped. "Follow me."

Anger and shame went through her as she followed the man to the front door. Collecting her coat, she put it on and went through the door he held open for her. "Where are we going?"

"I assume you own a horse," he said.

"I do."

He grabbed her by the elbow and pulled her toward the stables. Once inside, he stopped and turned to her. "Which is yours?"

"The chestnut mare," she said, motioning to the prized beast.

Robert removed a saddle from a nearby rack and placed it upon the horse. As he readied the animal, the fear in Eleanor grew. Did the man mean to take her away? If so, she would refuse to go.

When he finished, he led the horse out of the stall and turned to her. "I am leaving and taking this horse with me." A small smile played on his lips, an evil smile. "You see, this horse, which once belonged to you, now belongs to me, as well. Everything you own is what I now own. Everything."

As his meaning settled on her, she realized the man would never stop. He would use her until she had nothing left to give him.

Before she could respond, he placed his hands on her face and leaned in to kiss her. She turned her head away, but he forced her to face him once again. "Kiss me!" he demanded.

"Hello?"

Robert's face turned an ugly red, and he released her so forcefully, she almost fell back. Eleanor turned just as the stable boy came around the corner. "Oh, Lady Lambert," he said with a startled bow. "I thought I heard a noise but wasn't sure. Is there anything I can help you with?"

"No, Daniel," Eleanor replied. She had never been so happy to see him. "Mr. Mullens is just leaving."

"Yes, I was," Robert replied. He leaned in and added in a whisper, "No more games; do you understand?"

He led the horse from the stables, and once he was gone, Eleanor let out a sigh of relief. Tears stung her eyes as Daniel walked toward her.

"Are you all right, my lady?" he asked. "Do you need a chair?"

"No, thank you," she said, offering the young man a smile. "Why are you here? I thought you went into the village with the others."

"I usually do," he said with a shrug. "But I'm practicing my reading today." He cheeks went a bright red. "I have to keep practicing if I want to read a book one day."

The innocence of the man clasped her heart, and with the recent events, she could not stop a single tear from escaping her eye and rolling down her cheek. "You will read a book in time," she assured him. "I have no doubt."

"Thank you, my lady," he said, his ears now as red as his cheeks.

He turned to leave, but Eleanor called after him. "Did you happen to hear what Mr. Mullens and I were discussing?"

Daniel shook his head. "No, my lady. I mean, I heard voices, but I couldn't make out any words. I don't eavesdrop on people's conversations."

Eleanor studied his face and determined the man was not lying. "Most women do not conduct business. I was simply curious if you had heard any of our discussion."

He shook his head again, and she stifled a sigh of relief.

Halfway to the house, she stopped. Scarlett Hall had stood for over a hundred and fifty years. What Robert wanted, she would not give him, but she was uncertain how to rid herself of the man. She considered asking Forbes to help, but a shudder went through her. She could not ask him to do the same as he had before, at least not yet. However, the more she thought of what Robert knew and the hold he had over her and her home, her anger grew.

What she might be forced to do sickened her, but perhaps it was warranted. She only hoped she could find another way.

Chapter Twenty-Three

Juliet applied perfume to her neck and wrists with a thoughtful sigh. She knew, beyond any doubt, she was in love, and she could no longer hide that fact.

"You mean to allure him with fragrance?" Annabel asked.

With a laugh, Juliet replied, "No, that is not my intention. Well, not all of my intention, at least. The lesson we have tonight will be special, for I plan on informing him of...something special"

Annabel's eyes widened. "That you love him?" she asked in clear awe. She threw her arms around Juliet. "I am so happy for you!"

"Thank you," Juliet replied with a wide grin. "It must be said, and I fear that, if I wait for him to say it, I shall be old and gray." This made them both giggle as they made their way out the door.

Juliet had to keep herself from running down the hallway. "Always maintain a ladylike appearance," her mother was wont to say, "even when your eagerness attempts to get the best of you." Juliet had never been one for patience, but she employed it, nonetheless.

Forbes waited at the bottom of the stairs, two coats draped over his arm, and Juliet's heart thumped in her chest. *He knows!* came the strangled thought.

"Miss Juliet," the butler said with a quick bow before he offered to help her into her coat, "how was your dinner this evening?"

"I enjoyed it very much," Juliet replied carefully. "The lamb was a bit tough, but I am not one to complain of such things anymore, am I?" She gave him a wink, and he laughed.

"No, you are a lady through and through." Forbes helped Annabel with her coat. "The wind is a bit fierce this evening."

Juliet gave him a mischievous grin. "It is why Annabel and I shall drink brandy all night in order to keep warm," she teased.

A smile spread on Forbes' face as he opened the door for them. As soon as Juliet stepped onto the stoop, the chill breeze proved the butler was correct; it was quite cold. And the sun had yet to set.

When the door closed behind them, Annabel asked, "You will ask Daniel about me, won't you? Concerning me leaving with you? I do not want to be left alone."

Juliet took Annabel's hand in hers. "Even if Daniel were to say no, which he would not, I would say yes."

"You will be able to convince him?"

"Of course. No man can resist my smile." This made them both laugh, and they made their way to the stables. Daniel was already waiting at the worktable when they arrived.

"I'm very excited for our lesson tonight," he said as he jumped up from the stool. "I've been practicing, and I think you'll be pleased." The way he looked at Juliet made her cheeks burn. She found it odd, but extremely pleasurable, that each time she saw him, she found him more handsome than the time before. Although her knees did not go as weak as they had in the past, a fire still sparked in her stomach whenever they were together.

"I am certain we will," Juliet replied with a smile.

As she and Annabel neared the table, he picked up one of the books she had given him, his eyes filled with pride as he flipped through the pages. He stopped, as if waiting for something, but as he looked at her expectantly, that spark began to build into a flame inside her.

"Whenever you wish to begin," Juliet said.

He gave her a wide smile and looked down at the page. It was a children's book, one of Juliet's favorites from when she was young. "'The cat lives in the stable.'" His reading reminded Juliet of Nathaniel as a child when he was first learning to read, and that only made Daniel's attempts that much more endearing. "'The cow eats in the field.'"

Juliet gave a pleased gasp. "Oh, Daniel! That is wonderful! You are doing so well!"

"It's because of your teaching," he said, his eyes bright.

"I will return in a moment," Annabel said, rising from her stool and giving Juliet a knowing grin. Once she was gone, Juliet turned back to Daniel.

"Are you wearing perfume?" Daniel asked.

Juliet nodded. "Do you like it?"

"I do," he replied.

Juliet felt her heartbeat quicken, not only for his words but for what she wished to tell him. "I have something to tell you," she whispered. Her head began to swim and she found breathing difficult. She had to tell him!

"Juliet?" he asked, a concerned look on his face. "What's wrong?"

She reached out and placed her hands in his and took a measured breath. "I have told you that I have come to have feelings for you," she said, pleased that her words did not fall out in as jumbled a mess as they sounded in her head. "I did not know what those feelings were at first, but now I have no doubt." She worked moisture back into her mouth. This was much more difficult than she ever imagined! "I often wondered why in the past you did everything I asked, even if it meant discovery could mean dismissal."

Daniel tried to respond, but Juliet shushed him.

"At first, I thought it was because you feared me, but I realize now that believing that was a silly notion of a girl. Now I see that it was not fear that guided you but rather a result of the same feeling I have for you." She sighed. Now that she had begun, she could not stop even if she tried. "You taught me to appreciate everyone around me. To see the beauty in things that cannot be found in a shop." A tear rolled down her cheek, and his calloused finger wiped it away. "What I feel for you is far better than anything I could ever own." She searched his eyes, looking for any sign of his reaction before allowing the words to spill from her lips. "You see, I love you."

Her heart soared when he smiled down at her. "I have seen you grow into the beautiful woman you are today," he said. "You're right that I did as you asked because I felt the same. The truth is, I've loved you for as long as I can remember, but I couldn't say so, not some simple stable boy." He shook his head and placed a finger on her lips when she tried to argue. "You know it's the simple truth. But like the house and servants' cottages you showed me, there's a gap that exists between two different worlds. I'm just glad we're able to build a bridge between them, a bridge built by, as you say, things that can't be bought in a shop. The greatest gift is love, and I've been given that gift, which I give to you. I do love you, Juliet."

He placed his hands around her waist, and Juliet thought she would melt right there.

"I'll provide everything I can for you as my wife. It won't be easy, but I promise I'll love you with every bit of my soul."

"That is all I need," she said, wiping tears from her eyes. "It is the gift I cherish most."

Daniel leaned in, and their lips met. Soon, this man would be her husband, and she his wife! Their love for one another was connected by a bridge that joined them together, and she knew in her heart it would never be separated.

"Juliet, come here this instant!"

Daniel took a step back, and Juliet nearly toppled to the floor as she spun around to find her mother glaring at her from the doorway. To make matters worse, beside her stood Lord Parsons, his face red with anger.

Juliet walked toward the pair as new tears of fright replaced those of happiness. "I can explain..."

"Lord Parsons," her mother said, "please escort my daughter to the drawing room."

"Of course, Lady Lambert," he replied smugly.

Juliet looked back at Daniel, who shook his head slowly, as if to bid her farewell.

"No!" Juliet mouthed, her heart breaking as she was led through the door. Sickness, fear, and worry overtook her. What would her mother do to poor Daniel? And how on Earth would Juliet explain her actions?

***

When Juliet and Lord Parsons exited the stables, Juliet took little notice of the fact that the sun had set and the moon cast a feeble light around them.

"I am confused," Juliet said, and he glanced down at her. "What are you doing here?"

"I heard a rumor that you had returned." His voice held a thread of anger. "Your mother explained that you had no sick aunt, and I learned that you had misrepresented me in much the same manner."

Juliet stopped at the bottom step at the front of the house. "I can explain. It was not meant..."

"I do not care. I am appalled by what I saw, and I know your mother feels the same."

Juliet searched her mind for the right words to soothe the man. "I did not mean to lie to you, Hugh."

The man snorted. "It is Lord Parsons," he snapped. "To think I have been waiting for your return like a fool. And what is my reward? To be embarrassed in the presence of your mother!"

Before Juliet could respond, he placed a firm grip on her elbow and propelled her into the house. Forbes took their coats. If he knew what had transpired, he gave no indication.

When they entered the drawing room, Juliet wished she knew what her mother was saying to Daniel. How unfortunate that such a beautiful moment should be ruined so quickly!

"Where is Annabel?" Juliet asked, realizing her cousin was nowhere to be seen.

Lord Parsons stood in the doorway, his face drawn tight. "Your mother sent her to her room."

"I am sorry for what you saw. I can explain if you would only give me the chance."

The man raised a hand, and she fell silent. "I am the least of your worries," he said. "It is your mother for whom you should be concerned. Her anger is far greater than mine."

It was not long after that her mother entered the room. She spoke to Lord Parsons in hurried whispers, and without another word to Juliet, he left. Her mother closed the door, and Juliet rose from her seat.

"Mother, I believe I can remedy…"

"You will sit and listen," her mother commanded, and Juliet did as she bade. "Your lies disgust me. First you lie to Lord Parsons, and then you lie to me. It was under the guise of charity that you tricked me."

"But I have helped him," Juliet said. "He is reading."

Her mother gave her a glare. "For years, I have endured your stories, often chastising you for them, and yet my attempts at correcting you have done no good; I have failed at every turn. You forged letters, lied to me directly, and I do not wish to know what else! All so you would be able to see that stable boy."

"He…"

Her mother ignored her. "You led me to believe you had an interest in Lord Parsons. I was pleased, for he is a gentleman, and he has treated you well. Imagine his embarrassment when I told him we had not left the house. And my embarrassment…" She shook her head. "When I told him that I had heard his aunt was ill and nearly at death's door…"

"I am sorry," Juliet said, fighting back tears. "It was never my intention to hurt you."

"Whether it was your intention or not, it matters not," her mother said angrily. "You can no longer be trusted." She walked over to place her hands on the back of one of the chairs. "Daniel will be leaving at the end of the month."

Juliet sprang from her seat. "No! He cannot leave!"

"Do not argue with me, child," her mother said in that tone that brooked no argument. "He can no longer be where you are able to cause him, or yourself, any more trouble."

"But I love him and wish to marry him."

The room fell silent, and Juliet could hear her own blood thumping behind her ears. Her mother seemed to be at a loss for words as she wrung her hands together.

"It is as I feared," she said finally. "Well, it does not matter. He will soon be gone, and you will resume seeing Lord Parsons, who will return in a few days. You will put this notion of Daniel behind you. Just be happy Lord Parsons has not given up on you completely!"

Rage like nothing Juliet had ever encountered washed over her. "You do not care that I love Daniel and that he loves me?" she demanded.

"He is but a stable boy," her mother hissed as she walked around the chair to stand in front of Juliet. "Do you believe I or society will accept such a union? You know better than that!"

Juliet snorted. "Yet, you see no problems in you seeing a cobbler?" she retorted. There was a sense of satisfaction at the drop of her mother's jaw. "Do not worry; Robert did not tell me. I saw him here with my own eyes. He comes every Tuesday! I do not believe you are one to tell me what is right and wrong!"

Juliet had never witnessed violence from her mother before, but when the woman pointed a finger in Juliet's face, she was certain her mother would strike her. "You do not know about what you speak!" she hissed. "Have you told anyone about this?"

Juliet could do nothing but cower in face of such anger. "No," she whispered. "I have told no one."

"Never bring that man's name up in my presence again!" Her mother turned and walked over to the fireplace. "You will continue seeing Lord Parsons and your lessons with Daniel will stop. If you make any attempts to see him, or if I catch the two of you even in the same room together..." Her words trailed off.

"What, Mother?" Juliet demanded. "You will keep me away from the man I love? What else will you do? What else *can* you do?"

Her mother spun around so quickly, Juliet took a step back. "Lord Parson wishes to marry you. I will accept his offer on your behalf if need be."

Juliet shook her head, unable to stop the wave of tears from washing over her lashes. "All my life, you have said that I should not think myself better than others. Now that I have come to believe that, what do I receive as a reward? Kept away from the man I love and threats of marriage to a man I do not love."

She walked over to her mother, a great sadness filling her. "Yes, I have told many lies. I cannot, and will not, deny that. I will do as you ask not because I respect you but because I do not wish to break Daniel's heart as mine has been broken."

Without another word, she hurried out of the drawing room and ran to her bedroom. Throwing herself onto her bed, she sobbed into her pillow, realizing that everything that was her dream had now been taken away from her. Unless she was able to devise a plan, and quickly, Daniel would be gone and Lord Parsons would be forced into his place in her life.

Chapter Twenty-Four

Daniel sat at the worktable and stared at nothing in particular. Four days had passed since he and Juliet had professed their love for one another, and the moment had erased any doubts he had possessed. The kiss they had shared had been passionate and sweet, reflecting a whirlwind of feelings. She had provided him with hope and strength, and for the first time in his life, he had felt more than just a simple stable boy but rather a man of significance, a man of importance.

Yet, that had all been stripped away when Lady Lambert and Lord Parsons entered the room. He had to admit that he was embarrassed at being caught holding a woman who stood so far above him in every way, but for a moment, he wished he could stand up to those who saw what they had as less than it was.

Lady Lambert minced no words and made it quite clear that he had one month to be gone from the stables. He would have no reference and no fond farewells, but he did not expect any.

With a sigh, he replaced the worn leather strap on Juliet's saddle. He traced the letters that made up her name. He had not been able to read it in the past, but now he could. Perhaps it was best he had to leave, for everywhere he turned, he was reminded of her.

"An unbreakable bridge," he murmured ruefully. With a snort, he shook his head. For so long he had not believed they had a future together, and how quickly he had been proven right. He had been a fool to believe that he would ever be allowed to love a woman such as she.

Once his replacement was found, he would be without work and a home. He would travel north—much sooner than he had originally planned, but that was of little consequence—and if he was forced to wait in order to safe more money, he would find another position there. He may not have a reference, but he had the skills to prove his abilities. However, without Juliet with him, what future did he truly have?"

"Stand up, boy!"

Daniel started and spun around to find Lord Parsons standing in the doorway of the work room.

"A stable boy caught kissing a lady," Lord Parsons said with an evil laugh. "If such a thing happened in my home, I would skin your hide." The man took a step forward, his eyes glinting with something Daniel did not like. "Do you not know that a lady such as Juliet would never be with a man such as you?"

"I do know that," Daniel replied, watching the man's hands formed at fists at his side. "It's not allowed."

"Oh, it is more than not allowed," Lord Parson said with a scowl. "The mere mention of it brings about laughter, as it should. You are an uneducated fool, a stable boy, and lower than the dung on my boots." The man lifted his foot to show the soles. "I should strike you for what you did to Juliet, but I will not."

"You do not wish to fight me?" Daniel asked in surprise.

The man's laughter was scornful. "No. I have desired Juliet for some time now, and you have virtually handed her over to me." The man grinned. "Her mother is allowing me to court her, and I have already asked for her hand. I am certain I will not have to wait long for a response." He clasped Daniel on the shoulder. "Therefore, allow me to thank you for being a fool."

Daniel wanted nothing more than to hit him, to pummel him to the ground and not stop until the man no longer could speak, but he could not do it. What purpose would it serve? It would only bring about temporary gratification and land him in prison—or hanging from the gallows. Although the thought of Juliet with another man sickened him, he wanted only for her to be happy, and he doubted his death would accomplish that.

"I have a question, my lord," Daniel said carefully. "About Miss Juliet." He was careful to use a formal address.

Lord Parsons raised his eyebrows. "Oh? And what is that?"

"Do you love her?"

"Love?" The man struggled as if the word was foreign to him.

"Yes. It's not just marrying a woman and providing for her. A man should also love her."

When the man laughed, Daniel caught the odor of spirits on his breath. "People in my position do not marry for love," he said with a snort. "We marry for land and wealth. Love is for the poor like yourself, who have nothing of value to offer."

"She needs to be loved," Daniel argued, unwilling to step down.

Lord Parsons glared at him. "*Miss* Juliet," Daniel did not miss the rebuke in the man's voice, "will wear the finest dresses and have the best of everything." He glanced around and lowered his voice. "A woman with such a beautiful face and delectable bosom must be kept happy in order to get her to perform her marital duty." The man's smile widened. "Which she will do as soon as we are married. And it is all thanks to you."

Daniel instinctively clenched his fist, but Lord Parsons grabbed him by his coat before her could lift his hand.

"You will never speak her name or look her way again," he hissed. "Do not test me, boy, for it will only drive her further into my arms."

The man pushed Daniel back so harshly that Daniel fell against the table and landed on the floor.

"If you reveal to anyone you kissed my soon-to-be fiancé, I shall take your head off myself!" The man reared his head back and spat on Daniel. "Water my horse, boy. I have a marriage to secure."

When Lord Parsons was gone, Daniel stood, humiliation raging inside him. Not only was he losing Juliet, but she would be forced to marry that man! A man who sought to use her for nothing more than a brood mare he could feed lovely apples when she performed well.

The thought disgusted him as he wiped the spit from his face, but he had no idea what he could do about any of it. No man of his position could take on a man like Lord Parsons and live to speak about it later.

***

Numbness. That was all Juliet felt in her body, heart, and mind. Her very soul had been torn apart by her mother's demand she never see Daniel again. A demand Juliet knew she could not change.

She sat in the drawing room wearing her best gown, a blue muslin draped with white lace and satin underskirts. It had been her favorite, but now, forced to wear it for Lord Parsons, she hated it. The man sat across from her, his smile wide and his clothing immaculate, but she heard little of what he said, for her thoughts were on Daniel.

What must he think of the arrival of Lord Parsons? The poor man must be devastated, and she wished to tell him that she cared nothing for this awful man.

Her thoughts were interrupted when her mother touched her arm. "Juliet, Lord Parsons asked you a question."

"My apologies," Juliet said. "I have not slept well as of late." That was not an untruth; she had spent the past four nights since her mother had forbade her from seeing Daniel tossing and turning, sleep evading her at every turn.

"It is the weather," Lord Parsons replied with a laugh. "As spring nears and warms away the last of the winter chill, it causes all to become drowsy. I had asked if you and your mother would like to join me for dinner Friday next. It would be an honor to have you both in my home." He smiled and took on a humbleness that no one would believe was real. "It is no Scarlett Hall, but I believe you will find it to your liking."

Panic gripped Juliet. The man wished to show her his home, the home he wished to share with her. However, she wanted nothing to do with him, but if she spoke her mind, her mother's rebuke would be scathing. Furthermore, she would still be in the same position afterward.

"That would be pleasant," she replied. "I look forward to seeing it." She took a sip of her tea to hide her grimace and was surprised when she saw Lord Parsons smile. It was not a smile that radiated kindness or love like Daniel had given her so often in the past. In contrast, it was a smile of conquest. The idea of marrying this man angered as much as it terrified her. Oh, how she wished she could simply run far away!

"I am pleased," Lord Parsons said. "I believe you will find the journey short, and the roads are well suited for travel at the moment." He turned to Juliet's mother. "Although it will be some time before the flowers return to my garden, I do hope it meets your approval."

"I have no doubt that it will," her mother said with a wave of her hand. "As it will meet Juliet's approval, as well." She gave Juliet a piercing look when she did not reply.

"It is Juliet's approval I seek above all others," Lord Parson said. "It is what I hope I earn during our courtship. As we progress in our relationship, I hope it will lead to other...arrangements."

Juliet wished to tell the man that Daniel was courting her, not he, and that her heart and soul belonged to her stable boy. However, she kept silent. She pleaded with her mother with her eyes, but the woman ignored her.

"I have taken careful consideration of your offer after our last conversation," her mother said. "I believe now is not the best time to discuss it. Perhaps when we are at your home for dinner?"

Juliet wished to wail, to scream, to shout that she did not want to marry this man, but she sipped her tea, her fingers gripping the handle of the cup so tightly she was surprised it did not shatter.

Lord Parsons nodded. "No, you are correct, Lady Lambert. Forgive my eagerness." He rose and Juliet and her mother did the same. "I shall see you in a week. Thank you again for having me here." He gave her mother a bow and then took her hand to kiss her knuckles. "I await your arrival with bated breath."

When he was gone, Juliet rubbed the back of her hand on her skirts. "I do not wish to marry him," she said angrily. "Do not make me do that. Not him."

Her mother shook her head. "If I allow you to turn away Lord Parsons, another will take his place, and you will reject him, as well. It will become a never-ending cycle of you refusing each suitor, and I cannot have that." She turned to face the fire, her back to Juliet.

"But you will leave your daughter heartbroken," Juliet cried. "The daughter who has changed and become who you wanted. I have always known how much the others have pleased you and that I was the daughter you disliked the most."

Her mother turned, her eyes reddened with unshed tears. "Never say such things," she said in a low voice. "Never!"

"I am sorry," Juliet said, wiping away her own tears. "I do not wish to believe it, but I have never been like my sisters. I have done nothing but disappoint you, and for that I can only apologize. But I have changed! Can you not see how much I have changed?"

Her mother closed her eyes. "You have no idea how much I love you," she whispered. "You have a special place in my heart that the others do not."

"Then allow me to marry the man I love," Juliet said. "Do you love me enough to allow that?"

Her mother opened her eyes. "It is because I love you that I cannot allow it."

Juliet turned and stomped from the room before she said something she would regret. As she made her way to her room, she knew the time had come. Tonight, she would inform Daniel of her plans to leave, and then, come morning, she would ask Robert for his help.

Stopping at Annabel's room, she opened the door and went inside. Her cousin rose from the bed as she set aside a book she had been reading.

"What is wrong?" Annabel asked.

Juliet could no longer keep back the flood of tears, and Annabel rushed to her side and wrapped her arms around her. "It is no use," Juliet said. "I must leave Scarlett Hall. Do you still wish to come with me?"

Annabel nodded. "I do. I will not be forced to marry Lord Agar."

Juliet took Annabel's hand in hers. "Then I will need your help tonight distracting Mother. Go to her after dinner and tell her that you have concerns about Lord Agar. Keep her occupied for as long as you can."

"I can do that, but what will you do?"

"I must speak to Daniel," Juliet whispered. "I must let him know we must be gone two nights from now."

Chapter Twenty-Five

S tanding in the hallway outside the dining room after dinner, Juliet did everything she could to appear calm and keep her face clear of the anxiety that boiled inside her. When her mother joined them, Juliet nodded to her cousin.

"Aunt Eleanor," Annabel said, "may I speak with you?" She shot an apologetic glance at Juliet. "It is a private matter."

"Yes, of course," Juliet's mother said, her voice bathed with sympathy. "Would you like to join me in the study?"

Annabel nodded. Now was the time for Juliet's part.

"I am happy to listen and offer any counsel I can," she said.

Annabel sighed. "Do not be angry with me, but I would like to speak with Aunt Eleanor alone about this."

Juliet gave an exaggerated sigh. "Oh, I see. Very well. I will go and find something else to do. Perhaps I will read in the drawing room."

Placing a hand on Juliet's arm, Annabel said, "Thank you for understanding."

Juliet smiled in return. "Of course. See you soon, and then maybe you will be willing to tell me."

The door to the study closed, and Juliet let out a sigh of relief. Annabel would keep her mother busy for at least an hour, which was more than enough time for Juliet to speak to Daniel.

Hurrying to the door, she ignored her coat, fearing her mother or Forbes would notice it missing, and stepped out into the cold wind. She wrapped her arms around herself and made her way to the stables. When she saw Daniel brushing one of the horses, she smiled.

"Juliet," he said, placing the brush on a nearby bench and rushing to her. "You cannot be here. Your mother..." His embrace was comforting, but it lacked the heat it once had.

"Do not worry. Annabel is keeping her busy, but I cannot stay long." She placed her hands on either side of his face. "You may smile; I am here now."

He nodded and gave her a small smile. "I don't know what to say." He walked over and patted the horse he had been brushing. "I assume your mother told you I'll be leaving?"

Juliet nodded. "She has already made inquiries for another stable hand. But that does not matter. We will be leaving in two nights."

Daniel turned, and Juliet could not stop the worry that crept under her skirts like the cold wind outside. She brushed it aside; there was no need to worry.

"Tomorrow, I will go see Robert and collect any funds that may be ready. The rest we can collect at a later point. I am ready to leave here, as is Annabel."

Daniel nodded and walked away, heading down the long corridor between the stalls. Juliet followed him and watched as he walked over to the worktable. "I still can't read the letter you gave me."

"It does not matter at the moment," she said. "Once we find a place to live, we can resume the lessons. We must plan our escape; that is what is important now."

It was as if time had stood still. Then Daniel turned, his smile gone. "There won't be an escape," he said. "You're staying here."

"What? Our plans have not changed except that we will leave earlier than we originally expected."

Daniel kept his head down. "Your mother wants you to stay here, and I can't defy her wishes."

Juliet shook her head. "My mother does not know what is best for me; I do. Do not speak like this, Daniel."

"It can't happen. Our dream is over." When he looked up at her, his eyes held a firmness she had never seen him possess before. "Even if we were to escape, she would send men after us. And you'll break her heart."

"This is my dream!" Juliet shouted, tears rolling down her face unchecked. "To be with you, the man I love. Nothing can be more important than that."

"I'd thought that, too. But that was the dreams of a foolish boy." He went to reach for her, but she pulled back, and his eyes filled with sadness. "Never doubt that I love you; I always will. But our lives are too far apart, and no amount of love will bridge that gap no matter how much we think it can be done."

Juliet wiped at her cursed tears in vain. "She will have me marry Lord Parsons, and if not him, then another man. Is that what you wish?"

Daniel shook his head. "I know the man doesn't love you, and I don't want to think about his true intentions, but you have to please your mother." He shrugged. "Maybe another man worthy of you will come into your life."

"No!" She beat her fists against his chest, and he did nothing to stop her. "I do not want to love another! I only wish to love you!"

Daniel gathered her hands into his. "Goodbye, Miss Juliet," he whispered. "This hurts me, but we were not meant to be. If you love me like you say you do, please don't make this any harder than it has to be."

He turned away from her, and she found herself staring at his back, her vision watery. "It is because I love you that I will do as you ask. But no man, be he Lord Parsons or any other, will ever have my heart. That only belongs to you."

When he turned back around, the pain in his eyes was so pronounced, she almost took a step back. However, instead, she lifted herself onto her toes and placed a kiss on his lips. The thought that this would be their last crushed her soul.

"Goodbye, Daniel. Thank you for showing me the best thing in life."

"It's a beautiful gift," he replied, his voice breaking. "One I'll carry with me forever." He turned back to the table, a clear dismissal, and Juliet left the room.

Tears continued to fall as she stumbled across the drive, her steps thudding against the hard earth. Soon, Daniel would be gone, and

Juliet would be alone, forced to marry a man she did not love. When she arrived at the steps, she paused to look up at the great walls of her home. The house had once been filled with laughter, but now it was full of heartache due to a mother who denied her daughter the very thing he wanted in life.

She was uncertain how long she stood there, but thoughts of Daniel and the life they could have had tormented her. It was not until she shivered from the chill in the air that she went into the house.

Her mother sat on the bottom stair of the grand staircase and rose as Juliet closed the door. "Where have you been?"

Juliet looked at her mother, no longer wishing to lie to the woman. "I went to speak to Daniel; to ask him to leave with me." When her mother gaped, Juliet shook her head. "Do not worry; he refused my offer. It seems he believes that, because of his station, he is not worthy to be with the woman he loves."

"Juliet..."

"It does not matter, Mother. We shall see Lord Parsons next week and we will tell him that I accept his offer." The words tore at her heart, but she had no other choice. She walked past her mother without looking at her.

"Do you hate me?" her mother asked in a choked voice.

Juliet shook her head. "I could never hate you," she whispered, although she did not turn back to look at her mother. Instead, she continued her journey up the stairs and to her room where Annabel waited for her.

"I tried..."

Juliet embraced her cousin, but it felt mechanical in some way. "It is all right. I have news for you."

"What is it?"

Juliet sighed. "We are not leaving," she said. "At least not with Daniel." She explained what Daniel had said; it was strange her voice lacked any emotion. That numbness had returned, but it was better than the anger. Better than the sadness. Better than the loss.

"It seems my life no longer has meaning," Juliet finished. "I am tempted to try again, to convince him that leaving together would be the best for us both, but I am at a loss as to what to do."

"Monday we will go to Rumsbury to speak to Robert." Annabel had a lilt in her voice that surprised Juliet.

"Whatever for?" Juliet demanded. "What can he do besides give me some of my investment returns? What good will money be if I am not leaving with Daniel?"

Annabel glanced at the door and then leaned forward. "He is friends with your mother," she whispered. "Perhaps he can sway her in this matter."

For the first time since leaving the stables, Juliet felt a twinge of hope return. "I suppose he may be able to," she said thoughtfully. "If the woman is jealous over him, he may do anything he asks of her."

The more she considered it, the happier she became. "Annabel, I do love you and your mind!" she said, wrapping her arms around her cousin. "Now, let us consider how best to approach Robert."

***

Sleep had not come easy for Juliet, and come Monday morning, she was bone weary when they arrived in the village. The streets were busy, and people moved in and out of the various shops, greeting one another as they were wont to do after being closeted away during the colder months.

Annabel was speaking with Robert about the ledgers, and Juliet was on her way to collect a few items Robert needed. When she entered the haberdashers, the only shop in the village that carried almost every item on her list, including stationery, unbelievably, the shopkeeper set about collecting her required items.

As she stared out the window at the passersby as she waited, she could not help but wonder why the cobbler's shop was always void of patrons. Yet, perhaps it was only coincidence; it was not as if she was there at all hours.

With a shrug, she turned her thoughts to Robert. If her mother cared for him, which Juliet suspected she did, the woman would listen to any advice Robert gave. Juliet had little concern for making the request of Robert, for he was her friend and enjoyed seeing her happy. The man would be calling on her mother the following day, which was an opportune time for him to speak to the woman.

Once her mother agreed, Juliet would give Daniel the good news—that the love they shared was not lost.

"Here you are," the shopkeeper said.

Juliet paid the man and left the shop with the items bundled in her arms, almost bumping into Caroline in her rush to leave.

"Oh, Juliet," Caroline said. "It is fortunate that I have run into you, for I have been wanting to speak to you."

Juliet stifled a groan. She was not in the mood to listen to gossip. "I am sorry, but I must hurry. I have a very busy schedule. Perhaps we can speak next week."

"It is about Mr. Mullens, the cobbler," Caroline whispered after glancing around them. "Rumors are he propositioned a servant of Lady Chambers."

Juliet scrunched her brow. "Propositioned?"

Caroline grabbed her arm and pulled her into the alleyway between the haberdashers and the jeweler's. "Shh! Not so loud." She glanced around them again, her face filled with worry. "He offered her a pair of boots for her virtue!"

Juliet had no time for such nonsense. "I will keep my wits about me," she said. "I promise. But thank you for your warning."

Before Caroline could add more rubbish to the heap, Juliet pushed past her and hurried back to the cobbler's shop. She wanted to laugh; Robert propositioning a servant woman? It was preposterous! If it were true, what servant girl would tell anyone, especially someone who would tell Caroline? No, it was simply more senseless rumors that were so common among the *ton,* and she would take no part in it.

As she entered the shop, she glanced over at Annabel, who stood in the corner, her arms wrapped around her stomach and her face nearly white.

"Are you ill?" Juliet asked as she set the package on one of the benches. "You look as if you are unwell."

"It is my stomach," Annabel said. Then she lowered her voice and whispered, "May we leave, please?"

Juliet went to speak, but Robert entered through the white door behind the counter. "Ah, the supplies," he said cheerfully. "Excellent."

Annabel touched Juliet's arm. "I will wait in the carriage."

Robert walked up to Juliet. "You are a wonderful partner, indeed."

Juliet smiled. "I am glad I am able to help," she said. "I would like to ask a favor of you, if I may."

"Yes, of course. We are business partners...and friends. I will do whatever you ask if I am able."

Relief washed over her. "Thank you," she said. "Much has transpired since I last saw you. I am afraid that Mother caught me and Daniel in a...let us just say that it was unfortunate and leave it at that, and Lord Parsons was with her."

"I see," Robert said with raised brows. "I imagine you have gotten yourself into all sorts of trouble?"

"Yes." Just the thought of what her mother wanted her to do pierced her heart. "I am no longer allowed to see Daniel, and he refuses to take me with him when he leaves. He fears upsetting Mother, and I need help."

Robert grimaced. "I'm not sure I know what I can do," he said. "This is a complicated matter."

"My mother risks everything to see you," Juliet pleaded. "Would you perhaps speak with her and tell her that she should allow me to see Daniel? Please, I do not wish to beg, but I am desperate. I need a friend right now."

"You do," Robert replied as he placed a hand on Juliet's arm. "And I am the friend you can trust. But I fear that I am also the friend who will hurt you by speaking the truth."

Juliet eyed him carefully. "Truth? What truth?"

He sighed. "I have never thought a lady half my age would teach me the merits of honor and friendship, but you have, so I will tell you what I know."

Juliet nodded. "Please."

"I have already spoken to your mother concerning Daniel. I tried to reason with her, to explain how much you care for him, but she refused to listen. You see, Lord Parsons is a wealthy man, far wealthier than many realize. Your mother wants to purchase a cottage at the seaside for when her children are gone."

"No," Juliet said with a gasp. "You mean, she…"

"Has taken some payment already from Lord Parsons?" He nodded. "She has. And he has promised the rest when you have married him."

Juliet shook her head in disbelief. "Then it is truly over," she whispered. Her heart ached not only for the loss of Daniel but for her mother's betrayal. "I cannot believe she did this. My happiness in exchange for money?"

"I am sorry to be the one to tell you," Robert said sadly. "However, I may have a solution."

"Oh?"

He nodded. "Threaten her," he said. "And use me as a pawn."

"What?" Juliet asked, aghast. "Threaten her? She is my mother, I cannot…"

"Do you wish to be with Daniel?" he asked. She nodded. "Then it is simple. Tell her that if you cannot be with the man you love, you will tell everyone about her relationship with me. She will have no choice but to allow you to see him."

The suggestion made her feel ill. "I cannot," she whispered. "I love her too much."

"You are kind," Robert said with a sigh. "To love someone who clearly does not love you is a rare being indeed."

His words stung her heart. "She does love me," she said. Then she paused. "Does she not?"

Robert shrugged as he walked around to the other side of the counter to grab a ledger. "I will not be seeing her tomorrow, for I am leaving for two days. But think about what I said. Either you marry Lord Parsons or the stable boy. It is your choice."

Juliet nodded, the numbness greater than it had ever been in her life. However, what he said was true. It was her choice. And she would do what was best for her in the end.

Yet, was what was best for her best for everyone else who was important in her life? That was the question that weighed on her mind as she left the shop, still uncertain what she would decide.

Chapter Twenty-Six

Candlelight cast a soft glow on the rain pelted window as Juliet lay in bed, sleep evading her. Her thoughts were of Daniel and the hope he was not as heartbroken as she. However, it was much to ask, she knew, for how could he not be? Their love was pure and beautiful, and Juliet had thought nothing could tear them apart.

Yet, her mother's wishes had been their undoing.

The fact her mother wished to purchase a cottage for herself was unlike her. She rarely left the house as it was, and Juliet had no doubt as to how much she enjoyed living at Scarlett Hall. Granted, Nathaniel would take over the house when he became of age, but that was years away; the boy was only fourteen!

Another issue that bothered Juliet was her mother's wish that she, Juliet, marry Lord Parsons. That concern was more understandable yet did not sit with Juliet any better than her separation from the man she loved.

Sighing, she moved back the covers and donned her dressing gown and slippers. With one of the candles in hand, she made her way toward the staircase. No other lights peeked beneath any of the doors, nor were any lit in the hallway.

The fire in the drawing room should still be burning, she thought. There, she would pour herself a glass of brandy and drink away her final days of freedom.

Her slippered feet made no noise as she made her way down the stairs. She could hear the wind howling outside the front door, and she shivered from a draft. When she reached the drawing room, she was surprised to see the door sitting open and her mother curled up on the couch with a book on her lap and a drink in her hand, the fireplace aglow.

Robert's suggestion came to her mind, and Juliet shook her head. The idea of blackmailing her mother made her ill; she loved the woman despite the hurt she had caused, and Juliet could not bring herself to do it.

Her mother looked up and smiled. "Oh, Juliet, you startled me." She set the book aside and placed her feet on the floor. "Would you care to join me?"

Juliet nodded, closed the door, and looked at the array of decanters on the liquor cart. "May I have a small drink?"

Her mother nodded her head, and Juliet poured herself a glass of brandy—a tiny measure for her mother's benefit.

"You have been especially quiet since your return from the village," her mother said. "It is not like you."

Juliet took a sip of the brandy before responding, giving herself a moment to collect her thoughts. "I have been thinking..." Juliet's heart tore as she turned to face her mother. She loved the woman, yet she loved Daniel.

No! I cannot blackmail her! she told herself once again.

Her mother placed her glass on the side table and rose. "What is wrong? I can see it on your face that something is bothering you."

"I cannot do it," Juliet murmured as she lowered herself into one of the large wingback chairs across from her mother. "As much as I love Daniel, I cannot do it."

"Do what?"

Juliet drank the remainder of her brandy—barely enough to wet her lips as far as she was concerned—and set the glass on the table. "Blackmail you. I was advised to do so in order to pressure you into allowing me to see Daniel."

"And what would you use to blackmail me?" Her mother's voice was guarded.

"Robert," Juliet replied simply. "I would threaten to tell everyone about your sordid relationship with Robert in hopes that you would allow me to see Daniel. However, I cannot do that, even if it means marrying another is the consequence of refusing to do so." She looked up at the woman she loved with all her heart as tears filled her eyes. "I do not love him, but if you wish that I marry Lord Parsons in order to purchase the cottage, then I shall do so. I will do anything to make you happy." The tears slipped over her lashes, and she did nothing to stop them.

Her mother's eyes widened. "A cottage? I have no use for a cottage."

Juliet clicked her tongue. "You do not have to lie, Mother. Robert told me everything. How Lord Parsons has given you money and…"

"The man is a liar," her mother spat. "You cannot believe anything he says, for every word he utters is a falsehood!" She turned and walked to the fireplace, her back to Juliet.

Juliet leapt from her seat. "Then why do you see him in secret?" she demanded. "You speak as if he is Lucifer himself, yet he has been nothing but kind to me. If he is so awful, why do you allow him into our home?" She did not care that she was nearly shouting.

"Juliet…"

"I do not want excuses, Mother," Juliet said, her anger rising. "Why are you allowed to see a cobbler but I am unable to see a stable hand? Why do you speak ill of him and yet want him in your arms? Is it your jealousy?"

Her mother spun around, her skirts swishing around her ankles. "Jealousy?"

"Yes, jealousy. Robert told me that you are jealous of my mind and beauty…" her words trailed off as her mother turned her gaze to the floor.

"He has lied to you," her mother said, her voice just above a whisper. "He has lied to you more than I would have ever thought he would. I am not jealous of him nor of you."

Juliet shook her head. "I am confused. Why all the secrecy?" When her mother simply looked up and said nothing, she raised her voice. She *would* learn the truth! "Tell me! What is so special about this man?"

Her mother wrung her hands. "He knows something," she said, and a chill went down Juliet's spine. "A secret I thought would never be revealed. It is this secret he threatens to expose that forces me to allow him into our home."

"A secret?"

Her mother nodded. "I make payments to him every Tuesday in exchange for his silence. It was why when I first saw him I ordered you to stay away."

"Is that the reason you changed your mind and allowed me to return?"

"It is." Her mother's voice was barely audible. "He wished to see you, and I had no choice. If I had denied him, he would have attempted to destroy you." She shook her head. "Now that I have allowed it, I am afraid he has come close to doing just that anyway."

"Mother?" Juliet could do nothing to calm the trembling in her voice. "Why did he wish to see me? What is it about me that is a secret?"

Her mother walked over to her and placed a hand on the side of her face. "My sweet Juliet," she whispered, tears streaming down her face. "I love you; you know this, do you not?"

"Of course I do," Juliet said, the words sticking in her throat. Did she wish to know what her mother kept hidden? However, if she did not learn of it now, would she ever? She had to know! "You are frightening me. What does Robert know?"

Her mother dropped her hands to her side. "That he is your father."

Juliet's stomach rolled and her heart leapt to her throat. "No, it cannot be!" she gasped. "My father died..."

"It is true. I am so sorry. I never wished you to ever learn of it. However, the man has been blackmailing me since his return to Rumsbury, and I cannot protect you any longer."

Juliet fell to her knees sobbing, and her mother dropped down beside her. She pulled Juliet into her arms, and Juliet could do nothing to stop the wracking sobs that took over her body.

The man who she thought her father, Lord Charles Lambert, was not. Her father was a simple cobbler, a man who blackmailed her mother.

"I love you, and I am sorry," her mother whispered as she ran her hand down Juliet's hair. "If he were to tell anyone, no gentleman would ever have you. You would be disgraced and ignored."

When the sobs subsided, Juliet rose from the floor and went to the liquor cart, this time without asking her mother for permission. She poured herself a hefty serving of brandy and gulped it down, not caring that it burned her throat.

Then she turned and faced her mother. "Your affair with the cobbler?" she asked. "Did Father know?"

Her mother walked to the window without a response, and Juliet's fear returned. "Mother?"

"Join me," she said.

Juliet wiped the tears from her eyes and joined her mother at the window.

Her mother put her arm around Juliet. "How many times I watched you and your siblings outside I cannot count. As I told you before, you hold a special place in my heart."

Juliet nodded as her mother began a story that would change her life forever.

"For one hundred and fifty years, Scarlett Hall has held strong. However, it holds many secrets in its walls, and if you listen carefully, the voices of shadows past will tell you all you wish to know."

Chapter Twenty-Seven

Scarlett Hall 1788

L *et us hope this time it is a boy. I do not want a house full of girls and no heirs.*

Those were the last words Eleanor had heard from her husband before he left for Glasgow a month earlier. From there, the man would go to Manchester and then Paris. He had other places on his itinerary, but she had been told in no uncertain terms that it was none of her concern. What had been her concern at the time was that she was with child, expected to arrive in five months when her husband was not due to return for six.

She took a deep breath and ran her hand over the tiny mound under her dress as she peered through the bedroom window. Her eyes soaked in the rolling green hills that stretched far across the horizon. All the land, for as far as eyes could see, belonged to her family, and she loved every bit of it.

Raising a glass to her lips, she took a large gulp of wine. Her consumption of the beverage began earlier each day, but she had no other way to bring relief from the numbness that plagued her. And it mattered not that the wine increased rather than diminished it.

"My lady," Anne, her lady's maid, said as she entered the room, "I must speak with you."

Eleanor took another sip of her wine and placed the glass on a table before turning to smile at the woman who had also become a close friend and confidante. The woman always wore a bright smile, and with her raven black hair and brown eyes, she was strikingly beautiful. However, it was the bond of friendship that had formed between the two that brought Eleanor comfort when she sought it. An ear to hear and shoulder on which to cry.

"What is it?"

Anne worried her bottom lip. "I'm worried about you."

Eleanor clenched her jaw. Confidante Anne might be, but she had no right to overstep her bounds. "I do not need your worry," Eleanor said curtly. "You may leave now." She picked up and drained the glass of wine before grabbing the opened bottle and pouring a new glass.

"You're my employer," Anne said, "but you're also my friend, and I'm worried. You spend your days drinking away your hurt, and I can't stand by and see you suffer anymore."

Eleanor turned. "Do you believe I will not send you away?" she demanded, although it hurt her to speak to the only person who would listen to her woes. "I do not wish to listen to you explain to me how I am feeling, for no one knows the pain I endure..." She wiped away the traitorous tears that escaped her eyes and belied her words.

Anne took the glass from her, set it on the table and took Eleanor's hands in hers. "When Lord Lambert returns, what will you do? The padding under your dress might fool the servants, but it won't fool him."

"Do you not think I know this?" Eleanor said in a sharp whisper. "My husband has left me with child, and now that I have lost it..." She shook her head. "It is as though a piece of me was lost, as well. It killed me inside, and no one knows my pain!" No matter what she did, the pain did not subside, and she wanted nothing more than the numbness to return.

"I may not know your pain" Anne whispered, "but I have my own painful news to share."

Eleanor wiped at her eyes. She was being selfish; Anne had always been there for her whenever she needed her. "What is it?"

Anne took a deep breath and placed her hand on her stomach. "I am with child."

With wide eyes, Eleanor studied the lady's maid. She *was* thicker around her middle! She had been so caught up in her loss that she never took notice that the woman who was typically as thin as a stick had grown at least an entire dress size.

"How long?"

"Maybe a week or so longer than you, my lady." She turned a deep crimson and looked down at the floor.

"And the father?"

Anne looked up at her, tears in her eyes. "Robert, the gardener." The tears she had been holding back dripped down her face. "He wooed me with promises of marriage, and I believed him. Then he convinced me that I should give him my savings so we could buy a home together. However, when I told him I was with child...he left."

Eleanor pulled the woman into her arms and held her tight. "I am so sorry," she whispered. "So, that is why he left?"

Anne nodded, and Eleanor recalled the man giving his notice, but until now she did not know why.

"He told Lord Lambert that his mother was ill, and he told me not to tell anyone, not even you, but that was over a month ago." She shook her head, her face filled with despondency. "Now I'm without money and burdened with a child I cannot look after."

Eleanor understood the maid's concern. When Charles learned that she was carrying a child, he would throw her out immediately, spouting concerns for being burdened with the results of a woman with loose morals.

The truth was the woman would never survive in the world with a bastard child. She would gain no employment in such a condition, and with no money, she would have no means on which to live.

"But you can."

Eleanor stared at the woman. "What do you mean?"

"I cannot provide for this child," Anne said, looking down at her stomach. "But you need a child to make your husband happy and to heal the hole in your heart with the loss of your own."

Eleanor closed her eyes. The pain of losing her child had led to many sleepless nights and to her drinking as heavily as a village drunk. "Charles would never allow it," she said finally. "Society would..."

"Never know. You can keep up your ruse, and I will leave today to somewhere safe. When the time grows near, make an excuse to leave."

The idea was tempting. "I...do not know."

"This child is a gift. One I cannot support, but you can. It is a gift from my heart that can heal yours."

Eleanor nodded, the thought of gaining her lost child more appealing with each passing moment. "You could never tell a soul. If Robert were to return and find you with no child..."

"He will not ever hear it from me," Anne insisted. "It is your child, if you will have it."

It was a risky endeavor, and Eleanor knew that if Charles or anyone were to learn of it, the lives of the child and Eleanor's other daughters would be ruined. However, God's hand had to be in this, for He had sent her a replacement child. "I will do this," she said with finality before wrapping her arms around the woman. "I promise I will love the child as my own."

"I have no doubt you will, my lady," Anne replied. "I ask just one thing."

"Yes?"

"In the years to come, if the time ever arises, let the child know that I loved him or her and that I only wanted what was best."

Eleanor smiled. "I promise," she whispered. "Tonight, you will leave for a cottage we have on our property that is currently not in use. You will be safe there, for no one ventures there."

"I will collect my things," Anne said with another embrace and then a quick curtsy.

After the woman left the room, Eleanor returned to the table where she had placed her glass. Her heart had been filled with pain with the death of her child, but for the first time in a month, that pain began to subside, and it had not been wine that had brought her relief.

***

The cottage sat alone amongst a thick covering of trees as Eleanor stepped from the carriage. Her usual driver had not been used on this journey, but rather it was the young butler, Forbes. He seemed much more trustworthy, and she was in no condition to take the carriage on her own, or so she appeared with the large pillow under her dress.

A gentle breeze blew Eleanor's hair as Forbes closed the door of the carriage. Besides Anne, who was inside the cottage, only the butler knew her identity, and it was of the utmost importance that she had his trust. Not even the midwife knew who she was.

"This journey to my mother's," Eleanor said, holding her hand against the padded bulge, "is of no concern to anyone except my husband. And the stop at this home..."

"Is none of my concern," Forbes replied. "I know of many ladies who often visit cousins and other relatives, and some do not have the same means as they." The butler dipped his head. "In fact, I do not recall even stopping anywhere save your mother's house."

Relieved, Eleanor nodded and turned to walk toward the cottage when the door burst open and a girl of perhaps ten rushed outside.

"Miss! It's happenin'"

Eleanor hurried down the path and she heard Anne's groans from outside. The butler was no fool, and she hoped he would ask no questions. All she could do was trust him.

The cottage had a small kitchen, a sitting room, and two small bedrooms. Why Charles bought the place, she did not know, nor did she care. Her only concern at the moment was the woman hunched over the splayed legs of the woman who had once been her lady's maid.

"You are here," Anne said, sweat dripping from her brow and her breathing heavy.

Eleanor rushed to the woman's side and took her hand. "I am."

"I am so glad you came." Anne leaned back into the pillows and closed her eyes.

"You knew I would," Eleanor said with a smile.

Anne gripped her hand with a sudden gasp. Soon, Eleanor was speaking encouraging words. She had birthed two girls already, so she knew what Anne was enduring, but it did not make it any easier to watch.

"You are doing well," Eleanor said.

Anne cried out, held her breath, and then grunted. Then the most beautiful of things happened. The wail of a child filled the room, a sound that rang in Eleanor's heart. The midwife placed the babe on

Anne's bare stomach, and Anne squeezed Eleanor's hand.

"You have done well," Eleanor whispered as she sat on the edge of the bed and kissed Anne's forehead.

"It is a girl," the midwife said as she took the baby and washed her in warm water before swaddling her, her head full of dark hair the only part of the babe to be seen.

Eleanor took the baby in her arms. "She is beautiful," she said.

When she looked up at Anne, the woman lay with her eyes closed. "She is," Anne said. "And I know she'll be happy and well-loved, and I couldn't wish more for her."

With a smile, Eleanor began to rock the lively bundle, and the baby calmed. "She will be my daughter, treated as an equal to her older sisters. I promise she will find happiness in life."

Anne gave her a weak smile. "I have no doubt you'll make her very happy."

The woman could not have said anything truer. Eleanor already loved the child as if she was her own. "Her name is Juliet, and I will do everything I can for her." She took Anne's hand. "You have given me the most wondrous of gifts, and I will never forget you for it." She handed her a purse. "This is everything I have saved." When Anne attempted to push the purse away, Eleanor gave the maid a firm glare. "No, you must take it. You will need money until you find a new position. I wish you would come back to Scarlett Hall, but I understand how difficult that would be for you."

"I don't know where I'll go next, but this will help. Thank you."

Eleanor remained at Anne's side, the bond between them bringing them that much closer, until the hour grew late and Anne glanced toward the window. "You should go; it won't be safe if you travel after dark." She grabbed Eleanor's hand. "I'll never forget you."

With a firm squeeze of her hand, Eleanor replied, "And I shall never forget you, my dear friend." She leaned over and kissed the woman on the cheek before heading toward the door.

Stopping with her hand on the doorknob, she glanced back and the two exchanged a smile, one that would remain in Eleanor's heart forever, for she never saw her friend again.

***

The days became weeks, the weeks became a month, and a letter arrived announcing that Charles was to arrive in three days.

With Juliet cradled in her arms, Eleanor kissed the soft tuft of dark hair on her daughter's head. "You are the most beautiful gift I have ever received," she whispered. "And you will always have a special place in my heart."

Footsteps from the hallway made her look up. Charles entered the room, a wide grin on his face. "My child!" he exclaimed as he hurried to her side. He gave Eleanor a small kiss and knelt beside her, and her love for him grew. She pulled back the blanket so he could see the baby. "She has my hair color," he said with pride. "And my eyes!"

"She is her father's child," she replied. "Do you wish to hold her?"

He nodded and took Juliet into his arms, the child gurgling with clear pleasure. "Juliet. Named after my mother," he said. "This child is special; do you not feel it?"

"Yes, she most certainly is," Eleanor said as she pulled herself up from the chair to stand at his side. She placed a hand on his arm and gazed down at their daughter. "I know she has filled a special place in my heart."

And the words could not have been truer.

Chapter Twenty-Eight

That is why you have always had, and always will, have a special place in my heart."

Juliet stood in shock doing everything she could to comprehend what her mother had just revealed. Who was she? She was no longer the person she thought she was all her life, a woman of better blood, the child of title who came from an affluent lineage generations long.

Now, however, she was the daughter of servants—a man who was once a gardener and a lady's maid. She looked up at the woman she had called Mother all her life and could not find words to think let alone speak. All she felt was shame and humiliation. How could anyone love her now?

Yet, the woman who birthed her, had she not had Juliet's own interests at heart? Juliet would never have lived the life she had as the daughter of a woman of the working class. Where would she be now if her real mother had not made such a decision?

"I know this is overwhelming to hear, but you must understand that you are my daughter. Nothing will ever change that."

With surprise, Juliet looked at her mother. "I...you still love me although I now know the truth?"

Her mother responded by throwing her arms around Juliet. "My sweet child, I love you more than you will ever know. Although I am not the woman who gave birth to you, I hope you love me as your mother as I have loved you as if you were my own child."

Juliet sobbed into the woman's shoulder. How could she consider this woman as someone other than her mother? "You are my mother, and I am thankful that you raised me. I hold no anger to my...birth mother. I understand why she did what she did."

Her mother held her at arm's length. "She loved you, you know."

"What was she like?"

Pushing back a strand of Juliet's hair, she smiled. "She was beautiful, strong, and raging with a fire much like yours. It is from her you get your spiritedness."

Although a thousand questions swam in her mind, those concerning Robert rose to the top.

"How did Robert," she was not ready to think of him as her father, "learn of all this?"

Her mother sighed. "The last time he was here, he explained that he found work two years ago, and Anne happened to be a lady's maid there. She had fallen gravely ill, and it was on her deathbed that she revealed the truth."

"But why would she do that? She had promised!"

"I do not know," her mother replied. "She always saw the good in people, so perhaps she thought he had a change of heart. He may have manipulated her into believing so."

Juliet nodded, but anger rose to push down her shock. "So, this man came in search of his daughter, but rather than introducing himself to me, he used the information to blackmail you. He attempted to ruin not only you but my sisters, as well."

"Yes," her mother replied. "I am afraid that is the truth of it. I wanted to protect you from him, for I knew how twisted the man's lies could be."

Juliet studied the woman. Her mother was strong, a woman who rarely cried, at least not where others could witness it. Yet, her eyes were red and filled with tears, and Juliet knew much of her distress came from what that man had done to her—or at least attempted to do.

"What will you do concerning him?" She would not use his name; he was unworthy of such courtesy!

"I will continue to pay him. There is nothing more I can do."

Juliet walked over and poured them each a drink. Taking a long sip from her glass, her mind began to race. Her true father was alive, but the man had attempted to pit her against the woman she knew as her mother. The thought of her mother suffering because of him made her anger turn into rage.

"You cannot pay the man forever," Juliet said finally. "His price will only increase until he has run you...run all of us...into the ground."

Her mother gave a contemptuous chuckle. "It already has caused us a considerable amount of trouble. The man is mad. He has asked for my hand in marriage—has demanded it."

Juliet shook her head. "His greed runs deep," she whispered. A new thought came to mind. "I now realize I have been fooled in more ways than one." She sighed. "I have been investing in his business, as has Annabel and some of our friends. I have fallen for his lies and led them right into it."

"Investing?"

"He approached me first..." She explained everything, including Robert's plan to open new shops. "I cannot believe I fell for his lies." A new sense of shame came over her as she realized she would now lose everything she had given him, as would the others who had trusted her.

"He is a gifted storyteller," her mother said. "A palterer of the highest caliber."

Juliet clicked her tongue. "Wooing women into his bed," she murmured. "To trick a lady into handing over her savings." She looked at her mother, a sadness overwhelming her. "I see now from where my ability to tell stories come. Of all the attributes I could have received from him...It sickens me."

Her mother hurried over to her and embraced her once more. "Your stories have always been delightful. If you use them for good, there is no harm in their telling."

Juliet snorted. "Like him, I have only used them for my own benefit. Mother, do you believe he has any good in him?"

Her mother's frown was answer enough. "Even after nineteen years, the man has not changed, so I would hazard to suspect that he does not."

Juliet nodded, downed the remainder of her brandy in one gulp and placed the glass on the cart. "I will see if there is," she said firmly. "I love you, Mother, and if I have ever disappointed you in any way, I am sorry."

Her mother smiled. "You could never disappoint me." She kissed Juliet's cheek. "I love you. Tomorrow, if you wish, we may talk more about this, especially any questions you have concerning your mother, if you would like."

Juliet nodded again. "I would like that." She kissed her mother. "Good night."

"Good night, my dear."

Juliet left the room and headed toward the main staircase. From the bottom step, she gazed upwards. How many times had she come down those stairs in a new dress, her hair perfectly styled and her jewelry in place, believing she was better than most? Although her true parents were not of title or wealth, it did not matter, for her heart had changed. She had already begun viewing those around her as equals, and although the news she learned this night numbed her, she felt a sense of joy. It was nothing like other women, for she had two mothers. And although she had never met the woman who had given birth to her, she loved her all the same.

***

That night, Juliet lay beneath the blanket thinking of her past. She thought of the mother she never knew, a woman who had chosen to see her daughter have the best life had to offer. What a loving gesture!

Yet, her father was different. How had he become so evil? As far as she was concerned, her mother, the woman who had raised her as her own, was in trouble, and it was up to Juliet to confront him and convince him to stop the blackmailing.

A light tap on the door made Juliet start. "Come in," she called out in a loud whisper.

Annabel entered, closing the door with a soft click behind her. The girl had been quiet all day, and Juliet had been so upset over her own situation, she felt a twinge of guilt for not checking in on her before coming to bed, especially after her complaints about her stomach aching her. Annabel did not fall ill often, and Juliet certainly hoped she was not ill now.

"May I join you?" Annabel asked.

Juliet laughed and pulled down the blanket. "You never have to ask!" Annabel climbed in beside her. "Can you not sleep?"

Annabel shook her head as she reached under the pillow to take out the bottle of brandy Juliet always had hidden there. Juliet laughed when the girl drank straight from the bottle.

"I wish to tell you something," Juliet said. What would Annabel think when she learned the truth about her?

"As do I," Annabel whispered. "But I am afraid you will be angry with me." She lifted the bottle to lips once more, and Juliet began to worry. Her cousin was not ill, but something was most definitely wrong.

"Tell me. I promise not to be angry with you. You could never anger me."

Annabel nodded and looked down at her hands. "When Robert sent you to run to collect the stationary, I remained to work on the ledgers."

"Yes, I remember. What of it?"

"He told me..." She looked up at Juliet, and the fear in her eyes made Juliet push back against the pillows. "He told me he had a surprise for me, for my birthday."

Juliet attempted to calm her racing heart. "And what did he do?"

Annabel's eyes welled with tears. "He kissed me."

"He what!" Juliet asked, coming close to vaulting from the bed. She had to take a calming breath. "I am sorry, for shouting. What happened after?"

"When I told him I didn't want it, he grew angry. He told me that unless I wanted to lose my investment and not have you angry at me,

I would have to allow him to kiss me whenever he wanted." The last came as a sob, and Juliet pulled her cousin in close. "I am so sorry!"

"You did nothing wrong," Juliet said, the now familiar anger rising within her. "I am not angry at you."

"You are not?" Annabel asked in clear surprise.

"Not at all." Juliet wiped the tears from Annabel's cheeks. "In two days, I will speak with Robert. And I promise you, he will never bother you again." Annabel smiled, and Juliet gave her another hug.

That man had ruined countless lives through lies, blackmail and now coercion. Well, he had hurt her precious Annabel, her cousin and her best friend. "No one hurts my family, especially my Annabel."

Annabel sniffled. "Thank you. I wish I was as strong as you."

Juliet snorted. "I am not strong," she said, taking the bottle and downing a large gulp. "Not like you."

Annabel smiled and wiped at her eyes. "Thank you."

Juliet's heart went out to the young woman who, after enduring what her parents put her through, had been forced to suffer the forwardness of a man such as Robert. A man who was her father. "Let us speak of happier things to lift our spirits," she said. She would do whatever she could to keep Annabel's spirits high.

"Like what?"

"Like what we are going to do next season when all the gentlemen of the *ton* are fighting over you," Juliet said with a wide grin, making Annabel laugh. "I still believe I should sell you at an auction."

Annabel slapped Juliet's arm, but she was laughing as much as Juliet. "You are terrible!" When the laughter had died down, she said, "I must admit, I am excited for the parties."

They talked late into the night, and although Juliet laughed and shared her stories, her mind continuously returned to Robert. The man who had ruined lives had to be stopped, and she, Juliet, would be the one to do it.

Chapter Twenty-Nine

Juliet studied herself in the mirror. After several hours of donning and throwing aside all of the dresses and gowns she owned, she settled on a borrowed dress from Annabel, white to represent purity. Her hair was styled just so, and she wore the gold bracelet Lord Parsons had gifted her. Yes, it was the perfect ensemble.

The day promised to be glorious with a clear blue sky and bright sunshine. Spring had arrived, leaving the last days of winter behind. There was no other way to view the day than as absolutely perfect in every way.

The woman who stared back at her was much changed. She was no longer a woman focused on beauty, but rather a woman of strength. It was a trait Isabel and her mother shared and one she had always desired. Now she understood what that strength entailed and what one must do in order to use it.

"You look wonderful," Annabel said, joining Juliet in the mirror's reflection. Then she frowned. "But I believe your bosom is much too exposed; it appears as if your breasts will pop out at any moment."

Annabel was right. The dress was much too tight for Juliet's more opulent frame, but the result was what she had hoped to achieve. She dabbed a bit of perfume on her décolletage and wrists and took a step back to reassess her reflection.

"Are you attempting to," Annabel swallowed visibly, "entice the man?" Juliet had not yet told her cousin that Robert was her father, and she would not until she had implemented her plan.

Juliet smiled. "Not at all. I am a lady of the *ton*, am I not?" Annabel nodded. "Today, I simply feel as if I should stand out, so everyone recognizes me. Let us just say that I wish to be seen." The truth of the matter was she did not wear the gown any more provocatively than any other woman in her station; she simply preferred to have a bit more decorum in her typical choice of clothing.

Annabel laughed. "Then you have done it well. You do look beautiful, as if you are to attend the most magnificent of balls. I doubt anyone will mistake you for anyone other than yourself."

"Perfect," Juliet muttered as she patted her hair one last time. "Come, we have much to do today." She took a wrap from her wardrobe and placed it over her shoulders. She wanted every villager to see her attire but preferred her mother to not take notice. The woman would march her back to her room and demand she change, thus ruining Juliet's plans, and she could not have that!

They made their way down the hall to the foyer. Daniel stood beside her mother at the door, his head bowed as her mother spoke. Juliet watched from the landing above them, wishing she could hear the words, but her mother spoke too quietly, even in a room that echoed most sounds.

Juliet squared her shoulders and descended the stairs. Daniel glanced up, and his smile warmed her heart. The love she had feared gone shone brightly on his face.

"Mother," Juliet said. "Daniel." It was difficult for her to keep the formal tone in her voice, but with her mother standing there, she had to force herself to do so."

Her mother turned to Juliet. "Daniel has informed me that he will be leaving a week from Saturday."

Juliet stiffened but said nothing.

"You may say your farewells."

Juliet nodded. She wished she could be alone, but her mother and Annabel walked to the edge of the room and stopped. Well, she could do nothing about it, so she turned back to Daniel, her heart in her throat.

"Will you go to the North?" Juliet whispered, hoping her voice was as quiet as her mother's had been. She preferred their conversation to remain private, even if they were not alone.

"Yes."

"You will be safe, I trust."

Daniel shifted on his feet. "I think so."

Juliet glanced at her mother, who continued her vigil. "I love you, and I am sorry we cannot be together."

"Just know I'll never stop loving you," Daniel replied. "Goodbye, Juliet."

She blinked back tears. "Goodbye." Without thought, she threw her arms around him; she needed one last embrace. Although her heart ached, she found peace in his arms and knew somehow that feeling would never leave her. She wished to weep, to sob, but she would not. She would create her own future despite what others put in her way.

When Daniel was gone, Juliet turned to her mother and cousin. "I have something important to do, but I will be back soon."

Her mother nodded. "Be careful."

"I will," Juliet replied. She held out her hand to her cousin. "I am ready."

***

The carriage stopped in front of an inn that had a small cafe. Juliet kissed Annabel on the cheek. "I would like to speak to Robert alone, if I may. Go inside and have some tea and cakes. I will be back to join you soon."

Annabel nodded. It was not an uncommon request, so her cousin asked no questions before entering the tiny establishment.

Juliet made her way to the cobbler's just as she had done so often before. This time, however, she did so alone and with a plan in mind. On her way, she made every effort to smile and greet every passerby. Many she knew by name, and most, if not all, knew her, as well. Today, her status of the *ton* would serve her as it had never served her before.

When she arrived at Robert's shop, she peered through the window. A couple she did not recognize stood near the counter, an oddity in itself, and after the man gave Robert several notes, they left the shop.

Juliet entered the shop. Once she had thought the place full of joy dabbled with a bit of mystery. Now, however, she saw the falsity of it all.

"Ah, Juliet," Robert said, a wide smile on his face as he leaned against the counter in that leisurely manner she had once considered endearing. "It is an honor to have such a lady in my shop. As it always is."

"You are too kind," Juliet said, forcing a smile as she walked toward him. "May I ask a favor?"

"Of course! What can I do for you?"

"It is this wrap." She removed the shawl from her shoulders. "I am afraid I paid much more than Mother would approve of. Would you be willing to hide it in your bedroom for me until I can come for it at a later time?" She folded it twice and placed it in his hands. "It is from India and worth a small fortune." She had to fight back a laugh when his face lit up. "Yet, I fear Mother will learn of it, and I am simply unwilling to let it go."

"I'll do it now," he said with a grin before slipping through the white door behind the counter. He left the door open enough for her to see him place it on his bed, and when he returned, she sighed.

"I do not have money for you today, I am afraid," she said. "However, I do have this." She removed the bracelet. "Will it be adequate?"

His eyes bulged as he took it from her. "I believe this will do just fine," he said, placing it in his coat pocket. "As a matter of fact, if you want to increase your investment, I would be happy to accept other pieces you might have on hand. At this rate, we will have shops all across England!" He seemed extremely pleased.

"How wonderful!" Juliet exclaimed.

He closed the ledger he had open before him on the counter. "And your mother? Did you do as I suggested?"

Juliet shook her head. She had to force her fisted hands into the folds of her skirts and summon every bit of strength and control she could muster in order to keep calm. What she wished to do was beat the man across the head and scream as loudly as she could! "I was unable to speak to her," Juliet said. "For the woman has been dead for some time."

Robert blinked. "Dead?"

Juliet's jaw tightened. "Of course." She narrowed her eyes at him. "There are no shops, are there...Father?"

To Juliet's surprise, Robert barked a laugh. "Eleanor told you, did she? It is true concerning your mother. I came across her some two years ago." The man did not even have the decency to attempt to appear mournful!

"Oh? And her dying wish was for you to know me and use what you knew to blackmail my mother?"

Robert snorted. "Eleanor has more wealth than any woman should possess. You have led a comfortable life full of leisure while I suffered. I simply want what I deserve."

"You suffer because you love no one but yourself," Juliet spat. "It is how I was. However, you can change! You can begin by returning the money to the women you have tricked into investing. Then you will stop hurting my mother."

"She is not your mother," he said, his lip curling. "She is merely the woman who raised you."

"Which is far more than you have done! She is a woman of honor and strength; not a coward like you."

Robert formed a fist and leaned forward, and Juliet thought the man would strike her. "You think you're better than everyone," he said through clenched teeth, "but you're nothing more than the child of a gardener and a lady's maid. Servant blood, the lowest of all."

Juliet refused to withdraw, her anger was that strong. "You are right. I once thought the same about the blood that flows through me, but it is not the truth. It is the heart that matters."

Robert laughed as he straightened. "There's nothing more to say on this matter."

"Are you saying you are unwilling to do as I ask? You will deny your daughter's request?"

"You might be my daughter by blood, but I don't care about you, not in the way you want. Nothing matters but my money." He jutted his chin. "Now, if you will leave me be, I have work to do."

As he turned to move behind the counter, Juliet realized that no good existed in this man.

"Annabel," Juliet hissed, and Robert stopped. "How dare you kiss her and then try to coerce her into more!"

Robert gave a wry smile. "It is what I do," he said with a shrug. "Tell your mother I will see her Tuesday. Do make sure Annabel returns."

Juliet closed her eyes for a moment. It was time to implement the plan she had hoped to avoid. It had been her hope the man would take the one last opportunity to change, but it was clear it would never happen. Somehow, she was glad he did not, for what she would do would give her great pleasure.

"I am a storyteller," she said.

Robert stopped at the doorway to the back room and turned, a look of disinterest on his features.

"It is a gift I seem to have inherited from you."

The man grinned and tilted his head as if what she said honored him.

"Like you, it has served me well in the past. However, unlike you, I will not use it for my own advantage any longer, but instead, I will use it for those I love."

"What are you rambling about?" Robert said, the disinterest now replaced by annoyance.

Juliet leaned down and pulled off her boot, smiled, and threw it in an arc over the counter where it landed with a *thud*.

"What are you doing?" Robert shouted, his eyes wide. "Have you gone mad?"

In an unhurried manner, she pulled two pins from her carefully coiffed hair. "My precious Annabel is the closest friend a woman could ever have." She pulled at several strands of her hair to loosen them. "You will never hurt her again."

"Juliet, what…" He shook his head.

Ignoring him, she grabbed her right sleeve near the shoulder and pulled hard, the soft fabric tearing at the seam so the sleeve hung at her elbow. "My mother, she is the woman you call Eleanor, has sacrificed everything for me." Thoughts of her mother hurt and scared brought forth the tears she needed so much at the moment. "And you sought to destroy her and my family. Well, I will do anything to protect them!" She reached for the opening of her dress and gave a sharp pull. "Anything!"

"No!" Robert shouted as Juliet turned, one foot bereft of a boot and her dress hanging in tatters on her body. "Come back here now!"

Pulling the door open, Juliet ran out into the busy street and screamed with all her might, putting all her frustrations into that scream as tears flowed down her cheeks. "Help me! Someone! Please, help me!"

Men and women gasped and hurried to her, and she crossed one arm over her chest as she wiped tears from her face with the other.

"Miss Juliet," one man said, his voice filled with concern, "what's wrong?"

"That man!" she shouted, pointing at Robert standing in the doorway to the shop. "He tried to take my virtue!"

Shouts of anger erupted, and two men in dark coats grabbed Robert by the arms. Robert fought them, shouting his innocence, but he was no match for them.

"He ripped my gold bracelet from my wrist as he attempted to undress me!"

"She's a liar!" Robert shouted.

The crowd grew angrier, and one of the men reached into Robert's pocket and produced the bracelet. "What's this then?" he demanded.

"My bracelet!" Juliet cried.

Another man came running out of the shop, her boot in one hand and her wrap in the other. "Look what I found! The shawl was on his bed!"

Juliet sobbed as she made a point of looking down at her bootless foot. A woman wrapped an arm around her protectively. "It's all right, Miss. We'll see justice's served, we will."

"She's a liar!" Robert cried again as the men led him away. "She's my daughter!"

"And I'm the King's uncle!" shouted one of them men while another said, "If that's true, then you're even sicker than I thought!"

The woman wrapped the shawl around Juliet just as Annabel pushed through the crowd. She threw her arms around Juliet. "What happened? Are you all right? did he hurt you?"

Juliet shook her head. "I am fine," she whispered, her heart now settling.

"Do not worry, you are safe now."

"Yes," Juliet replied, her anger now replaced with relief—and perhaps a bit of joy. "We are all safe now."

***

Juliet came through the door of Scarlett Hall, her dress in tatters and hair disheveled but in better spirits than she had experienced in days. She spoke with several people in the village, including one Lord Ezra Montague whose brother was a magistrate, and he assured her that Robert would be met with swift punishment. What that entailed, Juliet did not know, nor did she care. Her family was safe and that was all that mattered.

Dozens had witnessed the fiasco, had heard her cries, and seen the evidence; she doubted the man would ever return. If he did, he would be shamed out of the village by everyone there.

When Annabel asked what had transpired, Juliet simply told her cousin that one day she would explain, but that day was not today, and the girl did not ask again.

Now they stood in the foyer, and Juliet gave Annabel a nod before turning and walking down to the study where she found her mother gazing out the window.

Juliet cleared her throat. "Mother."

Her mother turned, but when she laid eyes on Juliet she gasped and rushed to her side. "What happened?"

"I confronted the man who is my father," she said quietly.

Her mother touched Juliet's hair. "Your hair, your dress…surely he did not try with his own…" Her words trailed off and her eyes went wide.

"Daughter?" Juliet asked tersely. "No. However, you and I are the only two who know he did not make such an attempt on his daughter. According to the dozens of witnesses, a lady of the *ton* was accosted by him in his shop and was able to escape."

"I do not understand," her mother said, the shock clear on her face. "What happened to him?"

"He was taken away," Juliet replied matter-of-factly. "Far away where neither you nor any member of my family must endure his threats any longer. You have nothing about which to worry, Mother. You are now safe." She explained everything that had happened, including her attempt to give him the opportunity to choose a different path.

Her mother listened without interruption, and when Juliet finished, she pulled Juliet into her arms. "Why did you do this?"

Juliet gave her a wide grin. "You have done everything to keep me safe and happy, and I wanted to do the same."

Chapter Thirty

Nearly a week had passed since Juliet confronted Robert, and surprisingly things had quickly returned to normal at Scarlett Hall. The servants continued their work, Juliet and Annabel spoke of their future, and Juliet still had yet to speak to Daniel. He would soon be leaving to begin a new life, and that thought still brought sadness to her heart. She wished more than anything to be with him.

Yet, that was not meant to be. Juliet had come to a new understanding, a respect not only for herself, but for the wishes of her mother. Therefore, it meant that Juliet would soon be required to accept an offer of marriage from Lord Parsons. She did not wish to wed the man, but after all her mother had done for her, Juliet could not decline.

The morning was still early as Juliet made her way to the dining room for breakfast and was surprised to find Forbes helping her mother with her coat.

"Are you leaving?" Juliet asked as she descended the stairs.

Her mother glanced up at Juliet and smiled. "I am."

The woman offered no further explanation, and Juliet looked at the butler. The man gave no more indication than her mother as to her intentions.

"But Mother, it is Tuesday. You have never left the house on a Tuesday."

Her mother smiled. "I will meet you at the carriage," she told Forbes, who replied with a bow before leaving through the front door. When the man was gone, her mother said, "I have been doing a lot of thinking over the last week. Thinking of days past and habits that I have. Habits that made it easy for someone to arrive unannounced to find me at home alone." She pursed her lips at this but did not mention the name of the man of whom she spoke. "Upon reflection, I decided it would be a nice change to see what the world is like on a Tuesday."

"I think that is a brilliant idea," Juliet said. "May Annabel and I remain here for the day, then?" The last thing Juliet wanted was to have people fawning over her after the incident at the cobbler's shop. She almost laughed at this; how many times in the past had she wanted nothing more than to have everyone fawning over her?

"I see no reason why you cannot." Her mother placed a hand on Juliet's arm. "And do not worry about the gossipmongers. Give them at least another week, and the rumors of that man will calm. Someone else will do something…unconventional…and you will be completely forgotten."

"I know," Juliet said with a weak smile as she held the door open for her mother.

After closing the door, Juliet wondered how she would spend the day. She had no one on which to call, and even if she dared to speak to Daniel, she could not, for he had gone into the village with the other servants.

The fleeting memory of her and Annabel—and Daniel—going riding brought a smile to her lips. Although there was a chill in the air, a short ride would be pleasant.

She went to her room and donned one of her riding dresses and an older pair of riding boots. She had burned the boots Robert had given her as soon as she had returned to the house; the sooner the man was a distant memory, the better.

The door opened and Juliet smiled as Annabel entered the room. "I am going riding. Would you like to join me?"

"I would rather not," Annabel replied. "It is much too cold and I noticed storm clouds on the horizon."

Juliet embraced her cousin. "I will not be long. When I return, we will discuss the dozens of men who will wish to marry you come next season."

Annabel giggled at this, and Juliet made her way downstairs. She donned her coat and headed outside.

The sky was indeed gray, and a light breeze blew, but the chill in the air was not terrible. Juliet took in her surroundings. Scarlett Hall was the only home she had ever known, but when her mother accepted the request from Lord Parsons, Juliet would no longer live her. However, it was not the chill or the fact she would leave Scarlett Hall that made her shiver; rather, it was the thought of never seeing Daniel again.

Shaking her head, she made her way to the stables. As she reached for the door, someone called her name. What she hoped was that it would be Daniel calling out to her, but when she turned, it was to see Lord Parsons riding up to her on his white stallion.

"I returned late yesterday and learned you were attacked," he said, clear anger in his eyes. "Is this a rumor?"

"No, it is not a rumor," Juliet replied. She had many things on her mind, and speaking with Lord Parsons was not what she wished to do. "What are you doing here?"

The man's eyes narrowed. "Open the stables so I am able to put away my horse." The words were a clear command, and Juliet considered telling the man to see to it himself. However, she had promised to honor her mother's wishes, so she did as he bade.

As Lord Parsons dismounted, Juliet asked, this time in a more conversational tone, "What brings you here? Mother is not here today, but Annabel is in the house."

The man did not respond right away, ignoring her as he led his horse to one of the empty stalls. He then came to stand before her. "The woman I care about was attacked. Of course I would come over as soon as I heard."

"Thank you, but I assure you I am well."

He placed his hands on her arms, and her stomach clenched. "I must ask you something, and the truth is imperative."

"Truth?" she asked. "Concerning what?"

"The friend who told me what happened. He said you appeared to be in a state of near undress. I must know; did anything happen?"

"You already know something happened," Juliet said, digging fingernails into her palms to keep from lashing out.

He cleared his throat as if he was uncomfortable. "What I would like to know is, did he...did the man..."

Juliet raised her brows. "Do you mean did he compromise my virtue?" When the baron nodded, anger blazed inside her. "Would it be a problem if my virtue had been compromised?"

He tightened his grip on her arm. "Do not play games with me," he said in a low tone. "What did he do?" The man's breath was hot, and Juliet's heartbeat increased.

"He tore my clothes and tried to have his way with me," she said, surprised at the calmness in her voice. "He did not have his way with me."

Lord Parsons took a deep breath of relief. "I am glad, for I worried that he had. I assured my friend that you were well and unspoilt, and it is good to hear my assumptions were correct." He lifted his hand to her face, and she had to fight to keep herself from taking a step back. "How could a man marry a woman who had been used in such a manner? Even a woman as beautiful as you."

Juliet knew more than ever the man would never care for her, not entirely, for he cared only for himself. Before she could respond, his lips were pressed against hers.

Juliet pushed against his chest. "Lord Parsons! I am not a woman to be kissed in such a manner!"

The man's face reddened. "Yet you kiss a stable hand?" he hissed. "Or tantalize a shopkeeper?"

She stared at him incredulously. "Tantalize?"

"Indeed. I heard the dress you wore was meant to entice a man. I will not have my future wife displaying herself like a harlot. Do I make myself clear?"

"How dare you!" Juliet gasped in anger. "You do not know what I..."

"I know that I will have your hand soon, and this behavior will not be accepted once you are my wife." He grabbed her wrist. "I shall speak to your mother about this."

"You are hurting me!" she said as she attempted to pull from his grip.

Then her eyes widened when another voice spoke.

"Let go of her!"

***

All worry and fear evaporated in Juliet, and her heart swelled with joy at seeing the man she loved.

Daniel marched toward them, his stride long, his head held high. She had never seen him so self-assured, and it only made him all the more alluring.

"You again," Lord Parsons growled. "Have you not learned that, as an ignorant stable boy, you have no right to interfere with matters of the *ton*?" The man brought his hand back, meaning to strike Daniel, but the stable hand grasped Lord Parsons by the wrist. He appeared at his leisure as he held the baron, and the man gaped at Daniel with a mixture of shock and anger.

"Yes, I'm an ignorant stable boy," Daniel stated with eyes narrowed, "from a long line of servants centuries deep. But I would never raise my hand to a lady."

Lord Parsons pulled back his arm—or Daniel released him, Juliet was unsure which—but the baron did not hesitate in throwing another punch.

Daniel ducked just in time, and when he rose again, his fist connected with Lord Parson's jaw, sending the man reeling backwards. "You may ridicule me all you'd like, and maybe you'll marry Juliet, but if you ever hurt her again, I'll come and find you."

Lord Parsons rose, dabbing blood from his lip. "You fool! I will inform the magistrates what you have done!" He glanced at Juliet, a gleam in his eyes. "And Lady Lambert will be very disappointed. You will be very sorry you were ever born."

Juliet gasped. The man could make more trouble than Daniel could ever imagine.

However, Daniel did not appear concerned in the least. "What? Tell the magistrates you were bested by a boy?" he said with a laugh. Then he shrugged. "If you want to be ridiculed by everyone in Rumsbury, then by all means tell the magistrates." He glanced at Juliet and winked. "And her mother? Maybe you'd like to explain what you're doing here and the reason I struck you. What will she think of that?"

Lord Parsons glared at Daniel a moment longer before a look of defeat replaced his arrogant expression. He turned to Juliet. "You I shall see as planned," he said with a finger pointed at her. "I will not forget this." He stalked to his horse and moments later, he was gone.

Juliet turned to the man she loved. What she wanted to do was throw herself into his arms, but she had hurt him enough. "I do not know what to say. You risked much by intervening."

"I mightn't be able to marry you, but that won't stop me from loving you."

She was uncertain if it was his words or a reaction to what had happened, but soon she was sobbing in his arms as he spoke soothing words to her.

"I love you so," she said when her sobbing calmed and he released her. "No matter what happens, I will always love you." She glanced around them, a sudden thought coming to her. "What are you doing here? It is Tuesday; I thought you would be with the other servants."

He shrugged. "They go to buy supplies. I'm leaving soon, so I don't need anything more, and I didn't feel like going into the village." They stood in silence for several moments, and then he said, "I wouldn't worry about Lord Parsons. He won't speak a word to Lady Lambert of what happened. He has too much to lose; especially his sterling reputation." His grin had an impudent look to it, and Juliet could not help but giggle.

"I suppose it would be best if I did not inform Mother," she said. "It would only cause a new rift between us, and I certainly do not need to make more trouble. I shall keep what happened a secret."

Daniel glanced around. "I should leave. If Lady Lambert returns and finds us speaking together, it won't bode well for either of us."

Juliet nodded. "May I ask one favor?"

"For you, anything you wish."

Juliet felt a twinge in her heart upon hearing the words he had said to her so often before, and knowing it would be the last brought on a sense of melancholy.

"I came here to ready my horse. Would you ready her for me one last time?"

"With honor," he said with a deep bow, making them both smile. He retrieved her saddle and began preparing the horse. It was a feat she had seen him do numerous times before, and now she realized how much it meant to her. How she had taken it for granted for so long!

When the horse was ready, Juliet walked up to him. "I am unsure what to say..."

"Then let's do what we've always done," he replied, rewarding her with one of his small smiles. "Miss Juliet, there's no woman as beautiful as you. My only wish is to help you onto your horse."

Juliet gave a small laugh, but her heart was clenched in her chest. "You may," she said with a feigned jut to her chin. "Even if you are only a stable boy."

Daniel took Juliet's hand and helped her mount the horse. Without releasing his hand, she stared down at him, a thousand words on her tongue. However, as she looked at him, she said only two words. Two words that summed up everything the man had done for her.

"Thank you."

Daniel smiled and gave a small nod, as if he understood everything behind those words.

"And I thank you."

Chapter Thirty-One

Light spring rain pelted against the window in the study as Eleanor looked out at the tree where her children spent a goodly amount of their childhood. She had been blessed with the most beautiful of daughters, especially her sweet Juliet.

Although she had many memories of this particular daughter, Eleanor thought of another woman, a lady's maid and a dear friend, a woman who gave a part of her soul—her own child—in order to heal the pain Eleanor had endured. And Juliet had done just that. The girl had grown into a woman of heart and mind, which had always been Eleanor's greatest desire.

"Mother? I am ready."

Eleanor turned to Juliet and nodded. The time had arrived for them to leave for the home of Lord Parsons, and upon seeing her daughter, her heart swelled with love. Juliet wore a green dress with tiny white daisies and white gloves. Her hair was curled and pulled back with a white ribbon. She made such a lovely woman, and she would surely make any husband happy to have her on his arm.

"You look beautiful," Eleanor said. "Lord Parsons shall be a fortunate man to marry you." Juliet nodded but said nothing, which surprised Eleanor. "You will not argue?"

"I only wish to make you happy," Juliet replied. "I will no longer fight or argue over your wishes. I may not love the man, but I will conduct myself as the lady you have brought me up to be."

Eleanor could not stop the knot that formed in her throat but said nothing. What could she say?

The door opened and Forbes entered. "Lady Lambert," he said with a diffident bow, "he is here."

Eleanor nodded. "Allow him to enter."

Forbes bowed once more, moved aside, and the stable boy entered the room.

"Daniel?" Juliet asked with a gasp.

The young man smiled at Juliet, and Eleanor could not help but see the love they shared. A love so great it was as if a fire burned between them.

"You leave tomorrow morning, is that correct?" Eleanor asked Daniel.

"Yes, my lady," the man replied, his hands gripping his hat. "I leave with the sunrise."

"You understand that I could never allow you to leave with my Juliet?"

Daniel nodded. "Yes, I understand."

Juliet shook her head. "Mother, please, do not make it worse!"

Eleanor ignored her daughter. "I was curious as to why you refused to allow Juliet to leave with you." She narrowed her eyes. "And do not lie. Was it because she has no money of her own?"

Daniel's eyes widened. "No. That's not the reason."

"Then why would a man who has romantic feelings for a woman not allow her to leave with him? Surely that is the action of a man who does not love her?"

Daniel raised his head and gave Eleanor a defiant glare. "I love Juliet," he said firmly. "More than I thought was possible. That's why I wouldn't allow her to go with me."

"Mother, please!" Juliet said, her voice breaking. "I beg of you, do not put him through this."

Once again, Eleanor ignored Juliet. "Explain yourself," she demanded.

Daniel sighed. "When I was but a young boy and came to work here, I knew where I stood. Juliet taught me that, although title and wealth separate us, love could unite us and destroy the chasm. But like you, my lady, I want the best for Juliet. And like her, I want to honor your wishes by staying away from her. I don't regret it," his voice croaked and he cleared his throat, "I only regret that the blood that runs through me is not noble. If it was, we could..."

"Thank you," Eleanor said, interrupting the man. "May your journey be safe."

Daniel nodded before giving a glance of longing at Juliet and leaving the room.

Eleanor returned to the window, unable to face Juliet, who choked back sobs that tore at Eleanor's heart. Her thoughts went back to Anne and the promise Eleanor had made to the maid. *I promise she will find happiness in life.*

"I could never allow you to leave with him," she said without turning to look at her daughter, "for it would break my heart.

"I know this, Mother," Juliet said between sobs.

"It would crush me to wake up tomorrow morning and find you gone." She turned, took a step to the desk, and opened a drawer. "To come into this study and find this box gone," she removed an ornate wooden box and placed it on the desk, "which contains the title and directions to the cottage where you were born."

"Mother?"

"It would break my heart," Eleanor said as she walked over to stand before Juliet, "to know that the *ton* would whisper rumors of you running away in the night to marry a stable hand, rumors that would persist for years to come—or until another scandal took its place."

"I do not understand..."

Eleanor placed a hand on the side of her beautiful daughter's face. "And it would break my heart not seeing you for some time. However, although my heart would be crushed and my spirit bruised, it would never stop me from loving you." She kissed Juliet's forehead. "Goodbye, my sweet daughter."

***

Tears rolled down Juliet's cheeks at her mother's words. "Oh, Mother!" she said as she threw her arms around the woman. "I do not understand! Why...?"

"A letter in the box," her mother whispered, "explains everything. Forbes has sent a rider to deliver word to Lord Parsons that I have fallen ill. Now, I must go to my room, and you must prepare for what you must."

Juliet nodded. "I love you, Mother."

"And I love you more than you can ever imagine." She pushed back a strand of Juliet's hair, kissed her cheek, and left the room.

Juliet hurried over to the box and pulled out the contents. Indeed, there was a land deed to a cottage made out in Daniel's name. Beside it was a piece of parchment with the location of the cottage and several pound notes. Juliet was stunned at it all; however, it was the letter that warmed Juliet's heart.

My Dearest Juliet,

You have always been a raging fire, and I believe the love you and Daniel share will burn brighter if you are together. I will never admit that I allowed this, and I know you will never tell anyone the truth.

As to why I did this? It is simple. It is a promise I made to an old friend, one who gave me the greatest gift I have ever received.

You.

Juliet wiped tears from her eyes, placed the contents of the box in the pocket of her dress, and hurried down the hallway. Once outside, she ran, joy and love carrying her feet, to the stables, calling out for Daniel.

The stable door opened, Daniel rushing out with a frightened look on his face. "Juliet?" he asked in shock. "What is it? What's wrong?"

She threw herself into his arms. "Nothing," she said as she held the man close. "Everything is perfect."

"What's happened?" he asked, although he did nothing to release his hold on her.

"Dreams," she whispered. "My dreams, your dreams, they will all come true." Then, as she had done in the past, she kissed the man she loved, and he returned the kiss with a matching hunger as the fire banked between them. There had been a gap between a lady and a stable boy that no amount of wealth could have joined. Yet, it was not wealth that had done so. In fact, it was love, a love so beautiful and pure Juliet now understood who she truly was and the lady she needed to be.

A lady of heart and mind who gave Daniel the strength he needed to learn to read and to realize that he was a far better man than he could ever have imagined. It was that same love that, as the two walked together hand in hand to the stable, Juliet knew would keep them together. Forever.

Chapter Thirty-Two

With just a small carpetbag containing two dresses and a few other essential items, Juliet left her bedroom for what would be the last time. She stared at the door for several moments, drinking in the memories, when a door down the hallway creaked open.

"Juliet?"

Taking a deep breath, Juliet set the bag on the floor and turned to her cousin, who wore a confused expression. "Hello, Annabel," she said, attempting to keep her voice level. It was not an easy feat. "I am leaving—with Daniel—but I am afraid I cannot take you with me." The words tore at her heart, but they had to be said.

"But I do not understand," Annabel said, her voice choked. "I thought Daniel agreed..."

Juliet took Annabel's hand. "That is not the reason. Our circumstances have changed. However, I promise to write to you, and if you ever need me, I will return as quickly as I can."

Annabel threw her arms around Juliet. "I will miss you," she whispered. "But I am happy for you."

"And I will miss you," Juliet said, kissing her cousin's cheek. "Mother will take care of you. You will always be safe here. You do believe me, do you not?"

Annabel nodded. "I do. I have nothing to fear."

Juliet smiled and picked up the bag. "Now, go back to bed before I change my mind and sell you to a gentleman of the *ton*." This made them both giggle, each covering her mouth to stifle the sound.

"Do write to me."

"I said I would," Juliet said, feigning annoyance.

Annabel hugged her once more before returning to her room and closing the door behind her.

Juliet stared at the door for several moments before heaving a heavy sigh and making her way down the hallway. How she wished she could take her cousin with her, but what kind of life would one such as Annabel live in a tiny cottage? It had been unfair of Juliet to offer to take the girl, for her cousin had a wondrous life ahead of her; Juliet's mother would see to that.

At the bottom of the stairs, Forbes stood waiting, his tall imposing figure giving her pause. Would he attempt to stop her from leaving? Cause a scene and wake the entire household in the process?

"Miss Juliet," he said in his deep baritone. "I will miss you."

Juliet stared at him in shock. "You know?"

The man nodded. "Do not worry; I will not tell. However, I could not allow you to leave without first saying goodbye."

Juliet embraced the man. "Thank you, Forbes. I will miss you. I do ask one thing, not for myself but for Mother."

"Whatever you request, I will do."

"Please be certain she is happy."

Forbes smiled. "Rest assured that there is nothing I will not do to see your mother happy," he said.

He turned to open the door for her, and she stepped out onto the stoop. The future was frightening—as well as full of excitement. From this day forth, life would be much different from the life she had known, and she could not wait to live it.

As she made her way to the stables, the door opened and Daniel exited, leading two horses—one her Penelope—saddled and already laden with several bags. The first light of day broke across the horizon as she gazed at Daniel's smile.

"Allow me," he said, taking her carpetbag and tying it behind her saddle. When he turned and gazed down at her, she wondered if she would be able to remain standing. "I love you, Juliet. Are you sure this is what you want?"

She turned and looked up at Scarlett Hall. "This house is so magnificent that I once desired one like it for myself. Now, however, I have come to realize that it was not the many rooms and the size of the place that made it great, but rather the love inside."

He put his fingers under her chin and turned her to face him. "I couldn't agree more," he whispered. "It's a gift no money could ever buy. Don't you think it's a wonderful gift?"

The world seemed to disappear as Juliet stared into the eyes of the man she loved. "Yes," she replied readily. "Such a wondrous gift."

She took Penelope's reins from Daniel, and he helped her mount. As they moved toward the drive, she glanced at the front of the house and was surprised to see a lone figure standing on the stoop, a heavy wrap on her shoulders. She was not the woman who gave birth to her, but Juliet admired and loved her more than anyone would ever understand.

Her mother raised a hand, and Juliet did the same, keeping it raised until the woman, and Scarlett Hall, disappeared from sight.

With a sigh, Juliet rode beside Daniel, off to their new life. Together.

***

They traveled four days, riding through the countryside and speaking of their future and their marriage.

"I am surprised," Juliet said, attempting to suppress a grin, "that you would wish for four children."

"Is that too many?" he asked, concern filling his tone. "I suppose you only want two."

Juliet pretended to think for a moment. "I hope for a dozen," she said with a firm nod. His jaw dropped, and she added with a laugh, "One for each month of the year."

He gave her a chuckle. "You, Miss Juliet, are nothing like other ladies." She raised a brow at him, and his eyes widened. "That is...you're far more beautiful in every way."

She smiled. "And you, are the most handsome." Then she turned up her nose and pursed her lips. "However, you are a pitiful horseman."

Before allowing him to respond, she heeled Penelope, who launched forward, Daniel shouting with frustration from behind. With tears of happiness in her eyes, she laughed as he raced his horse beside hers.

"I don't know what I'm going to do with you," he chided playfully.

"I have a wonderful idea," she replied, glancing over at him. "Marry me!" She urged Penelope to go faster.

"I plan on doing just that!" he shouted back at her as his larger and heavier Irish Hunter overtook Penelope.

She giggled; he had only won the race because she allowed him to do so. Although, she would never admit it.

They slowed their mounts as the road curved, passing several small cottages with sheep dotting the land. Then Juliet saw the most precious of cottages, whitewashed with a heavy thatch roof and door and window frames painted red. Behind it sat a small stable.

"Is that our new home?" she asked, looking at the directions her mother had left for her. "I did not expect it to be so wonderful!"

They dismounted beside a tree, where they tethered the horses, and hand in hand, they walked to the front door. Juliet closed her eyes and brought to mind the story her mother had told her, imagining the woman standing at this door so many years before.

"Juliet?" Daniel asked, his voice filled with concern. "Are you all right?"

She opened her eyes and turned to him. One day she would tell him the story of her birth, but today was not that day. Today, they would be making new memories, not reminiscing on the past. "I am wonderful," she replied, taking his hand and pulling him to the door. "Come! Let us explore our new home!"

The house was more than they could have ever wanted and more. It had a small kitchen, a sitting room, and two small bedrooms. "It is perfect."

Daniel was looking around as if in shock. "This house is grand," he said. "Far better than I thought..." He looked down at her. "It's perfect."

"It is," she replied. "It is a home in which a woman once lived, a woman who had dreams for her daughter."

"Is that true?" Daniel asked as he glanced around again.

"Yes. She dreamed her daughter would be happy, and her dream, much like my own, has come true."

***

Mrs. Juliet Haskins, formally Miss Juliet Lambert, was doing amazing things with her life. For one, she was keeping house. How one actually did such a thing was beyond her, for most often she simply moved the furniture from one place to another. She swept and mopped the floors, cooked meals—not wonderful meals to be sure, but at least after two months of marriage she no longer served food so blackened it was inedible—and washed dishes afterward.

Despite her unfamiliarity with the life in which she now found herself, she could not have been happier.

The sound of hoofbeats came to her ear, and she smiled as she watched her husband ride up the drive. Daniel had found work in a stable at a manor not far from their home, and he enjoyed his work as much as he did while at Scarlett Hall, or so he had said. With the wide smile he wore every day when returning home, Juliet had no doubt he spoke the truth.

Daniel dismounted, his cheeks covered in rough stubble and his dark hair falling over his brow. However, it was his handsome smile that she adored above all else.

"I was told a lady lives here," he said as he walked toward her. "A lady who enjoys adventure and is like no other lady in existence. Is this true?"

"It is true," Juliet replied with a laugh. "For I am she. And who, may I ask, are you?"

"Some call me a stable boy, but that is only partly true." He put his hands around her waist and pulled her close. "For I am a man in love with the most beautiful woman in all of England." He lowered his head and kissed her. The kiss had passion and urgency, and she returned it with the same exuberance as he gave.

When the kiss broke, he kept his hold on her, not allowing her to move away—not that she tried. "As a matter of fact," he said, "that woman wrote me a letter."

Juliet frowned. "Letter?"

He smiled, reached into his coat pocket, and produced a folded piece of parchment. He unfolded it and began to read:

My Dearest Daniel,

I know in my heart that, one day, you shall be able to read this letter, and if, for some reason, I am not there with you, know that I am truly proud of you.

Please know that you hold a special place in my heart and that nothing can ever keep us apart.

With love,
Juliet

"You were right, Juliet," he said, pulling her close once again. "Nothing can keep us apart."

She placed her arms around his neck. "Nothing," she agreed. "And it is our love that will always keep us together."

Chapter Thirty-Three

Scarlett Hall June 1806

As their horses came to a stop outside the familiar stable beside Scarlett Hall, Juliet stared up at the grand house. She and Daniel had received the letter of invitation three weeks prior, and she would not miss Hannah's wedding reception for the world.

The new stable hand, a boy several years younger than Daniel, came to take their horses.

"It has been only two months," Juliet said as she and Daniel made their way to the house, "but it seems like years."

"Do you miss it?" Daniel asked, and she did not miss the twinge of concern behind his words.

"I could lie and say that I do not. However, I love our home more." Daniel smiled. "I'm glad."

The door opened, and Nathaniel came bounding down the steps. "Juliet!" he shouted before lifting her from the ground and twirling her around in his arms. "I am so happy to see you!"

Juliet laughed. "As I am you," she replied. The boy had grown much since she had last seen him. "You remember Daniel?"

Nathaniel nodded. "I do." He put out his hand, and after some hesitation, Daniel shook it firmly. "It is good to see you again."

"Thank you, my lord," Daniel replied quietly.

Nathaniel raised his brows. "You are my brother-in-law. You have no reason to be so formal. My name is Nathanial, not 'my lord'."

Daniel's cheeks reddened, but he nodded. "As you wish, Nathaniel." He stumbled over the name, but Juliet's brother did not seem to notice.

When Juliet's mother joined them, Juliet threw her arms around the woman. "I have missed you so," she whispered as tears filled her eyes.

"Not more than I have missed you," her mother replied. She took a step back and placed her hand in Juliet's. "You look happy." She wiped the tears from Juliet's cheeks and laughed. "Are you happy?"

"I am," Juliet replied, and she could not have been more truthful. When she turned to her husband, she was surprised to see him looking at the ground.

Her mother stood before him. "It is good to see you, as well," she said and then surprised Juliet by embracing him. "Please, both of you, come in."

They followed her mother into the house and glanced around the foyer. "Where are my sisters?"

"In the garden," her mother replied. "Daniel, would you like to join Nathaniel in the drawing room for some tea? James and John are there, as well."

"That would be nice, my lady," he replied with a bow.

Her mother chuckled. "I thought my son set matters straight about your formality of speech. If you are able to address to a baron by his Christian name, would it not be better if you refer to your mother-in-law as Mother? If you are comfortable with doing so, of course."

Daniel smiled. "I would like that...Mother." He was now a bright red to his ears.

"Come, Daniel," Nathaniel said with the impatience of youth. "We can discuss interesting things. Such as horses."

With a smile, Daniel followed Nathaniel down the hall.

Juliet turned to her mother. "Have you told the others about...me?" Her mother shook her head. "Then, I wish to be the one to explain, if I may."

"Very well, if that is what you wish. However, I believe they will love you regardless."

Juliet nodded and made her way to the garden. Her heart was

overcome with joy as she watched her sisters beneath the large tree.

Isabel's white dress fluttered around her, her face and posture as noble as ever, appearing the grand duchess that she was. Hannah laughed in her blue muslin, her smile wider than Juliet had ever seen it. Gone was the timid wallflower, now replaced by a woman in love.

Then Juliet's eyes fell on her Annabel, her favorite, in a yellow dress and a hat with a matching yellow ribbon, who sat doubled over with laughter at something one of the others had said. They were Juliet's family, yet she had to explain to them that she was not a true Lambert, which terrified her more than anything she had ever confronted in her life. It scared her even more than when she confronted Robert Mullens, a man who was her father but not.

"Juliet!" Annabel sprang from the ground and rushed to her. Before Juliet could respond, the others were racing toward her, as well, and she was greeted with embraces from each woman.

"Hannah, you are married!" Juliet said with a shake of her head. "I did not believe you ever would."

Hannah laughed. "Nor did I," she replied. "However, I found love and simply had no choice in the matter." She gave Juliet a wide grin. "I understand that you have, as well."

Juliet nodded. "We are in love, and it is wonderful." She turned to their cousin. "Now we only have Annabel left to find someone special." This brought about nods of agreement. Then Juliet took a deep breath. "We made a bond here beneath this tree, and now I wish to share a secret." Her heart pounded harder than it ever had in the past.

"Of course," Isabel said, her face filled with concern. "Our secrets are safe here."

"Let us sit." Once everyone was seated in a circle, Juliet collected every ounce of courage and said, "In the past, I told stories that stretched the truth." When Isabel's eyebrow raised, she added, "Oh, very well, some were outright fabrications. However, I swear that what I have to tell you now is the truth." She took a steadying breath. "It began here in Scarlet Hall nearly nineteen years ago, a lady's maid became with child..."

She did not know for how long she spoke, but she told them

everything. Of her mother and father. Of how the woman she had known as her mother had come to taking on a child that was not her own. Of how she confronted Robert that day in his shop and her reasons for doing so. The only piece she kept from them was their mother's part in Juliet's leaving with Daniel, for she had a promise to keep, even if it meant keeping it from her sisters.

When she finished, she stared at a blade of grass that she had knotted together with another, uncertain if she felt shame or relief. It would all depend on her sisters' reaction to her story. "And now you know the truth. That I am not truly your sister, for I do not share your blood. I am sorry to have broken our bond."

Hannah snorted. "That could never happen," she said with a derisive sniff. "You are my sister."

"And you are mine," Annabel said. "Nothing will ever change that."

Juliet sniffled and turned to Isabel, and saw a single tear roll down her sister's cheek. "Isabel?" she whispered, fearing the worst. Isabel was strong and wise, and if she believed Juliet was no longer her sister, it would crush her.

"Juliet is right in her fear," Isabel said. "For sisters are bound by both spirit and blood."

Juliet nodded and her heart sank. She had been rejected, the one thing she feared more than anything. However, she did not blame Isabel, for what her sister said was true. She was not one of their sisters.

Isabel removed a pin from her bodice, grabbed Juliet's hand and held it open with the palm up. "This is going to sting." She ran the point of the pin across the palms of each of Juliet's hands and a thin line of blood appeared.

One by one, each woman took the pin and cut their palms, including Isabel, and when they finished, the took the hands of the women on either side, forming a circle.

"The bond we made before is now made stronger," Isabel said. "We are now all sisters bound together in blood and spirit, and nothing can break that bond."

Juliet did nothing to stop the tears from streaming down her cheeks as she nodded her agreement. Then they gave each other an embrace.

"Thank you," Juliet said, dabbing at the thin lines of blood on her hand. "Thank you for everything you have always done for me."

Isabel hugged her. "You are my sister, and I love you. There is nothing I would not do for you."

The embrace broke, and Juliet smiled when she saw Daniel standing beside one of the hedges.

"Ladies," Juliet said as she motioned for Daniel to join her, "I would like you to meet my husband, Mr. Daniel Haskins."

As her sisters congratulated them, Juliet could do nothing more than smile. Thoughts of the past made an attempt to enter her mind, but she pushed them away. The past was over, and now she and her sisters, save Annabel, were married, their lives their own and their futures before them.

And as Daniel turned his smile upon her, she knew that their future was brighter than ever.

Epilogue

Eleanor Lambert looked out the window, just as she had for many years. Her daughters were once again reunited beneath their tree in the garden, and her heart was finally happy. The past year had been full of heartache, misery, and vile acts that had threatened to destroy the lives of her children. However, those days were gone, and for the first time in a very long time, Eleanor felt at peace.

Faint footsteps made her turn, and Forbes came to stand behind her.

"Look at them," she whispered. "They are happy. It is what I have always wanted."

"You have done well," the butler replied, his hand coming to rest on her shoulder. "Your strength is what guided them and brought them hope, even in the darkest of days."

Eleanor nodded and she reached up and patted his hand. "It is you who I have turned to many times," she said. She turned to face him. "Thank you."

As he had done many times before, Forbes simply nodded.

"Did you learn of his fate?" She did not need to name Robert for him to know of whom she spoke.

"He was imprisoned for ten years," Forbes replied.

She winced. *Only ten years?*

"It does not matter. If the man is released and returns here..." He allowed the words to trail off, but she felt his grip tighten on her shoulder.

She had no doubt what he would do.

"Thank you," she repeated. She knew she could never say the words enough to cover all he had done for her.

He took a step back and gave her a diffident bow. Then he produced a letter. "This came for you. It is from Lord and Lady Lambert."

"Annabel's parents?" she asked in surprise. She took the letter and quickly opened it. Her eyes darted across the page, and with each word, her anger grew. "They mean to have Lord Agar court her!" she said with shock. "The man is older than I by ten years, and a scoundrel to boot!"

"What will you do?"

Eleanor folded the letter and put it in the pocket of her dress. "I will not have her suffer," she said, returning her gaze to the happy group beneath the tree. "Not my Annabel, and not with that man."

"Eleanor, you cannot interfere. It will only cause..."

She turned and glared at the butler. "I will do what I see fit," she snapped, her hand tapping the pocket of her dress to assure herself the ring was still there beneath the letter. It was. With relief, she softened her tone. "Will you help me?"

"You need not ask," he replied. "You know I will."

The butler walked away, and Eleanor returned her gaze to her daughters. Daniel had joined them, and Nathaniel was walking toward them, as well.

Her eyes fell on Annabel and she pursed her lips. She would do whatever it took to keep the girl safe, regardless of what her brother and sister-in-law thought!

Author's Note

I hope you have enjoyed the Secrets of Scarlett Hall thus far, beginning with Isabel's Story in **Whispers of Light**, followed by that of Hannah in **Echoes of the Heart**. Then we learn more about Juliet in **Voices of Shadows Past**.

More secrets are revealed in the next installment of the Secrets of Scarlett Hall Series, **Silent Dreams**, which will recount Annabel's story.

Jennifer

Like most Regency authors, Jennifer Monroe fell in love with historical novels of dashing dukes and women wishing to be swept off their feet. She believes that no matter how well a romance story is written, love must be the driving force behind the characters.

Born in France to parents who worked for the United Nations, she found herself traveling the world, until she settled down in New York whilst attending University. As she completed her degree in literature studies, she met and married her loving husband, and they soon had two wonderful daughters. She chose to stay home and raise her children, and it was not long before she began to wonder about the novels she loved as a young adult and began to reread some of her favorites. This led her to reading newer authors and eventually to try her hand at writing the stories that bounced around in her head for many years.

Regency Hearts Series

The Duke of Fire
Return of the Duke
The Duke of Ravens
Duke of Storms

The Defiant Brides Series

The Duke's Wager
The Spinster's Secret
The Duchess Remembers
The Earl's Mission
Duke of Thorns

OR
Get all 5 in one boxed set!